CROOKED RIVER CANYON

What set apart the run-of-the-mill town in Prineville in the Crooked River county of Oregon was Major Calvin Tarback and his hidden, but unrelenting, hunger to become the most powerful man in the Northwest.

Seizing the opportunity presented by a senseless mob lynching, Tarback began to build a secret vigilante organization. Cloaked in respectability, the well-organized Prineville vigilantes ruled in a reign of terror. It was a bloody plot that pitted neighbor against neighbor—until a few brave men dared to set right the grave wrong and give Tarback a taste of his own medicine . . .

D(wight) B(ennett) Newton is the author of a number of notable Western novels. Born in Kansas City, Missouri, Newton went on to complete work for a Master's degree in history at the University of Missouri. From the time he first discovered Max Brand in Street and Smith's *Western Story Magazine,* he knew he wanted to be an author of Western fiction. He began contributing Western stories and novelettes to the Red Circle group of Western pulp magazines published by Newsstand in the late 1930s. During the Second World War, Newton served in the US Army Engineers and fell in love with the central Oregon region when stationed there. He would later become a permanent resident of that state and Oregon frequently serves as the locale for many of his finest novels. As a client of the August Lenniger Literary Agency, Newton found that every time he switched publishers he was given a different byline by his agent. This complicated his visibility. Yet in notable novels from *Range Boss* (1949), the first original novel ever published in a modern paperback edition, through his impressive list of titles for the Double D series from Doubleday, *The Oregon Rifles, Crooked River Canyon,* and *Disaster Creek* among them, he produced a very special kind of Western story. What makes it so special is the combination of characters who seem real and about whom a reader comes to care a great deal and Newton's fundamental humanity, his realization early on (perhaps because of his study of history) that little that happened in the West was ever simple but rather made desperately complicated through the conjunction of numerous opposed forces working at cross purposes. Yet, through all of the turmoil on the frontier, a basic human decency did emerge. It was this which made the American frontier experience so profoundly unique and which produced many of the remarkable human beings to be found in the world of Newton's Western fiction.

CROOKED RIVER CANYON

D. B. Newton

GUNSMOKE

Western
New

First published in the UK by Gold Lion

This hardback edition 2007
by BBC Audiobooks Ltd
by arrangement with
Golden West Literary Agency

ISBN 978 1 405 68143 8

British Library Cataloguing in Publication Data available.

For My Parents

Printed and bound in Great Britain by
Antony Rowe Ltd., Chippenham, Wiltshire

FOREWORD

I am not aware that there were any families named Hunter, Tarback, Langley, Allen, or Wright living in the Crooked River country of Oregon between 1882 and 1884, when the events occurred on which this story is based. Nevertheless, most of these people had actual prototypes. Nearly every incident in the book really happened, more or less in the manner described. As usual, there are conflicting traditions; I have chosen the one that seems to me most probable, and have used guesswork to fill the gaps.

This was a raw and violent time. Even now—after eighty years, with the descendants of the Prineville Vigilantes and their enemies residing peacefully enough as neighbors—some of the scars are still fresh. In order to avoid offending living persons, I have employed invented names. The time scheme has been condensed and the sequence of events rearranged in some instances. But if *Crooked River Canyon* is fiction, I hope that it remains essentially true to a particular time and place in Oregon's frontier history.

DWIGHT BENNETT
Bend, Oregon

CHAPTER I

It was typical spring weather, for this Oregon range country—a cloud ceiling that stretched unbroken from the timbered Ochocos westward to the ghostly white peaks of the Cascade Range, a March wind that came tumbling out of it to comb bunch grass and mountain pine and juniper forest, or send tawny dust pillars walking across the high desert. The grim quartet of riders who'd left Prineville toward midafternoon, armed with hand guns and rifles, also carried windbreakers strapped behind their saddles. Come nightfall, they knew, a man could welcome a heavy coat in this country at almost any season of the year.

They had taken the wagon road that led away from the river toward Grizzly Butte; almost at once they began to climb with the slow tilt of the wide canyon floor. Their leader, a dark-haired man of thirty or so, seemed preoccupied and thoughtful, speaking little and frowning to himself as he gnawed a drooping mustache. Finally, during a pause to rest the horses, he dug a wad of folded paper from his pocket and scowled at it. "Bob," he said to the one next to him, "I got me a problem."

The other man eyed the paper. "That the warrant for Langley?"

"Thing is, there's *two* warrants," Jim Blake said. "And that's my problem. This second one has Bill Farrell's name on it."

"I didn't know Farrell had anything to do with the killings."

"Of course he didn't. He was in town—I was talking to him there, less than an hour before the word came." Blake slapped the paper with the back of a hand. "Just the same, the coroner's jury has put him down as an accessory after the fact."

"They have any reason to?"

"None, except they knew he'd been working for Langley. Yesterday at the inquest, Bill walked in and said some things about all the trouble his boss had been having with Story and Cook over property lines. Maybe some of their friends didn't

7

like the way he talked—but, you can't put the law on a man for talking!"

Bob Hunter, a sober-eyed young fellow still in his mid-twenties, gave his opinion. "Seems if it was me, I'd shove the thing away in my pocket and forget it."

"About what I'd already decided," Jim Blake agreed, and did so.

Jase Evans had been watching. Now he kneed his horse a shade closer to ask, "What the hell you two jawing about?"

"Private conversation," Blake said coolly, buttoning the pocket flap. Evans cut his suspicious stare back and forth between them while the fourth rider, Bob Hunter's older brother Chris, watched in silence.

Evans was big, with meaty shoulders and a perpetual scowl. His cheeks had been badly pitted by some sort of skin disease, and the scars shone faintly as he swung his head. "I don't see what we're wasting time for," he declared loudly. "Not that we're apt to find our man when we get there. That killer's on the run. He ain't gonna head straight back where he started."

"He's got to have a horse," Jim Blake explained patiently. "He's been afoot and without a gun ever since the Major and the rest of you jumped him last night at that cabin on Mill Creek. His own place is the nearest he can hope to pick up another mount. I think it's where he'd go—and I think we've got a good chance of beating him."

"I don't recall anyone saying you had to come along," Chris Hunter pointed out mildly. "If you think we've got it figured wrong, there's other posses beating the timber for Langley."

The big man whirled on him, then apparently bit back a retort. And Bob Hunter, studying Evans, felt a sudden odd suspicion.

Was it possible he'd come under orders? He rode for Calvin Tarback, the rancher that people in this part of Oregon generally called "the Major"; and from the first word of the killings his boss had been taking charge of this manhunt, lifting it right out of the hands of the deputy sheriff at Prineville whose job it was supposed to be. Tarback was the kind of man who took charge; maybe it was a holdover from the Modoc Indian war, when he was said to have won his commission. Yesterday he'd organized and led the first posse that tracked the killer to his brother's place on Mill Creek, then through a blunder let him get away. It could just be he was jealously worried lest Jim Blake and the Hunters should have better luck, and had ordered his man to ride along and watch them.

8

So, let him watch.

They moved out a[...]
them up now onto the [...]
a long day for Bob Hur[...]
night had found him c[...]
from a trip over to M[...]
registered bull for sale.[...]
Prineville and found the [...]
double murder on Willo[...]
already in the field. His bro[...]
to ride with Jim Blake's grou[...]
to change to a fresh horse at [...]

The whole thing bothered [...]
others who, for all he could t[...]
than a break in the monotony [...]
and lonely land. The killer, aft[...]
were the pair Luke Langley wa[...]
homestead claim adjoining. Hun[...]
his son-in-law well—they'd been [...]
acquainted with. He'd known of [...]
and Langley over the line dividing [...]
could lead to murder had struck hi[...]
startling vista into unexpected depths [...]

Up here on Grizzly Butte, the dirt[...]
still clung in the shadows, making ra[...]
feet deep in places. The coarse dark s[...]
from the seeping of melt water; the first [...]
through. The smell of the pines was he[...]
Hunter, who seemed to know his brothe[...]
close beside him once to ask, "Aren't you [...]
don't think you had any business coming. [...]

"I'm all right."

Neither of these Hunters was any strang[...]
hard work. They'd put in their sixteen hours [...]
a whipsaw mill—possibly the toughest job [...]
While still in their teens, they'd worked for th[...]
the Warm Springs reservation and had collect[...]
mail from The Dalles to points where the [...]
operate. They'd ridden a season for the Major. [...]
homestead claim of their own up here in the [...]
district, fourteen miles northwest of Prineville, wh[...]
in the process of building themselves a beef herd [...]
from modest beginnings.

They made a good team, Bob and his brothe[...]

9

seldom-speaking[...]
having died ea[...]
knocking aroun[...]
brothers could [...]
almost as thou[...]

The sun wa[...]
dusk filtering [...]
down off Gri[...]
ran north of [...]
Langley plac[...]
faintly throu[...]
under its roo[...]
well with a [...]
outbuildings[...]
a warning [...]

Startling [...]
There he [...]
A door [...]
horse wai[...]
run; fling[...]
and sent [...]
ahead of [...]
Jim B[...]

From [...]
metal a[...]
movem[...]
their s[...]
seemin[...]
should [...]
gust o[...]
gun h[...]
dirt. [...]

Bo[...]
his [...]
Perh[...]
perh[...]
geta[...]
bul[...]
dr[...]
"W[...]

man a couple years his senior. Their folks
ly, they had grown—throughout the years of
d a big, raw land together—about as close as
get, so that they didn't need to talk much. It was
gh they had other ways of communicating.

s gone from the high country, with chill, gray
into the last of the light, when the riders came
zly and through the rolling juniper country that
it. The wagon road brought them right to the
e. As the trees thinned they saw a lamp winking
gh the shifting trunks, and then the cabin itself
f thatched with rye grass and willows. There were a
weep, a corral of crooked juniper poles, a couple of
. A dog had caught their scent, and it began baying
hile they were still a couple hundred yards away.

y, Jase Evans loosed a sudden shout: "Watch it!
oes!"

of the house flung open, letting lamplight fall upon a
ing groundtied and saddled. A man broke out at a
ng himself onto its back, he pulled the animal around
it at the ditch, in a plain effort to cut into the road
the nearing posse.

ake yelled, "No guns, damn it!"

the corner of his eye Bob Hunter caught the glint of
Jase Evans's hand came up. But in almost the same
ent, Chris had reached an arm across the space between
ddles; his hand closed on Evans's wrist and, without
g effort, did something to it that made the big fellow's
ers hunch violently and his body bend at the waist. A
sound broke from the man's lips. His arm swung and the
e had dug from his pocket dropped with a thud into the
Evans swore in a strangled voice.

b Hunter, not touching his own gun, was already kicking
oan hard forward and shouting the fugitive's name.
aps Luke Langley thought he recognized the voice; or
aps he realized he was shaving things too fine to hope for a
way. Almost at once Hunter saw he was pulling up, saw the
k of the horse gleam faintly through the dusk as the rider
w it broadside. Langley's words came, thin with strain:
ho's that?"

"Your neighbor."

He was gratified when the other held his horse in, dancing
rvously on a tight rein. He closed the distance. Langley,

peering at him, spoke anxiously: "Bob? Thought it sounded like you. But it could have been some of that same crowd that jumped me last night at my brother's place. Who's with you?"

Hunter told him. "Jim Blake, and Chris. And Jase Evans—"

Langley interrupted sharply. "Evans! Hell, he was in the bunch last night! Bob, I dunno . . ."

"He'll make no trouble—that's a promise. Chris and I are your friends, Luke," he insisted. "And Jim's a fair man. Won't you come on back to the house and talk things over?"

Luke Langley was a long moment giving him an answer. At last Hunter heard him sigh raggedly. "I can't go on much longer," he admitted, in a beaten tone. "Yeah, I'd like to talk."

"That's being sensible."

They rode back to where the others waited. Jase Evans was down salvaging his gun out of the dirt; he blew into the barrel, gave the weapon a swipe against a sleeve, and Hunter heard him say tightly, "By God, don't ever lay a hand on me again!" But Chris appeared wholly unmoved by the warning, and Evans muttered something and put the gun away.

Jim Blake had kneed his horse forward a step. "Good work," he told Hunter; and to Langley he said earnestly, "You're saving yourself a lot of trouble, friend."

"I hope you're right," the man said without conviction.

Over at the house the dog at its tether was still baying. A woman stood in the door calling questions in a hysterical voice. Hunter assured her, "It's all right, Martha. This is Bob Hunter. Luke's here with us. Nobody's been hurt."

Jim Blake said, "I think we better get your wife settled, Langley, before she throws a conniption."

The two of them rode toward the house together, with the Hunters following and Jase Evans bringing up the rear afoot, leading his horse. The dog quieted when Langley spoke to it. Then Blake and both the Langleys had gone into the house, and the door closed behind them.

Waiting, Hunter looked at Jase Evans and found the man's eyes resting on him. Evans's mouth quirked and he said, "Just in case you Hunters didn't know it, I ain't liked either of you much from the time when we was all riding for the Major!"

"That upsets me!" Hunter retorted. The fellow's scowl deepened, but then he shrugged and bent to examine a shoe on his horse's near front hoof. Chris was leaning from the saddle, making friends with the dog, which was a lean, liver-colored hound.

11

The door opened again. Jim Blake called, "Come on in, boys. Miz Langley's offered to fix us some supper, before we start back."

"You go ahead," Bob Hunter told the others. "I'll give these broncs some grain and water, first. . . ."

It was full dark now, starless and black; the wind whipped strongly at him as he worked the well sweep and brought up water for the horses. He moved slowly, stiff and sore from his many hours in saddle, and with an unexplained hesitation about finishing the job and joining the rest of the people inside the house.

When he did he found it crowded to overflowing. It was no bigger than the Hunters' own bachelor shack, and ten people more than filled its main room. Three were children, two boys and a girl, seated on the edge of a bunk and solemnly taking everything in. A couple belonged to the Langleys; the third was the son of the hired hand, Bill Farrell—a decent sort, who leaned his shoulders against the wall and watched, with a sober and troubled expression, as the men of the posse took their places at the crude trestle table and pitched into the food Mrs. Langley dished up for them.

Langley seemed willing enough to talk about the shooting. "I never will know just how it happened," he told them, in answer to their questions. "The best of neighbors are going to have trouble if they can't keep their boundary lines clear. Bob, you know me and Al Cook have been rowing, ever since him and that son-in-law of his took up land east of me. Yesterday noon I found their blazemarks a good hundred yards on my side of the line, and I knew we had to have it out. I figured it would take a gun to make 'em hold still and talk reason, so I come home and got it and was waiting for them when they showed up again after dinner. We had words, and Al dug out a six-shooter and then young Story went for his. I didn't have no choice but to try and defend myself."

Jim Blake thoughtfully smoothed his silky mustache with thumb and forefinger. "If that's the way it happened, why did you run?"

"Why does a man lose his head? I was standing there looking at them, beginning to realize they were dead for certain; and then I heard someone coming fast, from the direction of the road. I jumped on my horse and got out of there."

"That was Garrett Maupin you heard," Blake said, naming the Trout Creek rancher who had brought Prineville its first word of the killings. "He just happened to be passing and heard the shots. And he got a look at you."

Langley nodded bleakly. "I figured as much. I didn't know anywhere else to go, so I headed for my brother's place on Milt Creek."

Thin lamplight gleamed from the scar tissue on Jase Evans's raddled jaws as he cocked a look at the man, across the china coffee mug propped in both hands before his face. "Me and Major Tarback damn near nabbed you there, too. Just don't think you're getting away another time!"

The other man gave him a slow stare. He demanded, "And, Matt? What did you do to him?"

Evans leered knowingly. "Wouldn't you like to know!"

"That's enough!" Jim Blake snapped. "Quit riding him. Your brother's all right, Luke."

The prisoner thanked him with a nod. He didn't have the look of a killer, just then. He was not a big man, and now he appeared crumpled in weariness. He hadn't shaved and there was a long, crusted scratch down one cheek where a branch must have torn it during his headlong flight through the mountains after losing horse and gun. His clothing was torn and filthy; his tired eyes held the caution of a hunted animal's. But his voice was level enough as he turned again to Jim Blake. "I'm ready to go in with you. I've had enough of running. I can see now, I owe it to my wife and my kids to get this thing cleared up."

Over by the stove, the woman's thin shoulders began to shake and she put her apron to her mouth. Bob Hunter felt acutely self-conscious, suddenly, to be sitting here eating beef and beans while he watched this intimate drama of people in trouble.

Jim Blake swung a leg across the long seat of the trestle table, came to his feet. "I got a warrant here, but I can't see any need for me to show it to you."

"No need, Jim," the man agreed. "I won't make any fuss." He pushed back his plate, rose and got hat and coat from a wallpeg. He slanted a look at his hired man. "Bill, will you look after things here?"

But then Jase Evans was on his feet, the table jarring as one heavy cowhide boot struck it in the act of rising. "Ain't you forgetting something, Blake? Where's the other warrant?"

Jim Blake looked at him. "Which one?"

"You know damned well which! With Farrell's name on it. And don't tell me you ain't got it. You were showing it to Hunter, on the way up here."

13

Luke Langley was staring. "There has to be a mistake! Bill had no part in the shooting yesterday. Either then, or after."

"I know it," Blake said.

"Just the same, you was handed a warrant," Evans told him doggedly. "Your only job is to serve it."

"Then, that's too bad." Blake was looking straight at him. "Because I reckon I lost it. On the way up."

Evans stiffened. His face turned brick-red. "Like hell you lost it! Why, I saw you put it—!"

His hand reached toward the gap in Blake's unbuttoned windbreaker. At once, the hard edge of a palm sliced against his wrist and slapped it aside, so hard the big man almost lost balance. "Keep your paws off me!" Jim Blake warned coldly.

The other caught himself, on braced boots; a storm of angry emotion burst across his craggy face. "By God—!" he began hoarsely.

"Shut up!" That was Bob Hunter, suddenly losing patience. "Jase, your language gets monotonous. If Jim says there's no warrant, then there isn't. What do you say, Chris?"

His brother nodded briefly. "Looks to me somebody's fixing to be railroaded, and I'll have no part in it. So, I reckon you're outnumbered here, Evans."

The big man's eyes smoldered; he rubbed his palm along the seam of his jeans leg for a moment. At last he said heavily, "That's all right—that's all right. This ain't the end of it. . . ."

Jim Blake leaned and got his hat where he'd hung it on the floor beside his boots. He looked at Langley. The latter nodded, pulled his own hat on and slung the coat across his arm. He looked at the children seated on the edge of the bunk. He put out a hand, laid it a moment on his wife's shoulder. Abruptly, he turned and led the way outside.

The horses had been left under saddle. As Hunter was tightening his cinch, his brother Chris rode over to him and asked, "You riding back to Prineville with them?"

"Figured I would."

"Well, I don't figure I'm needed, now the hunt's over. We're almost home; I think I'll go on in. All right with you, Jim?" Chris turned as Blake came up. The latter nodded.

"Don't see why not. One thing you might do—stop off and tell Miz Cook and Miz Story we got him. I guess they have a right to know."

Luke Langley put in, "And tell them I'm sorry it happened, Chris. God knows I got no quarrel with womenfolks."

There was a scornful sound from Jase Evans, but it went un-

14

noticed. Chris said, "I'll tell them that, too," and a moment later rode off into the darkness.

The door had opened and Bill Farrell came out, shrugging into a mackinaw. He said, "If nobody objects, I'm going to town with you."

Jim Blake hesitated. "I'm not sure it's a good idea. It's kind of a touchy situation there. Some of the talk I been hearing . . ."

"That's just what I mean. If there's a warrant for me, I want it straightened out. Besides, I'd kind of like to stick with the boss. Martha thinks the same," he added. "She and the kids will make out here, alone."

Blake, frowning, reminded him, "You're still not under arrest."

"He should be, by God!" Jase Evans growled heavily. Blake only looked at him.

"Get saddled then. We'll wait. . . ."

A minute later, when Bill Farrell returned from the horse shed mounted and ready to ride, a boy's small figure came darting out of the house, calling to him anxiously. The hired man reined over to look down at his son. "Now, it's all right," he said, with firm affection. "You're to stay with Miz Langley. You know your share of the chores. Mind the way you should, and I'll bring you a sack of licorice from Allen's—O.K.?"

The youngster nodded reluctantly. Farrell leaned and tousled his head with a palm, then pulled erect in the leather and reined over to join the waiting group. They cantered out of the yard, falling once more into the road that led back across Grizzly, to the canyon of Crooked River.

Turning once, Bob Hunter saw the woman looking after them, with the three children gathered about her skirts. They were still standing there as the timber moved in between and the Langley place was swallowed in the night.

15

CHAPTER II

A dozen years ago, as late as the early seventies, the canyon where Prineville stood had been an empty expanse of wild rye, pea vines, and rank meadow grass growing belly-high to the ponies of the Utes and Snake Indians who hunted game through its deep and sheltered bottom. Now a town of some two hundred people stood where Barney Prine had staked his original claim by squatter's rights. There was not much to it—a few dozen wooden buildings and one or two of brick, centered around a dusty main street that ran south across the canyon from the Ochoco Creek crossing to the iron bridge over Crooked River.

It was somewhere short of two in the morning, but the town was not entirely asleep. A couple of the saloons—Burmeister's and Kelley's—still showed lights, and there were a few horses tied out front, surely unusual for this hour of a Friday morning. Here in the broad, palisaded depth of the canyon the air was chill but quiet; the noise the horses made, moving slowly down the wide strip of dust, was loud in the stillness.

They put directly in to Hamilton's Livery, on the east side of Main next the hotel, where an oil lamp burned on a nail by the door. Halting their mounts in the runway, they let tired weight drag the saddles far over as they dismounted, to a protesting creak of cinches and stirrup leather.

Hunter placed his hands against the small of his back to stretch the ache that felt as though it would snap him in two. Jim Blake turned to the night hostler who came limping out of his cubbyhole of an office, rubbing sleep from his eyes. "Where's George Wright? Did he get back to town yet?"

The old man lifted a shoulder inside his frowzy blue sweater. He smelled of stale beer. "How would I know?"

"You know where he lives, anyway. Go look for him. That's all right—we'll take care of the horses." When the man only stood there scowling, Blake lost his temper. "Look! We're played out, do you understand? Now, you go fetch George and

16

tell him to get his deputy's badge over here, fast! I want to go to bed."

The hostler blinked from one to another of these tired, gray-faced men, and as though he had only now truly got his eyes open he appeared to see Luke Langley for the first time. His eyes widened; with no more protest, he nodded and shuffled away on his errand, throwing a last look over his shoulder as he went. The posse fell to work unsaddling.

They were waiting in the stable office, stupid with fatigue, when the deputy sheriff came in looking as though he had thrown on his clothes in considerable haste.

His name was George Wright; the sixteen-year-old who came slouching in after him was his brother Eddie. The deputy himself was a lean fellow, about thirty, a little stooped and with an intense and intelligent face. Ambition burned behind his eyes and seemed to have whittled away every spare scrap of flesh from the strong, bony structure of his cheeks. He was an attorney by training and intention, but he found little need for his calling in a town like Prineville with the county seat at The Dalles, a hundred miles north. In fact he was simply marking time, while representing the sheriff's office here for the small salary it paid; generally the duties were trivial enough—routine matters of serving writs and collecting a few taxes.

Wright had come across the mountains from the Willamette Valley a little more than a year ago, and decided to cast his lot with this Crooked River country. Now he was waiting—as everyone was, impatiently—for the day when the State Assembly cleared away the legal roadblocks and got around to carving up sprawling Wasco County, and making Prineville a county seat with its own administrative machinery. Everyone said George Wright had a real future when that day came.

In sharp contrast to all this welling ambition, there was his younger brother who lacked any fire whatsoever. The two looked something alike, but a glance at the eyes showed you the difference. George was strung fine; Eddie was slack, indifferent. He had given up all pretense at getting an education, seemed satisfied to do a few odd jobs around town or get by on his brother's generosity. He was a trial and a real problem for George—a pity, folks said.

The deputy looked at the separate faces now, and his stare settled on Luke Langley, standing slack-shouldered against the rough wall, as he listened to Jim Blake's account of the arrest. He asked a question or two and told the prisoner bluntly, "You did well to come in without a fuss. We'd have got you sooner or later. Now, put out your hands." He reached for a pocket as, frowning and hesitant, Langley obeyed; lantern light glinted on metal and a pair of handcuffs clicked into place on the prisoner's wrists.

Wright tested them, drew a gun from behind his waist belt. "Those are the only irons I got," he said, looking meaningly at Bill Farrell. "But don't let it give you any ideas."

"Now, just a minute!" Jim Blake said sharply, as a pleased grin began to show on Jase Evans's heavy face. "Let me tell you about Bill Farrell. He came in on his own hook, to be with his boss—I told him, as far as I was concerned he didn't have to come at all. I don't give a damn if there's a warrant!"

"Well, I do!" George snapped. He showed Farrell the six-gun in his hand. "So just remember, I have to treat you like any other prisoner. And watch your step!"

The hired man only looked at him. Hunter wanted to know, "Where you figure to take them?"

It was a good question, because Prineville had never boasted a jail. "Hotel's as good a place as any," the lawman decided. "I'll hold 'em there for what's left of tonight, probably take the morning stage for The Dalles." He flung the plank door wide. "Let's go," he said.

Langley, with a look that was both patient and resigned, moved out first, the others following; but in the barn runway they halted abruptly. There were a dozen men waiting, silent and motionless, just inside the wide street entrance. Their breath hung faint plumes of steam against the horse-and-hay odors of the place.

George Wright demanded, "And just what do you think *you* want?"

No answer, at first. Then someone said roughly, "So you caught the sonsabitches!"

Something in the voice struck Bob Hunter's ear almost like a warning note of a bell. He looked at George Wright, but the deputy's lean face was coldly inexpressive as he nudged his prisoner forward again.

Langley took a step and no more, when he saw that those who stood in the doorway showed no sign of yielding. Now a townsman spoke loudly. "Where'd you nab them?"

It was Jim Blake who answered, and his manner was hard and crisp. "No one had to be nabbed. Langley was just where I told you he'd be, Weckler—right out there at his own place— and he gave himself up. He's as anxious as anyone to see this thing settled."

18

"I'll just bet!" Gus Weckler said, with a short laugh.

Someone else muttered, "If he's in such a hurry to put a rope around his neck, I reckon there's some that'd be willing to oblige him."

"Who said that?" George Wright snapped. His sharp tone quieted a beginning murmur, and the group settled into sullenness. "This is a kind of talk," the deputy continued, his words falling with a stony weight of anger, "that we don't need here—and I won't have it!

"Do you have the slightest idea," he demanded, having given them a moment and got no answer, "what time of night it is? I can tell you it's no hour for a crowd like this to be standing around, making irresponsible talk about things that are none of your business. Now, step out of the way!" And he put his forearm against a man's chest and simply moved him aside.

That was all it took. Irresolute and with no real initiative of its own, the clot of men let itself be broken in two. They went through, Luke Langley with shackled hands in front of him and his eyes set straight ahead. The sixteen-year-old, Eddie Wright, lagged after as the group went tramping the short distance from the barn to the hotel adjoining, at the northeast corner where Third Street crossed Main.

The Jackson House was a long, white frame building. Its lobby was cold and deserted just now. While Bob Hunter got a couple of lamps burning, Bill Farrell, under orders from the deputy, proceeded to build up a fire in the space heater. As the flames began to crackle and to work at the chill, Hunter, who was still deeply troubled by that scene in the livery runway, went to take a look through the window.

The men were out there, and a few more might have joined them. He said, "You don't suppose anyone's got ideas in their heads?"

"Of course not," George Wright said calmly. "It was nothing but talk—probably meant to put a scare in the prisoners." He laid his six-gun on the desk and began to unbutton his coat. "Might as well make ourselves comfortable. We've got a night ahead of us."

Luke Langley had already taken a seat on the lobby's one leather-bound sofa, hat on the floor beside him and shackled hands in his lap. Bill Farrell, having adjusted the damper and got his fire roaring solidly, chafed his palms and held them up to warm them at the flames.

"Not you, boy," the deputy said, looking at his brother who

19

still lingered near the door. "You go on home and back to bed. Hear me?"

Hunter saw the youngster's face blacken with anger. "Like hell!" Eddie Wright exclaimed in furious protest. "I'm staying! This is the nearest to anything that's happened in this burg all the time we been here!"

"I'm not asking you!" the other snapped. "Now—you move!"

Eddie's hands bunched into fists, but if he meant to give his brother further argument the intention was lost in the thud of boots striking the porch outside. They heard a voice that spoke with a carrying resonance, and Jase Evans said quickly, "That's the Major." The door opened part way; there was a moment's wait as the newcomer paused to finish whatever he was saying to the group in front of the hotel. Then Calvin Tarback strode into the lobby, shoving the door closed with a solid thrust of his heel, and looked around him.

He was a big man, this Major Tarback—big in size and in the sense of his own importance here in the Prineville country; about forty, blond, with clean-shaven jaws, and a mustache he kept carefully trimmed by contrast with the usual practice of letting such ornaments run wild. He had money and liked to spend it. His ranch on Hay Creek, where he ran cattle and blooded horses, was one of the largest anywhere in this part of Oregon.

To Bob Hunter the man was something of an enigma.

Actually, ranching was an activity new to the Major; heretofore his career had been in other lines. It was said the pair of gold nuggets that gleamed on his watch chain were mementos of time he'd spent as a freighter in the Idaho goldfields. It was said he had influence in the State capital, where he had made and lost fortunes editing political newspapers—and where, it was rumored, he had killed a rival publisher with his own hand. His career in the Modoc War was known, if not in much detail. It was said he had been ambushed by Indians and left for dead. It was said the stiff way he habitually carried himself was due to a Snake bullet lodged in his neck. More likely, Bob Hunter was inclined to think, it was caused by pride and native arrogance.

And yet, for all this, Hunter had an odd feeling about this man. He wondered if he could be the only one who sensed something missing behind the façade Calvin Tarback raised to the world—in the pale, repelling stare that didn't let you look into him for any real distance. . . .

Tarback walked forward, now, into a waiting silence. It was

20

certainly like him that he'd taken time to dress completely, despite being wakened at such an hour of the night. He came to a stand directly above the seated prisoner. "Well!" he said. "You gave us a chase. But you didn't actually think we'd let a murderer get away from us?"

Langley met his stare. "I'm not a murderer," he said quietly, and got an automatic response from Jase Evans—the heavy snort of disbelief with which Evans greeted every word he tried to say. "I didn't mean to kill anyone, Tarback. That's the truth."

The Major's shoulders lifted in a shrug. "Then you shouldn't have run. You'd have saved yourself and all of us a lot of trouble by surrendering last night when you had a chance."

"Give myself up to you? And that lynch mob you called a posse?" Luke Langley shook his head. "I knew better than *that!*"

The Major's face darkened at the thrust. Jase Evans commented, "Fellow actually thinks he's going to beat the rope. He's already counting on a jury up to The Dalles letting him off."

"You said that before," Bill Farrell reminded him tartly. "I think you better find a different string to play on!"

Lamplight shone on pock-marked jowls as the big man's head jerked around. He swore with feeling and took a reaching step toward Bill Farrell, as Jim Blake rapped out, "Stop this!"

Tarback nodded. "Sounds as though there's a lot of short tempers around here. Truth is, this business has everyone worked up. More than anybody would have supposed. . . ." He turned to George Wright, then, with a glance at the prisoner. "I see you have the cuffs on him. That's good. Remember—I'm holding you responsible."

Hunter wanted to ask: By what authority do you figure to hold anyone responsible? But he kept his mouth shut. He noticed the deputy himself didn't appear to take exception; George Wright, apparently, had put up very little argument from the first moment when Tarback took over the running of this man-hunt. Now he merely nodded and said, "Don't need to worry, Major. He's not going to get away from me!" It seemed to Hunter he was a little too anxious that Tarback should be reassured.

A man eaten by ambition, it was only natural George should be an admirer of the Major—who, after all, might seem to embody all the success and assurance he so coveted. Hunter found the whole business distasteful; but then, he had to admit, it was hard for him to view George Wright with any degree of

21

objectivity, since they both happened to be courting the same girl. . . .

"I'll leave you with it, then." Major Tarback, turning in that stiff-necked way he had—as though his head and shoulders had been cast in one solid piece—walked to the door. He looked at Jase Evans. "Come along," he said.

The big man shrugged inside his heavy sheepskin. He tramped out behind his boss, and the door slammed with a force that made a pane shake and rattle in its frame.

An impulse carried Bob Hunter across the lobby. Through the glass of the door he could see Tarback talking to the men in the street outside. When he opened the panel a crack, fragments of their speech came to him. "—Might as well turn in," the Major was saying in his heavy voice. "The deputy appears to know what he's doing, and he has things under control. I don't think the prisoners are very likely to get away from him."

Somebody asked a question that Hunter couldn't hear. Tarback's voice answered, "Yes, the morning stage, I suppose. After that it becomes the sheriff's problem. . . ."

He closed the door, shutting out the chill breath of the March night.

In the silence, Jim Blake stretched his lean length and said, "I don't know about anyone else, but I'm beat out. I don't reckon anyone will miss me if I head for home." Like the Major, and a number of other ranchers, Blake lived in town though his ranch was a dozen miles or so east of Prineville, up the canyon. He looked at Hunter. "You've had a longer day than any of us. Why don't you come along? I can bed you down on the parlor sofa—the wife won't mind."

Hunter hesitated, seeing no good reason he shouldn't accept. If George Wright had been dealing with hardened criminals, bent on escape, there would have been some grounds for believing he might need help with them; but, plainly, neither Langley nor Bill Farrell had any idea of giving trouble. Outside, meanwhile, the crowd was already beginning to split up—it was as though they had simply been waiting for the Major to announce his satisfaction with the arrangements.

Yet a prickling uneasiness bothered Hunter. He found himself shaking his head. "Thanks. But I reckon I'll stick awhile."

"Suit yourself." Jim Blake picked up his hat. At the door he turned for a word with Bill Farrell. "Don't worry, Bill. I'll be talking to the justice of the peace, first thing in the morning. I'll

22

either straighten out this silly warrant they've got charged against you, or I'll know why not."

Farrell thanked him, and the rancher pulled on his hat and went out.

Minutes later young Eddie Wright, too, had left, under protest: "And see you go home!" his elder brother ordered flatly. The excitement which had seemed likely for a while to rouse the whole town apparently hadn't disturbed any of the hotel's guests. Now a stillness settled on the lobby that was broken only by the ticking of a wall clock behind the desk, the roar and crackle of fire in the stove.

The spreading warmth began to have its effect. After a while Luke Langley stretched full length on the old sofa and, making himself as comfortable as he could with the manacles on his wrists, promptly fell asleep. Bill Farrell and the deputy were seated by the stove, talking quietly. Hunter, for his part, had taken over one of the lobby's few remaining chairs—bristling, cane-seated rockers that generally lined the veranda in summer weather. It was a singularly uncomfortable chair, with a straight back and no arms, and he couldn't actually achieve a position to fit it. Even so, the dragging minutes and the warm stillness began to work on him. He started to nod.

He roused with a start, to the touch of a hand at his shoulder; he jerked up his head on a neck that felt stiff and cramped, and found Bill Farrell standing over him, gently shaking him awake. "What's wrong?" he demanded, his voice a little slurred.

"Nothing's wrong—except you look like you're about to break your neck. It makes mine ache just to watch you!"

Hunter rubbed the back of his neck, and winced. "What's the time?"

"Crowding four," the other said, after a glance at the dim face of the wall clock. "Look. Why don't you lie down? That second room off the hall is empty. George Wright's in the kitchen heating up a pot of coffee. Leave the door open, and you can hear if anything happens. But I don't think anything's going to, now."

Hunter looked up at him. "*Now?* Why—did you have a feeling it might?"

The only answer he got was a shrug. He pushed himself to his feet, went to the window. Main Street lay silent and deserted. Kelley's Saloon, opposite, was dark. It really looked as though he had been worried about nothing.

Farrell said, half seriously, "Of course, maybe you'd rather not leave George alone here with Luke and me, in case we're figuring to make a break."

"You know me better than to think that." He straightened cramped shoulders, ran the back of a hand across his mouth and discovered the scrape of bristle. His eyes felt as though they had been sanded. "I'm not much good to anyone, in this shape," he admitted. "Just stretching out a few minutes would help. Which room did you say?"

"Second one on the left."

"Thanks. . . ."

He was stumbling a little, heavy-footed, as he made his way toward it along the hallway.

He roused to an impression of noisy confusion, and a room-trapped pair of gunshots that brought him pawing up through cottony layers of sleep, his heart pounding wildly and the conscious thought jarring through him: This is it! This is what I was waiting for!

Rolled to a sitting position on the edge of the bed, even before he could have been called fully awake, Hunter sat a moment blinking at gray dimness, hearing the continuing boil of shouting voices, the heavy trampling of boots. His own gun lay on a chair where he had laid it; he fumbled and grabbed it up. And then he was off the bed, and hurrying into the corridor.

Cordite sting hit his nostrils. There'd been no further shooting, however, and now the tide of sound appeared to have swept outside—through the hotel entrance, onto the veranda and the street beyond. To Hunter's first glance, the lobby itself seemed deserted in the light of the oil lamps. The windows and the street door, which stood wide open, showed a first grainy hint of dawn.

Then it was he saw the body thrown in a grotesque sprawl across the old horsehair sofa, head and shoulders trailing toward the floor. He stepped and laid a hand on it; at his touch, the head rolled loosely and the man's whole body gave a sudden lurch and slid off onto the worn linoleum, face down. Metal clinked as lamplight gleamed dully on the shackled wrists.

With a feeling of strong distaste, he leaned and turned the man over. Luke Langley had been shot in the chest. He had only just stopped breathing.

Straightening, Hunter felt as though his own chest were bound by iron bands. Nearby, against an overturned chair, George Wright sat on the floor with head hanging. He didn't seem to hear his name. When Hunter took him by the chin his head came up without resistance; though the eyes were open it was plain they didn't see him at all. The deputy looked stunned, probably knocked down by a blow from a gunbarrel. Hunter let him go and his chin sank slowly forward again onto his chest.

No sign of Bill Farrell. But now the racket in the street outside reached to his shocked senses; Hunter dragged a long breath, turned and made quickly for the veranda door. Gun in hand, he shouldered through and halted with the splintered floorboards cold beneath his stockinged feet.

The vaguest rumor of daylight, layered with filtered dust, stretched from black earth to steel-gray sky. Figures moved through it dimly—men and milling horses. Suddenly the dust screen shifted and for that moment his slight vantage point gave him a view of the street—and of a man staggering and reeling about with both hands clawing at his throat, as though to tear free of something that tormented him. Hunter saw the rope then, and saw how it ended in a dally on the horn of a saddle whose rider was hardly more than a blocky silhouette.

There was only this brief glimpse. In the next moment heavy boot heels drummed the horse's barrel. The shouting swelled, to a new frenzy. Hoofs struck the earth, and as the rope sang taut Bill Farrell was wrenched bodily off his feet. Hunter could see him twisting and turning at the end of it, before dust boiled up and enveloped him. After that other horsemen closed in and they all were whooping and yelling and pounding away southward down Main, in the direction of the river.

Hunter's throat distended on a cry of protest, as he started blindly forward. But on the edge of the wide steps a figure materialized suddenly, at his elbow. He felt breath against his cheek, caught the sour whiskey smell—tried to turn, as the first blow struck his shoulder, numbing his entire arm and knocking the gun from his hand. He caught at a roof brace, missed. The clubbing arm swept across his vision a second time and the edge of a fist, like a plank, connected with the base of his skull. White fire exploded as it tumbled him forward, headfirst down the steps.

He scarcely felt that he'd lost consciousness. Only minutes could have passed, before he managed to clear his head enough to push himself up. Yet the light was already noticeably stronger; the clouds that capped the sky were beginning to take on a flush of sunrise color now. There was a taste of blood in his mouth. When he had groped to a sitting position on the steps he dabbed a wrist to his cheek and found where he had cut it in falling. His whole head ached miserably from the blow that had

25

struck him down. His shoulder felt almost broken.

The men and the horses were gone; the street lay utterly empty and quiet now, but here and there faces were beginning to appear at doors and hastily opened windows. A man came bursting out of the hotel—he looked like a drummer. He had on shirt and trousers, but his galluses were dragging and only one shirt tail was tucked in. His voice held a note of hysteria. "Mister—you hurt?"

As his head began to clear, Hunter became aware of a sense of desperate urgency. "I'm all right," he muttered.

He climbed to his feet, remembering then that he was in his stocking feet. He looked for his gun and saw that it had slid, or else been kicked, into the weeds below the porch rail. Stooping he got it. "There's a man dead in there!" the drummer cried. Hunter merely brushed past him, and hurried back up the steps and into the lobby.

Luke Langley's body lay as he had found it, but George Wright had disappeared. Hunter wasted no time wondering about him. He rushed back along the hallway, to the room where he had left his boots under the bed. He thought he would never manage to get them pulled on. Afterward, pausing only to grab up his windbreaker, he made for the street again where he turned toward the river, south of town across the broad canyon bottom, and a good part of a mile distant.

Someone yelled at him but he went grimly by, intent on what he was looking for and didn't want to find. Crossing Third, he bore south past Hodges's store and Moore's saddlery and Gil Haze's saloon. All Prineville seemed to be coming alive around him. Horsemen galloped past, scattering dust. He found he was only part of a straggling tide of movement, pulled in one direction as though by a magnet.

With every moment the sky was more afire with sunrise. Directly ahead, the high southern rim of the canyon palisade shone golden from the morning sun. Hunter had left off running; he had a feeling there was not that much hurry any longer—that it was too far, and much too late for running to do any good. Walking fast instead, each jar of a bootheel stirring sick residues of the clubbing blow that had curdled his wits, he left the last of the town's buildings behind; and presently he became aware of the crowd of people gathering on the river bank, where the road swung to cross on its narrow iron bridge.

He halted finally, with laboring lungs and with pounding head, to stare at the bloody thing that hung from a bridge railing above silent, dawn-tinted water. Bill Farrell's body showed the punishment it had taken. Wreckage of his garments still clung to it; even the bootleather had been ripped open. Wind that swept along the river plucked at the ragged red shirt, caused the body to sway and twist slightly, as the rope creaked. It seemed the only movement in this whole silent tableau.

A man who stood next to Hunter said, in a shocked voice, "My God! He must have been dead even before they strung him up!"

Someone else exclaimed, "What kind of a man would do a thing like that? To put a rope on a man and drag him . . ."

No one offered an answer.

With every moment the crowd was growing, each new arrival falling silent and motionless at sight of the thing that had been done here. Finally a voice spoke. "What the hell! We just going to leave him hang?"

There was a belated movement, then, out onto the bridge, where a couple seized the rope and began the grisly task of hauling the body up by the noose around its grotesquely disjointed neck. Other hands were waiting to lay hold. Just as they lifted Bill Farrell across the bridge railing, the bell on the town schoolhouse began tolling wildly, the sound of it drifting thinly down to them—some idiot was spreading the alarm.

Suddenly Hunter caught a glimpse of George Wright; a fury descended on him and expended itself in the move that sent him shouldering forward, plowing through the trampled weeds, pushing men out of his path until he confronted the deputy and put a hand on him to haul him around. George had a confused and hapless air about him. The skin across his cheeks and temples looked as though it had been stretched tight, and it held a pallor of shock. "I been wondering where you'd got to!" Hunter exclaimed. "Now suppose you tell us about this!"

The deputy shook his head as he mumbled, "I don't know anything."

"The hell you don't! You were there. It's your job to know!"

The other man appeared too dazed to take anger. His stare was fastened on Hunter's cheek, as though fascinated by the seepage of blood from the place that had been laid open in that tumble he took down the hotel steps. He said, in the same dead tone, "Everything went too fast. One minute Bill Farrell and I were sitting there by the stove, talking; Langley was asleep. Then, they were coming through the door in back of me. They were all over me before I had time to think."

By now the crowd had closed around the pair of them, but not before Bob Hunter caught a glimpse of Farrell's body being carried up the bank; he saw the dead face—the protruding eyes, the mark of the rope—and something rose, hot and nauseating, in his own throat. He swallowed hard.

A newcomer had shoved his way forward. It was Jim Blake; the rancher's eyes, and his mouth under the drooping mustache, were grim. "We're waiting for you to tell us, George. We want some names. Who did this?"

"I don't know," George Wright insisted, his voice rising. "I tell you, I didn't see any faces." Something in the way he said it grabbed at Hunter's attention, sending the sudden thought through his mind: Why he's lying! "They jumped me," the deputy continued, "and threw me on the floor and got my gun away from me. I remember hearing a couple of shots—that must have been when they killed Langley. Then Bill Farrell was struggling and yelling, and they were dragging him out."

"And what did you do?" Jim Blake prodded.

"What could I do without a gun? There must have been fifteen or twenty of them! I tried to put up a fight—and something hit me."

Bob Hunter said sharply, "And you're certain, during all that, you never saw anyone to recognize him?"

George Wright looked trapped, harried past endurance. "No! You might understand, if you'd been there!"

That caught Hunter up, cooled him a little as he thought of that nightmare in the street—the confusing moment before someone laid the edge of a fist across the back of his own neck. It was only fair to admit he'd seen nothing sure, no single face he could testify to.

"I *was* there," he said slowly. "The shooting fetched me—and I didn't see much more than you did. But I still don't understand how you could have let yourself get taken by surprise. You were supposed to be on guard!"

George Wright's chest started to swell. Before he could answer, Jim Blake interrupted in an effort to settle roiled tempers. "Look! Let's not forget, George thought his only job was to keep a prisoner. He wasn't looking for anything like this. Me, either. If I had been, I'd never for a minute have gone home to bed."

"That's true," Hunter admitted grudgingly. "I gave out and went to sleep, myself. I never really thought any of that crowd around the hotel would go so far as a lynching."

Somebody said, "What crowd? Who were they, Hunter?"

He hesitated, then shook his head. "I won't name names. I don't see any of them here. But they know who they were; so

28

does George Wright. If I was the law, I think I'd start by letting a few people try to say where they were about five o'clock this morning!"

He turned away, fed up with useless talk, his head throbbing miserably. And Jim Blake was there to drop a hand upon his shoulder and say, in a sympathetic voice, "I know how you're feeling. I feel the same way—a little sick at the stomach. Come on along to the house and let's put something on that cut. You're bleeding like a stuck pig!"

CHAPTER III

The split in Hunter's cheek was painful but in no way dangerous, not bad enough to need stitching; though Jim Blake told him it might leave a scar. In the kitchen, he sat at the table and submitted while Blake cleaned it thoroughly and dabbed it with peroxide, which smarted like hell, and a square of court plaster.

About this time the rancher's wife, an attractive woman beginning to show the signs of pregnancy, came in removing a shawl from over her head. She was sober-eyed and alarmed over the lynchings. "I've been out gossiping with the neighbors," she told them. "I've never seen people so worked up. Only thing anybody can talk about is, who could have done it? Most everyone acts as though he thinks he knows but ain't saying. And poor Sarah Meeks . . ."

"What about her?" Blake demanded quickly.

"She's near out of her mind with worrying. Len was away all night, got in a little while ago drunk and hungover—and when she tried to ask questions he stomped out again without saying where he'd been, or what he was doing. She'd almost rather she knew he was with that horrible woman over on Third Street, than what she's afraid of."

The men exchanged a meaningful glance. Len Meeks, who worked in Stewart & Pett's grist mill on the river, had been part of the crowd at the stable and, later, in front of the hotel.

Hunter borrowed Blake's razor and gingerly scraped off a

two-day stubble of beard. Afterward, over a breakfast Mrs. Blake put together, the two men sat at table and soberly discussed matters. Bob Hunter had fairly well recovered by now from the sick ache inside his skull, though it left him with a neck so stiff and sore he hated to turn his head. He drank down two cups of coffee, black, and with that his head felt clearer.

But a mood of severe depression had settled on him; the picture of Luke Langley's body—and of Bill Farrell hanging, torn and bleeding—refused to leave. "Jim, how could men do a thing like that?"

Stolidly working at his steak and biscuits, Jim Blake said, "Who knows what a bunch of drunks will take onto themselves?"

"Then you figure they were drunk?" Hunter remembered the reek of whiskey on the man who had knocked him down on the steps of the Jackson House. "You think that's the explanation?"

"What else makes sense? Hell, nobody had enough reason to care about a killing out on Willow Creek. They were just letting off steam. It's been a long winter; a man gets restless."

"Restless!" the other echoed. "Oh, my God!"

"You noticed they waited out most of the night before they did the job," Blake continued, sawing at a tough piece of steak. "It took them that long to work up to it. The only question I can't answer: Why'd they shoot one man and then hang the other? That doesn't make sense."

"Maybe it does. Langley got it while he was asleep; Farrell, though, put up a fight and that made them mad. You aren't forgetting what went on, earlier, between him and Jase Evans. . . ."

Blake slowly lifted his head. "Evans! Are you laying this to—?"

"Jase is a violent man," Bob Hunter continued stubbornly. "He tried to pick a row with me and my brother Chris, but we wouldn't oblige him. I figure he found another victim to take it out on."

Jim Blake was frowning. "This is pretty strong talk."

"I don't expect you to repeat it. But I got a look at the one who dragged Bill off to his death. Maybe it wasn't much of a look, and I admit the light was bad; maybe I don't really know anything I'd be able to swear to in court. But you'll have to prove to me there's another man, in this stretch of Oregon, who shapes up that big in a saddle!"

Before he spoke again Jim Blake gave himself time by getting up and going to the stove for the coffee pot, with which he

30

refilled both their cups, and then set it back on the fire to heat. He took his seat again, and Hunter waited while he spooned sugar from the bowl.

"Let me say one thing," he remarked finally, laying his spoon down again. "This is a new country—a rough one. You've knocked around some; I'm sure I'm not telling you anything you don't know, when I say that lynchings have happened plenty of times before, other places, and they're bound to happen again. Here, the trouble goes back to one thing: We live in a county that's gotten too damned unwieldy, now that Oregon's filling up. And wherever men start thinking the law won't give them what they need, you can look for them to do something about it themselves."

Slowly, Hunter ran a palm across the back of his neck and winced as it touched a tender spot there. His eyes brooding, he nodded.

"Maybe you're right. Could be it was just being there, and seeing it, that makes the difference. But—I don't know!" He swung to his feet and paced to a window that gave him a view of backyards and rooftops, of clouds sweeping above the canyon rimrock. He put a hand against the edge of the windowframe, looking out at these familiar things but really seeing only his own thoughts.

"The hell of it is, Jim, I'm only a little less guilty than the men who actually killed them. I was the one talked Langley into giving himself up. And afterwards, at the hotel, if I'd just followed my hunch and stayed awake . . .

"I got a feeling about this," he went on. "Maybe there's times when vigilante rule can be justified. Maybe that mob can even bring themselves to excuse what they did to Langley. But, in killing Bill Farrell they hanged an innocent man. That was murder! They know it, and so does everybody else." He turned to face the other. "Jim, there's no use in kidding ourselves. If we stand by and let this end here, then you—me—this whole town's guilty.

"A town can fester and rot on that kind of guilt. You know it as well as I do!"

Jim Blake, frowning, couldn't seem to find an answer.

Before he could leave that morning there was someone he wanted to see, and Bob Hunter walked over to Main Street alone. He found exactly what he had expected. The normal life of the village had been broken short, and no one seemed to know how to pick up the pieces. He saw townspeople gathered

31

on street corners and in doorways, heard excited voices tumbling out of business houses and saloons. Every kid in town appeared to be playing hooky, and nobody seemed to notice.

He wondered what had been done with the bodies, and if it had occurred to anyone to see about notifying the survivors— Langley's brother, and his widow and the three children waiting out at the ranch on Willow Creek. He doubted that George Wright would have thought of it, and no one else would feel any responsibility. As a neighbor, he supposed the job was going to end up falling to him.

The last thing he wanted just now was to get himself involved in any of the futile gossiping, and he stayed deliberately aloof from it as he walked through the streets where cloud shadow moved, shutter fashion, and the mild spring morning was laced by a tang of woodsmoke from all the village chimneys.

When he turned the knob of Walter Allen's brick-fronted mercantile, a freak of wind seized the door and tried to wrench it out of his grasp; he stepped inside, causing a bell to tinkle on its spring, and careful not to release the knob until he heard the latch click. Apparently the store had just opened for the day; in spite of a fire in the big space heater, the room with its ceiling of pressed tin and its high banks of shelves and tall, narrow windows was still cold.

It was empty at the moment, but he heard voices behind the curtain that draped the partition doorway at the rear. He started toward this, past counters and bins of hardware and general merchandise, and the grilled window where Walter Allen, as postmaster, handed out the mail that came to Prineville on the daily stage. The curtain was pushed aside now and the storekeeper emerged, ushering George Wright ahead of him.

He laid a hand in friendly fashion on the deputy's shoulder and he was saying, "If I see your brother I'll be sure and tell him you were looking for him." He noticed Hunter then, and became stiffly formal as he added, "Good morning, Robert."

"Morning, Walt."

The difference of manner didn't surprise Hunter or bother him too much; it was no secret that Walter Allen, knowing they both were interested in his daughter, happened to favor George Wright who was, after all, a townsman like himself. Allen probably saw in George an ambition he thought lacking in his rival; or, perhaps, he preferred a lawyer for a son-in-law, to a knockabout rancher who showed little prospect, so far, of getting rich from the spread he shared with his brother out on Willow Creek.

Allen himself was a good businessman, and a successful one. His enterprise had paid off well enough that he had been able to put up the first solid brick building in Prineville to house it; recently he had been elected mayor. He was a man given somewhat to fussiness and anxiety. His color was bad and his graying mustache tended to have a ragged look as though from being chewed at.

"I want you to keep me fully informed," the storekeeper went on, turning again to George Wright. "This has been a terrible business—simply terrible! But let's hope, now, things quiet down so that it can blow over."

George seemed preoccupied; he nodded shortly. "Let's hope so." And Bob Hunter felt his temper slipping.

He heard himself saying, too loudly, "Do you really call this something that should be let blow over?"

The storekeeper stiffened and shot him a look through silver-rimmed glasses. "Of course not! As the mayor of this town, I share a responsibility with George. We both deplore the thing that happened last night, and naturally we mean to get to the bottom of it."

George Wright's sallow cheeks were touched with color. "I'll give you to understand once and for all, Hunter: I know my job—even though you apparently think I don't!"

Coldly, Hunter said, "You'll never have a better chance to prove one way or the other."

"Why, damn you—!"

George Wright's fists tightened, and he actually took a step toward Hunter—a foolish move, if he really thought of making a fight of it, because he was no match for the rancher even if they stood almost of a height.

There was a cry of alarm from the girl who had appeared, just then, in the curtained doorway. But even as Hunter found himself wondering what he would do if the man took a swing at him, Walter Allen was shouldering between. "Here—here!" the storekeeper cried nervously. "This has got to stop!"

George Wright stood glaring, the angry breathing swelling his narrow chest. It was left for Hunter to say gruffly, "You're right, Walt. I'm sorry. I don't want to be the cause of making anyone's job harder than it is."

Allen wagged his head in obvious relief. "Thank you, Robert," he said crisply. "We're all of us keyed up this morning; but it can't do any good if we start losing our tempers."

The deputy said with poor grace, "All I know is, I've had a good plenty of his heckling. I won't put up with much more of

33

it!" George turned to the girl then, abruptly changing the subject. "Tell your mother thanks for asking me tonight, Jen."

She nodded, almost absently; her troubled glance was past his shoulder, on Hunter's face. She said automatically, "We eat at six. You know we're always glad to have you."

"I'll make it if I can." He turned abruptly away, brushing past Hunter with the merest flick of a glance. Walter Allen went with him as far as the door, leaving Hunter and the girl alone. She looked after her father, then caught at Hunter's hand and, turning, led him back through the partition opening.

He ducked under the curtain and followed her into a tiny cubbyhole of a room that served for an office. It contained filing cabinets and a cluttered rolltop desk and a few other odd pieces of furniture. A crackling fire in the stove pushed out welcome warmth. In one corner was the high stool and the bookkeeper's desk where Jennifer Allen worked to keep her father's business records in order. "Bob!" she said suddenly, facing him. "You've been hurt. I didn't know."

"You mean, this?" He touched his cheek. "It's nothing to fret about. I—stumbled and laid it open. Jim Blake fixed it up for me."

Plainly the explanation didn't satisfy her.

She was normally a merry person, rather small of stature, with dark eyes and shoulder-length brown curls and a heart-shaped face that showed no great resemblance to her father's blunt and jowly features. Just now her brow was puckered with concern, her ripe underlip thrust slightly forward as she frowned up at him. Despite his many distracting concerns, he felt the expression made her look about the most delectable creature on earth.

"Tell me what happened last night," she said. "Were you really there? Right in the midst of it?"

"I was there—not that it makes me a hero or anything. I tried to stop it, but I just didn't do any good."

"But, tell me, who in this town could have done such things? People just aren't like that. Not Prineville people!"

His mouth was grim. "That's what I would have said. . . ."

They drew quickly apart as Walter Allen joined them, shouldering the doorway curtain aside. He was worried and businesslike as he motioned Hunter toward a sagging, black leather armchair near the stove. "Sit down, Robert. I want to know everything you can tell me about this miserable business—every single thing you saw or heard. I want it all." He himself dropped into the barrel chair that he pulled away from

34

the desk and leaned attentively forward, ready to listen, his pale, broad hands resting on plump knees.

Hunter was reluctant, actually, to go through it all again. But Walter Allen had an official interest and a right to know what he could tell. Crossing his legs to hang his hat on a boottoe, he gave the story. Beginning with the finding of Luke Langley at his place on Willow Creek, he laid very special emphasis on what Langley himself had had to say about the double killing that started the whole thing. The older man heard him out with frowning attention, gnawing at an end of his mustache and casting frequent looks at his daughter who perched primly on the tall bookkeeper's stool, intently listening.

When Hunter had finished, there was silence for a moment except for the roar and crackle of a pine stick burning in the stove. Walter Allen stirred himself, and ran a palm slowly down across his face. He looked like a very troubled man.

"I hope this jibes with what George told you," Hunter said. "I don't really want to call him a liar, if he claims he never saw their faces. I couldn't take an oath to what I saw, either, out there on that street! It was the first dim light, and I hadn't had much more than a glimpse of what was going on when the ceiling landed on me." He put a hand to the back of his neck, gingerly.

Jen said, "But you think it was Jase Evans on the horse . . ."

"He was as big as Evans. That's all I know, and it's all I'm going to say."

Walter Allen frowned at him, fingers drumming silently on his knees. He said, "One thing you left out. Just who were the men you saw earlier? The ones you say made threats against Luke Langley?"

Hunter hesitated, unwilling to speak. "Why don't you ask George Wright that? He saw them, and heard them."

"Just now, I'm asking you."

He took a long breath, glancing at Jen. "All right . . . Besides Evans, Gus Weckler did the loudest talking. But there were others. Hack Gorham, for one—" He broke off, suddenly, as he reached back and felt his neck again. "You know, come to think of it, whoever it was dropped me must have had an arm like a blacksmith. Of course, that doesn't prove it was Hack. . . ."

"No," Allen agreed crisply. "It doesn't. . . . Who else? Go on!"

Reluctantly, he named half a dozen more. "Those are all I can remember."

35

The eyes behind the polished lenses probed his. "You're sure?"

For an instant he held back. He was thinking of Eddie Wright. The boy had been there, at the start, and though George had ordered him home, Hunter had no proof of his going. If he'd taken any part in what happened, that might go a long way to explain the fact—if it *was* a fact—that George was telling less than the whole truth now.

Still, he had nothing but vague suspicions, and he'd already let them build antagonism enough between George Wright and himself. He shook his head and said firmly, "No, that's all. And even though they were around when we brought Langley in, I don't suppose that necessarily means these were the ones that lynched him."

"I'm glad you see that," Allen said quickly.

"But I still say," he went on, unyielding on this point, "it's the best place to start looking! After all—where else is there to start?"

Walter Allen's chair creaked faintly under him. His lips were compressed and his face was somber as he rose to frown down at the younger man. "Look," he said at last. "Will you do me a favor? Go home!" He nodded at Hunter's quick frown. "That's what I'm saying, Robert. Go on out to that ranch of yours, and give George and me a chance to investigate. It's our job, you know—and it's not an easy one."

"I never claimed it was."

"Your behavior is making it no easier! One of these days the legislature's got to quit stalling on this business of creating new counties. But until they do—until we've got our own court, and our own county officer—Prineville has to make out the best way it can."

Bob Hunter came to his feet. "If that means lynch law and murder," he snapped, "it's not good enough!" He saw real anger harden the older man's face then. Walter Allen's lips set tight. He was about to make some answer when the street door opened and closed, and the bell leaped and jangled on its spring. Allen made an irritated gesture. With a last meaningful look to pin his message home, he turned away and went out through the curtain to attend to his customer.

Hunter watched him go and afterward, taking a deep breath, turned back to the girl. "Now," he said, dispiritedly, "I've got him mad at me!" He shook his head. "I suppose he's right. And, yet—"

Quickly, Jennifer slipped down from the stool and came to

36

him. She laid a hand on his sleeve. "Bob, whatever you do you mustn't let anyone make you lose faith in what you believe. Not even my father!" She hesitated. "Still, I hope you'll do what he says, but for an entirely different reason."

He frowned. "What do you mean?"

She blurted it out: "I don't want anything to happen to you. I couldn't bear it!" She reached up, touched the court plaster covering his hurt cheek. Her eyes misted. "Oh, darling!" She was in his arms suddenly. She lifted her mouth and he kissed her, and then she had wound her arms about his waist, inside his jacket, and put her cheek against his shirt; she held him tight. He felt her trembling.

"Hey! Why, honey—what is it? What's wrong?"

Her answer came, a little muffled. "I'm sorry. I can't help it! When I think of what could have happened, with you facing that lynch mob . . ."

He stroked her shoulder gently, within the trim shirtwaist. "Don't worry. I can generally take care of myself." He added, "Look! Supposing your father comes back and catches us like this!"

She shook her head against his shirtfront; her curls brushed his cheek. "If Papa doesn't know how I feel about you, he had just as well be finding out!"

Hunter reached behind him, took both her hands and gently freed himself. He stood looking down into her troubled eyes, her hands still in his. He smiled a little. "I think he has some sort of an idea, all right. And I think he'd rather it was George."

"Now, you're not jealous, are you?" Her eyes widened, still bright with unshed tears. "Just because my folks insist I be polite to him, and let them invite him to the house for supper? *You* know whose girl I really am!"

"I reckon." He kissed her again. "And I'm going to do what your father asked me. There's a pile of work waiting, and Chris home alone to do it. So, I'm heading out there. I've said my say; now maybe it will be easier on your father, and on George Wright, if I get out of the way for awhile."

"But you'll be in town again soon, won't you?"

Bob Hunter grinned. "It would take more than your father, or George, or even a lynch mob to keep me away from here for very long!" He gave her shoulder a squeeze, then picked his hat from the chair seat where he had laid it and went out through the curtain. Walter Allen, glancing up from the package he was wrapping for a woman customer, paused to frown and watch him pass through the building and out the street door.

37

As the door closed behind him, Walter Allen shot a glance toward the partition and saw his daughter there, holding the curtain back, looking after Hunter. He read the expression on her face; his mouth tightened, and the string snapped with a deft move of his soft hands.

CHAPTER IV

Upon leaving Allen's, George Wright continued his searching up and down the length of Main Street, masking a growing storm of panic behind an unapproachable manner. It was at almost the last place he could have asked, that he finally got the word. Gil Haze, polishing an expanse of bar that was already spotless, gave it to him. "Eddie? Why, yeah—he was in here, with some other fellers. You know I never sell your brother nothing, George; but I can't very well stop him from coming in. And if somebody else calls for a bottle, and then passes around the drinks—well, it's a free country. . . ."

"All right. I understand," the other cut him off. "You said he was here. How long ago?"

"Not more than an hour; maybe less than that. Jase Evans came and got him. Seems to me I heard Jase tell him the Major wanted to see them both."

"The Major? You mean, at his house?"

"That's what I thought he said," Gil Haze told him. It was one possibility George hadn't thought of. He nodded his thanks and turned and walked rapidly out of there, brushing past those who would have interrupted him with their idle and impertinent questions about the affair last night.

The town residence that Calvin Tarback maintained, a couple of blocks off Main Street, was one of the largest in Prineville—two stories, built of milled lumber, painted white and seemingly all porches and railinged balustrades and scrollwork under the eaves; the window of the big front door pictured an antlered stag, done in colored glass.

When George Wright tramped the wide steps and twisted the bell knob, the door was opened to him presently by Gus

Weckler. The feed store owner, who always reminded him somewhat unpleasantly of a ferret, blinked and sucked in his cheeks in startled surprise. "This is a private meeting!" he cried, as he saw the deputy looking past him, and tried too late to shut him out. But George Wright had already caught a glimpse of his brother Eddie, stumbling quickly up out of a chair. He elbowed Gus Weckler from his path.

He scarcely saw any of the others who filled the Major's living room. He was aware only of his brother's face; and at the look of him, Eddie blanched and drew back, the legs of the chair scraping on the carpet. The boy shook his head. He blurted quickly, his voice a little wild, "I—I had nothing to do with it. . . ."

"You'd try to tell me that?" George said between his teeth, and hit him—a backhanded blow across the face. Staggered, the youngster tremblingly lifted a hand toward a cheek that had gone ashen. "Damn it!" his brother cried. "I *saw* you! You were dancing around that hotel lobby, yelling like an Indian!"

The boy's lips worked but no sound came from them. And then, amid the tense quiet, George Wright caught an unmistakable sound of metal brushing against cloth.

He turned, hastily, to see Jase Evans standing before the fireplace where a small blaze of pine and juniper logs crackled brightly. In the man's big hand was the revolver he had dug out of a pocket of his unbuttoned windbreaker. George stared at it as Evans said, in a voice heavy with warning, "You better start forgetting whatever you think you saw." The eyes glaring at him over the faint gleam of the gunbarrel were bloodshot and ugly. "Or you'll get worse than a clout on the skull!"

George Wright cursed his own terror, as his chest wall seemed to collapse inward upon his lungs and hamper his breathing. But he forced his look to meet the other's and his voice was steady as he said, "Remember, you're talking to the law."

The big man's mouth shaped into an ugly sneer. "You and that deputy's badge! Why, you mealy-mouthed sonofabitch! Maybe you impress some folks, but not me. It wouldn't take anything at all to give me an excuse to smash you!"

"No one's going to smash anyone," Calvin Tarback said from the doorway.

He had a decanter in one hand, empty glasses in the other. He said, "Put the gun away, Jase." Evans scowled but, without an argument, shoved the weapon again into his pocket as the Major turned to George Wright and told him, "I'm glad to see you. This will give us a chance to get some matters straightened out."

Weckler muttered, with a hostile look at the deputy, "I suppose he's come here thinking to arrest the lot of us!"

"He'll arrest nobody," the Major answered quietly. "He knows there's no way he dares touch any person in this room, without hurting someone he can't afford to." And Tarback's pale stare touched Eddie Wright, meaningfully, afterward swinging back to George as though inviting contradiction. The latter swallowed in a dry throat, but said nothing.

Seeing defeat mirrored in his eyes, the Major's whole manner changed; he became all at once the genial host. "Have a seat, George. And a drink." He had set the glasses on the sideboard; he filled one and the deputy accepted it with a trembling hand. Suddenly he knew whiskey was what he needed, and he drained it off and closed his eyes a moment, waiting for the jolt.

"Who else?" Tarback said, and calmly set about refilling glasses and china teacups. George Wright watched him, from a depth of trapped and sullen depression.

The room was big, and yet it was nearly filled by the heavy furniture of the period, brought by wagon freight all the way across the mountains from Portland. The charges must have been steep, indeed, on such items as the huge center table, the chesterfield and the massive wing chairs and the big breakfront that stood against the wall opposite the stone fireplace; but Calvin Tarback could have well afforded them.

Following the Major with his eyes as Tarback passed among his guests, George Wright considered the other people in this room. There were ten, all of them men he knew well—and every face, one that he had seen in the nightmare of the hotel lobby, or glimpsed in the dust and dawn-streaked street outside.

How did you explain a thing like this?

Jase Evans, of course, he knew for a bully, hard and brutal. Gus Weckler, too, was one who had a definite mean streak—an officious man, a little man, who might have been expected to hang at the edges of violence and gleefully egg others on. Then there was Hack Gorham, seated awkwardly on one end of the Major's sofa, with a whiskey glass engulfed in one broad hand, narrow figure made grotesque by the weight of massive blacksmith's shoulders.

Gorham was all dull wit and slow reactions—one would almost have thought, too phlegmatic and docile for a part in a lynching. Probably he had liquored with the crowd, had his sluggish instincts roused and found himself swept along, lacking the will to do otherwise. On the other hand, George Wright had seen the look on his stolid features as the blacksmith stood over Langley's bleeding body . . .

George saw Tom Ridges, a sullen and pugnacious sort who barely made ends meet on a quarter section of homestead ranch up on the sage flats south and west of Crooked River near Powell Butte; he saw a townsman, a fellow named Len Meeks who, he thought, did day labor at Stewart & Pett's flour mill. And more, of different types, but all bearing this one terrible thing in common now. Observing them coldly, George Wright saw in each the marks of the sleepless night, of the liquor that had carried them through, of the spent emotions that left them drained and empty. Some appeared palely remorseful, some hungover and defiant, some merely a little sick. . . .

The Major turned to Eddie with glass and decanter ready to pour. "Not for the kid!" George said sharply. Tarback looked at him, and at the boy; he nodded, turned away. As he stoppered the decanter and set it aside, color leaped into Eddie's thin cheeks. And a sneering laugh broke from Jase Evans.

"Major's right," he said pleasantly, teetering on his heels before the fire. "Big brother's too busy being nursemaid to let anything hurt the kid. So, you can bet the law ain't going to hurt any of the rest of us, either!"

George could see the same thought begin working at the rest of them—or else it was the whiskey had served to cut through the air of gloom that hung over these men. He watched looks and nods of relief pass from one to another; for some reason this set him to trembling so with fury that he had to rest a hand on the table top.

"Listen to me! Even if I didn't happen to see which of you it was put the bullet into Luke Langley, that makes no real difference. You were all there, you're all equally guilty—every damn one of you. You should be real proud, this morning! Maybe that's why you're all sitting here, hiding from the talk you know is beginning to go around. Ashamed and afraid to show your faces to the town—even to your own families!"

This had some effect. One or two appeared a little less sure of themselves, suddenly; while Len Meeks actually broke gaze and cut his glance aside, as though something George said had really struck home.

"Don't think for a minute," George Wright persisted, "that this town doesn't already have a pretty good idea just who you are—a secret like that doesn't keep. What I'm wondering is, will your sleep ever be bothered? Will you ever wake up seeing

41

Langley lying dead in his own blood—or Bill Farrell, the way he begged for mercy as you dragged him out into the street? I know I'll go to my grave remembering the way he cried, *'Please—please! I got a little boy . . . !'* "

He broke off, suddenly, reaching for breath. He had swung about and was looking directly at the guilty horror in his brother's face.

Then Tom Ridges sat forward, rope-burned fingers clasping denimed knees. "Damn it," he said hoarsely, "we done what we had to. . . ."

"Exactly!" said Calvin Tarback.

All their eyes swung to the Major. In the center of the room he turned slowly, with that peculiar and stiff-necked manner, letting his stare touch each face in turn while the fire crackled lightly, and a spark snapped out in a bright arc to die upon the hearthstone.

"That, I'm afraid," Tarback said smoothly, "is the issue! You all know I'm a peaceable man, one who hates any sort of violence. I was ready to leave punishment of those murderers to the court, even though I realized how little chance we had of seeing justice done. Turned loose by some jury at The Dalles, they would have come back here, bolder than ever, and ready to take up where they left off!

"But I'm glad to say there were some that knew an example had to be made. Perhaps what you've done will be enough to stem the lawlessness in this country—perhaps not. But I'd say all Prineville owes you a vote of gratitude."

George Wright had been listening, in growing amazement. One part of his brain could admire the man's ability to handle words and the emotions of his hearers; but at the same time he found himself mentally protesting: What is this talk of lawlessness? Surely, if there was anything out of the ordinary going on, I would know about it. After all, it's my job . . .

"Now wait a minute!" he exclaimed.

It brought all their eyes back to him, but he found himself unable to continue. Suddenly, meeting his brother's guilty stare, it struck home just how effectively he had been trapped and his hands tied. A sick load of helpless shame settled on him.

The Major said gently, "You were going to say something, George?"

With an effort he filled his lungs, pulling back his shoulders. His words tasted as heavy as lead on his tongue. "Whatever you want to call the thing that happened last night," he said, looking directly at Tarback, "the real question is going to be what the sheriff decides to call it. He's going to have to know. Don't forget, it will be up to me to make a full report."

There was a stir. The Major frowned, but he was nodding. "A good thing you mentioned this," he said. "You're perfectly right. The sheriff has got to be made to see the facts in the right light. We're fortunate that you're the man who's in a position to do it."

George Wright said coldly, "Any suggestions?"

"I have one or two. If you'd like, the two of us can sit down together and discuss this report of yours. In fact, I'd suggest that we do it right now."

The deputy considered, and then he shrugged. "If you say . . ."

Suddenly the meeting, if that was what it was, seemed to be over. The men were finishing their drinks and getting to their feet, stirring about to collect hats and top coats they had laid aside; the Major lifted his voice in a final word to them all. "Before you go," he said, "look around you. Take a good, long look. Remember—every face you see here belongs to a man who helped make sure a pair of murderers didn't escape what they had coming. Unfortunately, a thing done once sometimes has to be done again."

Jase Evans said, grinning, "Now you're talking *my* language! Looks to me like, next time, we might have to go after Jim Blake and them Hunters." He seemed wholly unrepentant and unabashed at having dragged an innocent man to a bloody finish at the end of his tie rope.

The Major silenced him with a stern look. "All I'm saying is, if things should come to the point where some kind of an organization is needed—the nucleus is here. Each of you keep in mind who you are—who you can count on. That's all. . . ."

He finished with a curt nod and, turning, placed a hand on George Wright's shoulder, to press him toward a chair at the big center table. George, however, pulled away and threw a word toward the group that was already moving through the door someone had opened. "Kid!"

His brother Eddie, among the others, paused to look at him sullenly. Heads turned, bodies went motionless. "Where are you off to?" George demanded sharply.

The youngster shuffled his boots. "I dunno," he said, scowling. "With them."

Jase Evans was eyeing the deputy, wearing a grin of open mockery. George Wright's thin mouth drew out long and a muscle leaped beneath the tight-drawn flesh of a sallow cheek.

He felt suddenly tired, unable to cope with the massive resistance he had been encountering. He took a breath and told Eddie, "I won't go chasing over town a second time looking for you. When I'm through here I want to find you without any trouble. You understand?"

Eddie looked at him, and then to the other men for reassurance. He shrugged narrow shoulders. "Why not?" he said gruffly, and shoved his way through the door. George let him go that time; a moment later the last man was out and the door closed behind them. Silence descended, broken by the snap and crackle of the fire.

George Wright moved over to the table, pulled back the chair his brother had left and dropped slackly into it. He glanced up briefly to find Tarback with the whiskey decanter ready to refill the glass he had been drinking from; he shook his head, covered the glass with his hand. Tarback stoppered the bottle and replaced it on the sideboard. Taking a cigar from his waistcoat pocket, he bit off the end, walked over to the fireplace and spat into the flames. He leaned and picked a burning stick from the coals, got the cigar to burning. Afterward he returned to the table and let himself into a seat facing George Wright. Without looking up, George thought he could all but feel the steel-gray eyes studying him—picking him apart, calmly reassembling him again.

The Major said suddenly, "You know, this is all very unfortunate. I have a great deal of respect for you, George. You seem like an ambitious young fellow, with considerable ability. Just now, you're over a barrel, and I don't blame you if you don't like it. You don't like having your brother used as a lever against you."

"That damn fool kid!" George said bitterly. "He let himself get mixed up in this horrible business, and I should let him take the consequences. But I can't!"

"You're that fond of the boy?"

He shrugged. "Let's say I feel responsible for him. I came over here from Portland because it looked as though this would be a good place for a lawyer to get a start, as the country builds up. The folks couldn't keep Eddie home; he tagged after me. All his life he's been tagging after me. Yet he'd never do a damn thing I told him!"

Tarback carefully knocked a bit of ash from the end of his cigar against the rim of an empty glass. It occurred to George Wright that the man was letting him do the talking, letting him reveal himself without offering any slightest grain of information in return.

"What I don't understand," he blurted, "is you getting yourself so deep into this. *You* weren't involved in that horror last night—or if you were, at least I never saw you. The men who were murdered out on Willow Creek meant nothing to you. I can't figure any reason why you're trying to save the drunks who lynched their murderer—let alone, an innocent man who hadn't anything to do with it at all!"

He broke off. The pale eyes held on his own, without any flicker of emotion. "We have a statement to prepare," Tarback said finally, the words leaving his lips on a blue stream of tobacco smoke. "I think you'll find pen and paper there in that drawer, in front of you."

George Wright could not believe for a moment that his questions were to be so bluntly shoved aside; but he saw then that he was going to get no answer from this strange man. Well, he could be stubborn, himself. He made no move toward the table drawer. Instead he folded his hands deliberately and leaned forward. "Suppose we talk about it a little, first. What are you suggesting I could put in a report, beyond the plain facts?"

"I've always found it's best," the Major said coolly, "to let the facts speak for themselves. Certainly you don't want to give the sheriff any reason to suspect you're telling him more than is strictly true. Like any good legal brief, the report should be concise, detailed—from the finding of the bodies, right up to the moment when the prisoners were taken out of your hands by this masked group of armed men. . . ."

The deputy's head jerked slightly. *"Masked?"*

"Why, of course." Tarback spread his hands. "How else do you expect to keep the sheriff from asking how it was you never saw anyone you could identify? You must know, people here in town have already been raising the question. To spare yourself, I think you'll be smart to remember, suddenly, that every man you saw in the confusion had a cloth tied across his face." He nodded meaningly. "Think it over."

George Wright considered the thought. He had to admit the sense of it; he asked heavily, "What else?"

"Once you've made it clear there's no real chance of ever knowing who the lynchers were, you've next got to convince your chief what they did was simple justice, and that the best thing is to let the whole matter drop. After all, these were

45

murderers, and almost certainly involved in horse and cattle stealing on a large scale. . . ."

George Wright straightened. He laid his hands, palm down, on the table in front of him. He drew a breath. "You keep saying this as though you actually believed it. You know it's not true!"

"For our purpose, it is," the Major answered. He tilted his head a little, gray eyes studying the deputy. "You're interested in politics; surely you know, by now, it's always easier to out-talk an opponent than debate facts with him. Repeat a lie often enough and loud enough, and it might as well be true. Farrell and Langley are dead," he pointed out as the other continued to stare at him. "You can't hurt them with a lie—but, you just may be able to save your brother!"

The sound of the Major's voice died; George Wright was left with the look of a man who had had a distasteful but convincing revelation. And then, as he opened his mouth to answer, his eye was drawn to the hall doorway. Catching the direction of his glance, Tarback turned stiffly in his chair and scowled, as he saw the woman.

Nothing had announced her; she might have been standing there for almost any length of time—a slight, tall figure, head erect, one hand lifted against the edge of the jamb. Suddenly remembering his manners, George blundered to his feet. "Mrs. Tarback . . ."

She still did not move, though her eyes touched him gravely. She would be some years older than he, who was not quite thirty; there was beauty in her, but something had tampered with it. You had the feeling a brightness must have vanished from the pale hair she wore in a coil about her neat, patrician head. Her cheeks held no bloom or luster. Her figure was good, but she seemed indifferent to the fact; her dark dress, with its wrist-length sleeves and high collar, did nothing to set it off.

Ada Tarback was something of a riddle to the people of Prineville. In the three years she and the Major had been here, she had held herself aloof from the life of the village; one seldom even saw her.

Her husband rose more slowly than the other man. His voice held displeasure. "Did you want something?"

"If I'm not interrupting . . ."

"I'm very much afraid you are," the Major answered, in a tone so lacking in civility that George Wright felt compelled to contradict him.

He said hastily, "Not at all—I was just about to go." Turning

46

to the Major he added, with curt finality, "I'll think over everything we've said. It's too late now to make the morning stage with this report. That gives me tonight to get it written and on its way. I'll be careful in what I write."

The gray eyes considered him; Tarback nodded. "I'm sure you will."

Taking up his hat, George spoke again to the woman who heard him without any show of interest or attention. After that he walked to the door, and Major Tarback followed to open it for him. The March sun was warmer, with the nearing of midday; the wind still moved along the palisade escarpments, hurrying the broken clouds across the sky, but down here on the broad floor of the canyon the air was still. After the deputy had turned from sight down the slight hill, toward Main and the heart of the village, Tarback stood a moment contemplating the town with a thoughtful narrowness to his eyes, and the cigar clamped between his heavy jaws.

He turned suddenly, as he heard the stopper chime faintly against the neck of the whiskey decanter, in the room behind him.

The door went shut to a thrust of his heel and he strode quickly across the room, reaching the sideboard as his wife tilted the decanter to pour. When he moved to take it from her, she resisted for a moment, while their eyes met. Under the pressure of his pale stare, her own broke away, and she let him take the whiskey from her. Tarback replaced the stopper, put the decanter away behind a door of the cabinet, which he locked with a key from his pocket. The woman stood with arms at her sides, her head a little fallen; all the resistance and the momentary aliveness had slipped away from her.

The Major said coldly, "You've been told often enough that I will not have you drinking! You know what always happens."

Ada Tarback made an answer; her words were muffled and indistinct.

"Yes?" he prodded. "What was that?" When she didn't repeat it his face hardened. He brought a hand up under her chin, forced her head up sharply and around. "Look at me!" he snapped.

She did, for a long moment. Then a small flare of defiance sparked her eyes. She pulled her head away, giving him a single hating look before she jerked from him and moved to the big center table. There she laid her hands upon the back of one of the stiff chairs; the hands trembled a little.

The Major watched from beneath lowered brows as she

stared about her at the room that had been nearly filled with men a moment ago. The evidences were there, in the disarrangement of the furniture, the empty glasses, the smell of tobacco smoke, the dirt that had been tracked in and ground into the carpet. Ada Tarback looked upon the wreckage and said, in a voice empty of emotion, "You were right in your element, weren't you?"

The cigar rolled between his lips; his pale stare narrowed. "I'll ask you to explain that! You certainly aren't accusing me of having anything to do with those killings last night?"

"I know you hadn't. But now the thing is done, I also know you wouldn't be above using it to your own advantage." She turned quickly, facing him. "I heard everything. I could just see those scared fools sitting here drinking your whiskey—letting you put on your show of saving them from the results of their own stupid violence!"

Coldly he said, "When friends of mine get themselves in trouble, naturally I'll do what I can to help."

"What do you know about friends! They're nothing but an excuse; all that counts is this—this *need* you seem to have, for playing God. Never mind what it does to other people's lives!"

Tarback had stood listening, his eyes pinned on her, and making no move except that one hand went slowly to his mouth and plucked the cigar away. His wife's pale cheeks were touched with a faint flush of color, now; her breast lifted to a long indrawn breath and her hand tightened on the chairback, until the knuckles showed white.

Suddenly she was speaking again, with feeling that had plainly been bottled up too long. "When we first came here, I actually hoped that leaving a man dead by your own hand, over in the Valley, would have shocked you into some sense of right and wrong. Things have gone well for you in this Eastern Oregon. You've made money; you're respected. I don't understand why you can't be satisfied. But, you'll never change—I see that now. After nine years, a woman should begin to know something about the man she married."

A savage gesture flung the cigar into the fireplace. Three solid strides brought the Major to a stand before his wife. There was a fierce yellow gleam behind the flat gray surfaces of his eyes, but his voice was quiet enough as he said, "Go on! This should be interesting. Just what is it you know about me?"

"I know by now it's power you want," she answered, not flinching. "When that young man—that deputy sheriff—sat in this very chair and asked, point blank, why you're interfering in

48

a horrible thing that's none of your concern, you wouldn't answer; but I could have told him. And the men who came to you for help, admitting the thing all the rest of this town is only guessing at . . . I don't doubt you've already decided how you mean to use them. I only wish I knew of a way to warn—"

"You bitch!"

Next moment his hand was at her throat. The square-tipped fingers, their nails yellowed by tobacco, spread against the soft flesh and tightened until he felt the wild beating of a pulse; her eyes, widening under the pressure, looked at him with the first hint of panic.

After that the hot fury eased, the red haze thinned before his eyes and he shook the stiffness from his shoulders. He released his grip on the woman's throat, transferred it to her upper arm where his fingers dug deep into the soft flesh beneath the blue cambric.

There was a fleck of spittle at the corner of his mouth as he said, in a tight whisper, "Think what you like about me. But let me know of you saying one word against me in public—just one word—and I promise you'll be sorry for it!"

Her throat swelled with effort as she swallowed, painfully. There were beads of moisture at the roots of fading hair along her temples. Her eyes held terror, but a kind of beautiful defiance as well. She said levelly, "I don't doubt that, for a minute. Any more than I doubt you'll go on, now that you've started, spreading your poison, telling your lies until all the men around you start to believe the things you say. Until you even start believing them yourself. . . .

"And then, God help this Prineville country. God help us all!"

CHAPTER V

The Hunter brothers had chosen to build their cabin where they did because of the view it gave them—the sweep of the Ochocos rising close on the one hand and, far to the west, Mount Jefferson's white cone pasted flat against the sky above the Cascade foothills. In between lay miles of government land, unmarred by any fence except where other homestead ranchers had put up an occasional rail enclosure to guard their hayfields.

This was rich country, open range shagged with bunch grass that nothing could beat. For water the Hunters had a stretch of Willow Creek, in addition to the springs that rose on the timbered swell near the house. Their cabin and barns were made of hand-hewn timber, the roofs topped with shakes and steep-pitched against the heavy snows of this high plateau country. They had built everything themselves, from pole corrals and horse pens to the stone springhouse, where they kept meat and dairystuffs and the root crops they took from their vegetable patch. They had cut and stacked along the bottoms the wild hay that they used to winter-feed their growing herd; the stacks had dwindled to nothing now, as the coming of spring greened up the range and beef stock could once more forage freely for itself.

It was a fine, clear morning, with ground-frost sparkling in the shadows of juniper and fence post, and steaming where the sun touched it. Bob Hunter was stretching his muscles, knocking up some firewood at the chopping block, when he saw the single rider approaching. He quickly sank the axe bit into a chunk of pine and walked out to meet his visitor.

He said, "Hello, Matt," trying not to show alarm at the change in this man since he last saw him.

Matt Langley had aged as no man should in a few brief weeks. His shoulders seemed rounded within the weight of his canvas coat, his cheeks had taken on deeper hollows as though they had fallen in upon the bones of his skull, making the nose and forehead stand out sharper under the weathered skin. His hands fiddled with the reins, and his glance moved restlessly from Hunter's face to the ground littered with wood chips, and to the house with the pine trees behind it shining in the sun and the smoke whipping at the chimney. He told Hunter, "I rode over a minute to say we're leavin'."

It took a moment for it to sink in. "Leaving?"

"Wagon's about loaded. We'll be pulling out, soon as Martha's fixed up something for us all to eat."

Hunter dragged off his hat, ran a hand through his hair as he thought about this. He said heavily, "I'm truly sorry. I'd been wondering what she was going to do—left alone like that, with the place, and the children. Last time we talked, the day of the burying, she was still in too much of a state over Luke to tell me much."

Langley said, "She asked me to let you know, if there's

anything there you can use, you're welcome to help yourself. There's some cut poles that might come in handy, a bunch of odds and ends I couldn't get in the wagon. But you better be taking what you want before somebody else beats you to it."

"Thanks." Pulling on the hat again, Hunter asked, "What about Bill Farrell's youngster?"

"Why, we're taking the boy with us. He's a good little kid and he's got no other folks now."

"That's mighty decent of Martha. Where does she intend to go?"

Her brother-in-law said, "I have an idea we'll try Portland. Looks like I ought to be able to find some kind of work to help keep us all floating."

Hunter felt his attention come to a sudden sharp focus. *"You're* not leaving?" He received, for answer, a wooden look that brought the protests pouring out of him. "But you can't just walk off and leave your own place! You got beef stock. You got—"

"A hundred head. I sold 'em."

"You couldn't have made much on them, this time of year. And what about all the work that's gone in there?"

The other eyed him doggedly. "Better to take what I can get, than die trying to hang onto it!" And with Hunter's stare pinning him, Langley added: "I went into Allen's to ask for my mail, day before yesterday. I found this." Reaching through the gap of his coat, he dug into a shirt pocket and brought out a scrap of paper, which he passed down from the saddle. It was crumpled and thumb-smeared, as though it had been wadded and unfolded and read a lot of times since day before yesterday. Hunter spread the thing out, holding it against the wind that tried to pluck it from his hands.

The writing had been penciled in rough block figures. There was no heading, no signature:

THE CROOKED RIVER COUNTRY DON'T NEED HORSE THIEVES AND MURDERERS. TWO OF THEM HAVE BEEN TOOK CARE OF. YOU CLEAR OUT IF YOU DON'T WANT US TO FINISH THE JOB. THIS IS ALL THE WARNING YOU GET.

The message was completed by a very crudely drawn skull and crossbones.

Astounded, Bob Hunter lifted his head and saw that Langley was trembling—plainly a badly frightened man. "Have you

51

shown this to anyone?" he demanded. "The law, for instance?"

"George Wright, you mean. What the hell good would that do?" He lifted a hand from the saddlehorn, pointed to the paper. He said explosively, "You know there ain't any truth in what it says, though, don't you? About Luke, or Bill Farrell. Or—me!"

Hunter's fingers tightened hard on the paper, became a fist. "The whole thing's ridiculous! Why don't you forget it?"

Langley dropped his hand, shook his head a little; his lips were stiff with fear. "I dunno," he muttered. "I'm no hero. I got no family to worry about, like the others did. But—I can't help it. Fact is, I'm scared! And I'm licked!"

"Wait!" Hunter moved a step nearer, reaching for the bridle as he saw the other man shift in saddle and start to take the reins. "Think a minute! Don't you see? If this really came from somebody in that lynch mob, it can only mean they're afraid of *you*. They're worried what you might do, to raise feeling against them and maybe even the score for Luke."

But the man in the saddle could only shake his head, his eyes vacant, as though this suggestion was beyond meaning. "I dunno," he repeated dully. "How can I fight 'em, alone? I don't want to end up with a bullet in me, or hanging from a tree somewhere. . . ." There was no persuading him. Hunter let go of the bridle and stepped back; he watched as Langley gathered the reins.

"I wish you'd change your mind," he said. "Scaring you out is just what they're aiming for." Remembering then that he still held the paper he added, "Can I keep this?" His voice was grim. "I'd like Chris to see it."

Matt Langley gave the note the barest of glances, shrugged indifferently. Already he was turning his horse, and Hunter stood and watched him ride away as he had come, with an old and beaten look about his sagging shoulders.

Hunter went back to work, but a sense of outrage troubled him and put an extra vehemence into the swing of his shoulders as he wielded the axe. He finished knocking up this batch of kindling, and carried it inside to dump in the woodbox. He replenished the blaze in the iron-bellied stove and poured himself a cup of coffee from the pot that was always kept heating. He stood drinking it, looking about the cabin's interior but hardly aware of the familiar homemade furniture—crude but serviceable trappings, similar to those in Luke Langley's house except that the beds were merely a pair of wooden bunk frames built against the wall with blue denim ticks for mattresses.

There was a patch on the barn roof that needed attention, and Hunter got out the tools for the job; but he left them on the table, his mind too full of other things. Chris had not returned from the business that had taken him out on the range that morning. Meanwhile, it was Saturday which meant that at Prineville a good many people would be in town, including some that he would like to talk to. Suddenly reaching a decision, Hunter scrawled a word of explanation for his brother and afterward went out to catch and saddle his roan horse.

At the last minute he remembered to shove his gun into a pocket of his windbreaker.

He rode by way of the Luke Langley place and found it deserted; Matt Langley, with his sister-in-law and her children and Bill Farrell's orphaned youngster, had already left. The wheelmarks of the wagon showed in the mud before the door. There were all the evidences of hasty flight—the belongings discarded at the last minute and left behind because there was no room for them in the wagon. The cabin door stood open, and that one detail somehow gave the place an air of having been empty for a long, long time, instead of an hour or two. It was, Hunter thought, the most forlorn and desolate sight he had ever seen.

Because of the protecting canyon where it sat, with steep palisades to collect the brilliant light and hold it as in the bottom of a bowl, Prineville basked today in nearly summer warmth. The loops of Crooked River flashed the sun like beaten metal; the town's shimmering, dirt streets were busy with Saturday traffic. Indeed, it looked to Bob Hunter as though there were more than the usual number of saddle horses and wagons tied the dusty length of Main. He drifted past the Jackson House, where Luke Langley had died, and on south across the Third Street crossing; now that he was here, he wondered where he should start with the business that had brought him in.

A couple of men he knew stood under the swaying wooden sign at the saddlemaker's. One, a stocky, blunt-jawed German named Schrader, who had a homestead ranch some dozen miles from Prineville, called Hunter's name and came out to the edge of the boardwalk. Squinting in the sun as Hunter pulled over, he said, "You been something of a stranger, past week or two. Reckon you're here for the meeting?"

Hunter scowled his puzzlement, letting a glance move from Schrader to the second man and back again. "What meeting?"

"Why, at Haze's. Ain't you heard? That's funny. Everybody was notified—by mail."

"We haven't been in to get ours," Hunter explained. He asked, "Just what would be the purpose of this meeting?"

The two men exchanged a look. Vern Larkin, owner of one of the bigger spreads along the Ochoco, said, "I guess you *ain't* been around town much!"

It wasn't pleasant to admit the truth: Walter Allen asked me, as a favor, to stay away! He said briefly, "I been busy."

"Who ain't?" Dutch Schrader agreed. "Still, there's some have been finding the time to campaign for organizing a stockman's association in Eastern Oregon. Everyone that's interested has been asked to show up at Gil Haze's this morning, and hear a reading of the constitution and bylaws."

"Who thinks we need a stockman's association?"

"Major Tarback, for one," Larkin said. "It's mainly his project. He'd like to put something together here, modeled after the ones they've got operating back in Wyoming and Montana. The idea is that an association can manage the range better—register brands, set up rules for the handling of roundups and the disposal of strays and such matters."

"I've heard something of what they've been doing in Wyoming," Hunter agreed, nodding. "It might be a good thing, and again it might not. Personally I wouldn't have thought we were in so much of a rush. We ain't that crowded yet."

"Well—maybe. They do tell me one of the main things behind this is a hope that it'll help in putting down lawlessness, and in running the stock thieves out of this Crooked River country."

Bob Hunter stiffened. The words had a familiar ring to them; he felt himself turn a little cold, thinking of the paper in his pocket. His voice was sharp as he demanded, "What stock thieves? I never knew we had any!"

"The Major says we do. According to Tarback there's what amounts to a ring of 'em. Those two killers that got lynched a couple weeks back is supposed to have been in it—up to their necks. And since then, they tell us some others have had their warnings to leave or take the consequences, and word is they've already started clearing out."

"Who, for instance?" And when his informant appeared stopped for names, Hunter added coldly, "This all sounds pretty damned vague to me!"

54

Peering at him with mild blue eyes, Dutch Schrader said, "You surely ain't thinking the Major—"

"I'm thinking I just might take a look-in on that meeting!" Hunter was hardly aware that he had cut the man short; a dangerous mood was on him as he booted the gelding in to Gil Haze's hitching rack, shouldering room for it among the horses tied there. He swung down, tethered his mount, and joined the others on the plankings. They walked inside together.

A saloon might seem an odd place to call a meeting, but there were few other buildings in town large enough to hold this one. The bar had been closed for the occasion apparently. Haze, the saloon's owner, stood leaning against the backbar with arms crossed and a sour look on his face—sour, perhaps, at thought of all the business he was missing—for the long, low-ceilinged room was very nearly full, every chair at every cardtable occupied and a surplus of men lining the walls. They seemed to be listening, in fairly good order, to the monotonous drone of a single voice.

Hunter quickly recognized the unpleasant nasal tones of the storekeeper, Gus Weckler, who was one of those he was virtually certain had taken part in the lynching of Luke Langley and Bill Farrell. He stood alone before the bar, reading haltingly from a few scrawled sheets of foolscap that apparently contained the bylaws of the proposed organization. Hunter turned to ask Dutch Schrader dryly, "Since when is Gus Weckler a stockraiser?"

The German shrugged. "I understand he's volunteered his services as secretary-treasurer. Says anything that helps his friends is good for business. . . ."

Hunter let his stare prowl the room, which smelled of horse and man-sweat and whiskey and of the pungent drift of blue tobacco smoke that hung in layers below the pressed-tin ceiling. He had already noticed that Jim Blake wasn't there; he wondered if this had any significance. Unlike the Hunters, Blake would surely have known about the meeting; but he was the sort who would simply ignore it if he thought it wasn't worth his time. Hunter made a careful and deliberate check then, and somehow wasn't surprised to discover that with one or two exceptions, every face he could remember seeing outside the hotel the night of the lynchings was present in this room.

Yes, there at a table close to the bar, big Jase Evans sat like a lump, hitched around in his chair with one bent elbow resting on the back of it and a limp hand dangling before his chest. The kid, young Eddie Wright, was here, too—and, seated between

55

the pair of them, Major Tarback, himself.

In the same moment Evans had caught sight of Bob Hunter. He sat a little straighter, lowering his arm to nudge the Major's elbow as he murmured something. Calvin Tarback's head came slowly around. His eyes settled on Hunter and their looks met and silently held.

Hunter was beginning to like this less with every minute.

At last Weckler had finished. The drone of his voice broke off, and he turned to straighten up his sheaf of papers by tapping their edges on the bar. In the following silence, someone coughed and a boot scraped the floor. And Calvin Tarback pushed back his chair and got to his feet.

He swung his body in that stiff way he had, surveying the whole room as he said, "You've heard the proposed constitution and bylaws. I think they're clear enough. Now, who has something they want to say—pro or con? Let's hear a discussion."

Nobody spoke. Hunter had a feeling that each man was waiting for the next to begin it. Tarback must have sensed their reluctance; his face darkened impatiently. "A few of us have put a lot of work into trying to get this launched. The rest must at least have some opinion. Somebody start the ball rolling."

"I'll vote for it," a voice said promptly. Hunter was not surprised when he saw the speaker was Tom Ridges, a sullen-eyed, hardscrabble rancher who could be counted on to belong in Tarback's camp. Perhaps even more to the point, unless memory played him false, Ridges had been another of that crowd in front of the Jackson House. "Looks clear to me," he said now, "if we want to see things run orderly, in this Oregon range country, it's up to us to get together and organize for it."

Again, silence.

The crowd wasn't responding yet, Hunter thought, with too great enthusiasm; for all his prestige, the Major was going to have to do better than this—somehow manage to put on more pressure than he had so far. He saw this knowledge work on Tarback. The man's chest swelled on a long breath. But before he could speak someone in the room said, "Now, wait a minute . . ."

His name was Jed Starns, and he was a silent sort who wouldn't have been expected to sound off in public meeting. He seemed more than a little taken back at what he had started, but as every eye turned his way he got slowly to his feet, chairlegs scraping under him. He was gaunt, work-toughened, his bony features red-scored and his yellow hair bleached out nearly

56

white by the sun of Oregon's high desert where he ran his horse herd. He carefully hung both thumbs into the waistband of his faded jeans, as though he were uncomfortable without some place to put them.

"One thing I'd like to get straight," Jed Starns said. "I've heard rumors that some of the men pushing this organization idea were mixed up in the lynchings here in Prineville a couple weeks ago. If that happens to be true, I for one reckon I don't want any part of it! I hope I ain't talking out of turn," he went on doggedly, looking around him, "but what about it? How can we be sure this is a real Stockman's Association we're forming, and not some God damned vigilance committee?"

"I'll try to answer your question," Major Tarback said calmly, quieting a stir among his hearers with a lifted hand. "I've heard the rumors, and I don't doubt some of you are concerned. Perhaps I can't entirely blame you." Hunter heard the words, but he was observing, just then, the expression of Jase Evans's raddled face. The big man was staring straight at Jed Starns, in a way that made Hunter think to himself: You might learn it's risky, my friend—talking up to the Major like that!

"I have never," Calvin Tarback was saying, "called any man to account as to whether he might have had a part in what happened the night of March 16. That's between each man and his own conscience. What they did wasn't pleasant—but it happens that there are some who thought it was important for a couple of murderers not to be let off scot free.

"The regrettable thing is that, now, we may never know just why the murderers' victims were killed. Was it really no more than a boundary line dispute? Or could it be they'd learned too much about their neighbors?"

But Jed Starns was persistent: "That just ain't too clear, Major. Seems like I been hearing it said that Luke Langley was maybe none too careful about other people's livestock. Could that be what you're hinting at?"

"I'll say this much," Tarback answered blandly. "I'll admit I'd had my eye on both those Langleys for some time, thinking I might catch them up to something they could be definitely saddled with."

"But you know damned well you never did!" Bob Hunter had been listening to all this, hardly believing his ears. Now pure anger propelled him forward, shoving past someone who stood in his way. His boots struck echoes from spur-scored floorboards, and Tarback swung stiffly to watch him come.

57

"While we're talking about the Langleys," he said in a voice that trembled slightly with poorly controlled fury, "maybe you can tell us if it was someone in that vigilance committee of yours who had the writing of this!" He held up a crumpled bit of paper.

Tarback's pale eyes showed nothing; he seemed to look at Hunter from somewhere behind them, as he held out his hand. Hunter shook his head and drew the paper back before he could touch it.

"I'll read it to you," he said. "Better yet, I'll ask Gil to read it—in case anyone here should get the notion I'm making this up!"

Gil Haze had pushed away from the backbar; he frowned as he came forward to take the letter. The saloon man was a Prineville character—tall, balding, and cadaverously lean; a musician of sorts, who played the violin for soirées and the cornet in the seven-man town band he had organized. There was another side to his character, though: Men knew he had killed more than once with the ivory-handled six-shooter that hung on a nail on the cherrywood backbar.

But above all, he had a reputation of fairness; and so the room waited as he smoothed out the paper and tilted it for better light, his mouth drawing down under the heavy mustache while he ran a scowling glance over the words. Slowly he began to read, the words falling like stones into the silence of the room. Concluding, he raised his head to spear his audience with a fierce glance.

"Damn thing ain't even signed!"

"Such things are never signed!" Hunter snapped. "Matt Langley gave it to me this morning, just before he took his sister-in-law and her family and cleared out of this region for good. But what's been said here gives me an idea Tarback could maybe name the coward who wrote it!"

The Major seemed wholly unperturbed. "What does it matter who wrote it—or if it's signed or not—so long as it's done the job? For this man to break and run, after no more than a warning, sounds to me like a fair proof of guilt."

"It proves nothing except he was scared out of his wits!" Bob Hunter retorted. "Like he told me himself—he was no hero. How could he be expected to stand up to some faceless group of vigilantes who'd already lynched two helpless men?"

The Major shrugged slightly. "So you defend murderers. Well, it's your privilege, of course. I don't doubt you have your reasons."

"Are you going to say next," Hunter demanded, having trouble keeping his voice under control, "that *I'm* part of this rustling ring?"

"*You* said it—not me," the Major pointed out crisply. "I call on every man in the room to be my witness to that!"

"That's right, mister!" big Jase Evans said from his place at the table. "You be careful how you go putting words in another man's mouth!" Hunter favored him with a brief, cold stare.

"I'm still waiting to see one shred of evidence against either of the Langleys—or against Bill Farrell, either."

It was obvious Tarback felt confident he had his audience safely with him, for he spoke calmly enough. "I don't see much profit in arguing a closed case. Two of these men are dead and their secrets with them; according to you, the third has left the country. But I'm not optimistic enough to think that this ends the matter. Our job has only begun—and we'd do better to get on with it."

Jed Starns was still on his feet, his pale brows knotted in earnest concentration. He spoke up now, switching Tarback's attention back to himself. "I ain't one that likes to argue, but I don't know nothing except rumors of any stealing going on. Sure, we all stand to lose a horse or a steer now and then—to wolves or cougars maybe. There's always loose riders passing through, or sometimes an Indian off one of the reservations helps himself to a free beef. But I seen no sign of anything worse than that."

"Then I suggest you look a little deeper," the Major snapped, spearing the man with his stare. "I'm personally short a dozen head of prime saddle stock within the past month alone; I won't even begin to know how many cattle until after roundup. Oh yes, friend! This is more than cougars, or a bronco Indian or two at work! You'd better believe it!"

There was a murmur of agreement that time, swelling quickly as more of Tarback's hearers joined in. At last the Major's talk was having effect. Angry looks sought out Bob Hunter, and men who were standing near turned on Jed Starns to shout him down. Starns lost color, stammering a word or two; then, his nerve crumbling in the face of such opposition, he backed down and dropped into his chair—silenced, if unconvinced.

Hunter scowled back at the crowd, yet he thought he could understand their readiness to believe. Losses such as the Major was talking about could be a serious matter in a country given over, as this Eastern Oregon rangeland was, to cattle and particularly to the breeding of fine horseflesh. When it was

59

possible for a man's whole wealth to be cleaned out in a single moonless night, he could hardly be blamed for taking alarm over the idea.

Tarback was saying now, "If we don't want to throw away what's already been accomplished, we'll vote in this association, and we'll back it with the authority to assess dues and issue permits. We'll make sure no man works the range without having first been recognized as a member in good standing. And we'll know exactly what to think about any man who refuses to sign the articles."

Hunter looked at Jase Evans, at Gus Weckler and Eddie Wright and the other remembered faces that seemed to leap at him from the crowd. He said abruptly, "I can tell you, for one, *I'm* not signing—now or ever! This Stockman's Association looks like nothing more than what Jed Starns called it—a front for a vigilante mob. And if anyone thinks I'll tie myself hand and foot and turn myself over to it, they can damn well think again!"

He was beyond caring about the stir his words created, or the danger peering at him through Jase Evans's narrowed eyes. He merely scowled as Tarback demanded, "You'd go against the will of the majority?"

"If it comes to that!" Suddenly he dug into the pocket of his windbreaker; there was a scattering scramble behind him, as his hand brought out a six-shooter and laid it on the bar.

"Just to make everything clear, I'm serving notice now—this is the only permit I'm going to need or ask for, anytime I've got business on the range I figure wants taking care of. And I suggest the rest of you'd be better off, doing the same."

He waited, letting the challenge hang, then picked up the gun again and shoved it back into his pocket. And as he turned to go, in a continuing stillness, Gil Haze spoke from behind the bar.

"You forgot something."

He was holding the note that had frightened Matt Langley out of the country. Expression grim, Bob Hunter looked at it. "Tear it up!"

"Tell you what," the saloon owner suggested pleasantly. "Any time one of these things should show up in your mailbox, you just bring it around. You and me'll stick the blamed thing up and have us a little target practice—with old Emily, yonder. . . ." He jerked a thumb toward the ivory-handled Colt hanging on its nail behind the bar; his words were mild but his eyes were completely humorless. He was really issuing a warning—

60

serving notice that, for what it might be worth, he was on Bob Hunter's side.

Coming from a cautious man, one who by profession was a neutral in other people's quarrels, that was going pretty far. There wasn't a man in the room but knew that the same strong, lean hand that could draw you a beer—or a bow across a fiddle's strings—was equally skilled with that gun.

Bob Hunter thanked him with a nod. "If anybody sends me one of those things," he said, rashly blunt, "they better start looking for a hole!" He let a challenging stare touch on Gus Weckler's pallid face, moving on deliberately to Jase Evans who sat leaning forward a little now with both his hands spread before him on the table top. Evans's pock-scarred chin was sunk upon his chest, his mouth pulled out into an ugly line and his eyes meeting Hunter's with a disturbing hostility.

He had made his statement and it seemed a good note to leave on. He turned his back on the Major and shoved his way through the disordered crowd of men; some of them appeared to think he was out of his mind. In the doorway Dutch Schrader gave him a worried stare and put out a hand as though to stop him, but Hunter shook his head and shrugged past. Anger carried him on into the bright, clear sunshine of Prineville's Main Street.

CHAPTER VI

The Hunter brothers wintered their small beef herd on the high Central Oregon plateau that stretched north from Crooked River Canyon to the Columbia, between the Ochocos on the east and the deep gorge of the Deschutes to westward. There was no finer horse and cattle range anywhere, well fed as it was by a dozen good-sized creeks, and with bunch grass that in some places reached to a rider's stirrup. Being government land, it held—except for the scattered quarter-section holdings of other homesteaders like themselves—not a fence or structure anywhere, other than an occasional juniper-pole corral put up by stockmen for use during roundup season.

The brothers worked without a wagon, there being just the two of them. Each carried cold grub on his saddle, and a running iron for use when he found a new calf following a cow in their brand, which was Slash 7. Since this was precisely the same area where Major Tarback ran his own beef and saddle stock from his ranch headquarters north and west on Hay Creek, there was good reason to expect they might be hearing the aftermath of the meeting at Haze's before this job was finished. But they were undeterred. After all, it was the optimistic, the hopeful time of year. The winter past had been a cold one, with no real snow until after New Year's. Now the range bloomed; as soon as their cattle was gathered, it would be moved up into the Ochocos on summer grass. The changeable and patience-wearing moods of early spring were giving way to an unbroken succession of fine days that would continue, with few breaks, during the few short summer months ahead.

Coming down through a break in the rimrock, Bob Hunter jumped a Slash 7 cow and her slick-eared, unbranded calf and put them through their paces, turning them when the cow tried to dodge past him and lead her bawling calf back into the safety of the lava breaks and thick rabbit brush. He drove them at last into a deepening, sandy-bottomed cut that had been a creekbed at some time past, and coming past a shoulder of black lava found he had struck a real bonanza. This cut funneled out into a draw that had grass and some water in it, and there almost two dozen head of cattle were feeding. All but three were Hunter stock, and half of them had calves.

Working carefully so as not to startle the rest, Hunter cut out those that didn't belong to him and sent them on down the draw—it took considerable slapping of a coiled rope across stupid bovine faces to persuade them to go. Afterward, stepping down and ground-reining his horse, he proceeded to collect material for a fire. He got his running iron from the saddle lashings and laid it in the flames to heat.

He was about to mount and use his rope on the first calf, when the ring of a hoof on stone gave him a warning that lifted his head.

They were Tarback riders—four of them, moving up the draw at an easy walk with soft sand slurring the noise of their approach; Hunter watched a moment, through heated air that shook above the snapping flames. They all wore belt guns, and one had a rifle laid across his lap. That reminded Hunter his own revolver was in a pocket of his saddlebags, a couple of yards from where he stood. Quite casually, he moved a step toward his roan horse.

Just as casually, that rifle shifted and the barrel flashed sunlight as it swung in a short arc; the muzzle was pointed now at a spot between him and his horse, which he would have to cross in order to reach it. It seemed to be wholly by accident, but Bob Hunter weighed everything and so stood where he was as the four riders came to a halt, facing him across the fire.

One said, with a gesture that took in the fire and the bunch of grazing cattle, "Burning some strays, Hunter?"

He had to fight against a sudden flare of anger. "They're not strays. It happens every calf in that bunch is following a Slash 7 cow."

The man looked at him without emotion. His name was Bud Morrison, and Hunter was pretty certain he must have some Indian in him—he owned the broad face, the smoky eyes with the slightly oriental cast, the dark skin. He was in fact a good deal more inscrutable than any Indian Hunter had known when he worked on the Warm Springs reservation.

He sat one of Major Tarback's prime saddle horses, hands crossed on the horn and an unlighted cigarette pasted to the corner of his lower lip. He spoke over one shoulder. "Dallas, go check them brands."

Hunter stiffened. "No need of that. There were a couple of your animals in the bunch; I already cut 'em out—you must have passed them as you came up the draw. These here are all Hunter beef."

"Dallas will check them," Morrison said bluntly, and the man he'd named pulled out of the group and walked his horse over for a closer look at the cattle. It was all Hunter could do to hold in his temper, but that rifle muzzle still covered him like the black eye of a tunnel. He wondered grimly if there would be an apology when they found he had told the truth.

Waiting, Bud Morrison swung easily from his saddle and went down on his ankles, to pluck a burning twig from the fire and touch it to the shapeless twist of paper and tobacco between his lips. With the cigarette burning, he tossed the stick back into the coals and then, quite casually, took up the iron Hunter had heating. With the latter watching narrowly, the dark-skinned rider turned the brand in one big fist, squatted there looking at the glowing end of it. No expression showed in his smoky eyes.

The man called Dallas rode back, now, saying curtly, "Well, they look clean enough—all Slash 7's."

"That's good." Morrison's cigarette bobbed as he spoke. "That's very good—for Mister Hunter!" he said, and the words had something sinister about them. He straightened to his feet, then, still holding the heated branding iron—and, with no further comment, proceeded to kick apart and scatter Hunter's fire.

Hunter shouted something and took a step forward. At once the glowing end lifted threateningly almost into his face, halting him. "Careful!" Morrison held the iron like a cocked gun, and the heat of the glowing iron caused beads of sweat to break out upon Hunter's cheek.

Hands clenched, he demanded hoarsely, "What the hell do you want from me, anyway?"

"Why, *we* don't want nothing," the other man said. "It's what the Major wants—and the Association. You was warned, mister. The Major told you, himself, there'd be no time wasted on holdouts."

"And I told him I wasn't asking anybody's permission to round up my own stock!"

The dark-skinned man didn't answer. He stepped back a pace, and looked at his companions. He said loudly, "Scatter 'em!"

"You'll keep your hands off my cattle!" Only the rifle pointed at him could have held Hunter back, even in spite of that glowing branding iron.

Morrison spoke tightly, fiercely. "You don't like anybody moving your beef? All right, mister! Let's see if you like this any better. . . ." He flung the cooling iron away into the sage, at the same moment signalling to the man who held the rifle. The weapon was tossed down and caught out of the air. Before Hunter could do so much as cry out in protest, Morrison drew a casual bead and fired.

The rifle's voice slapped thinly against the lava rim of the coulee, and a steer dropped. The man flipped the lever, settled the Winchester to his shoulder again while he picked a second target.

Blind fury swept Hunter and sent him wading right through the scattered brands of his fire. He got a hand on the barrel of the rifle and pushed it up, just as the weapon spoke a second time—a rush of explosive energy tearing through the metal tube clutched in his fingers. The little jag of beef took panic. Hunter could hear them bawling, feel the drum of their hoofs through the floor of the arroyo as they broke into scattered flight.

64

Nearer, the Tarback buckaroos were shouting and their horses were moving under them.

In their midst, the pair of dismounted men struggled for possession of the rifle that they both clutched—Hunter by the barrel, Bud Morrison at the trigger action. They were evenly matched; their free hands exchanged wild blows that mostly missed as they reeled about through the stunted sage, stumbling over their own boots but somehow keeping their feet under them.

Then, quite by accident, a twisting yank by Hunter at the barrel caused the rifle's heavy stock to swing up and slam Morrison alongside the jaw, with force enough to break his grip and send him to the ground in a rolling topple. Hunter was nearly swept off his own feet but he managed to retain his grip on the rifle. He came swinging around with it to work the lever and jack a fresh shell into the breech.

Nobody was even looking at him. The Tarback men—the ones still in saddle—were staring toward some point a little beyond Hunter; and now he heard sound of a rider moving up behind him.

It was his brother Chris. He came at an easy walk, and the hand that rested on his thigh held a six-shooter—Hunter realized now what it was that kept these others motionless. Chris drew to a halt and looked at all of them, at the smoldering brands of the scattered fire, and the rifle, and the dead steer and Bud Morrison who had climbed to his knees. He took a long breath and moved the barrel of his six-shooter slightly. He said, "Maybe you better get rid of those guns. . . ."

Without a word they let them drop into the sandy dirt at their horses' feet. Even Morrison, scowling furiously, pulled the weapon from his holster and threw it down. Now Chris looked at his brother's sweating face as he demanded, "So, just what's going on here?"

Hunter filled his lungs, suddenly aware he was shaking. He explained the situation, curtly, as Chris frowned, his honest face looking more bewildered than ever. Afterward the older brother put a mild look on Morrison and asked, with a shake of the head, "Now, why should you want to kill our beef? What good could that do you—or the Major, either?"

"It would make an example, I figure," Bob answered, bitterly. "Show us and the range it ain't permitted for anyone to breathe the air, nowadays, unless he gets the word of the Association!"

Chris Hunter rubbed a hand across his jaw. "Damn!" he said,

and shook his head. "Well, I guess we're only lucky it didn't come to anything worse. Put Morrison back on his horse, and send the bunch of them about their business."

"Just like that?" Bob protested. "We didn't start this."

"Somebody has to finish it. What do you want to do—shoot one of them, to make up for the steer? Set them afoot? That would only push things one step further."

As usual, his younger brother had to admit the sense of Chris's calmer judgment. It pained him to give way; he ground his jaws and said angrily, "All right. I'll give you this one steer, Morrison—just to show we're not spoiling for a fight with anybody, not even Vigilantes. But, that was the end!" He closed the distance between them, and let the muzzle of the rifle nudge the other man's breastbone. The swarthy skin of Morrison's face lost some color and a nerve pulled at the corner of his mouth a time or two.

"Pass this on to the Major," Bob Hunter said. "And the four of you keep some for yourselves: If there's a next time, nobody's going to be caught off guard. Tarback may get it into his head to hurt us some more—but he's vulnerable, too, just because he's bigger and we can hurt him even worse!"

"All right, Bob," Chris said. "You've made your point."

With quick motions Hunter levered the rifle dry, kicking out a spatter of bright cartridges, and tossed the empty weapon up to its owner. He told Morrison, "Now, climb on that horse and all of you ride out of here. And don't bother us again!"

"What about our guns?" Bud Morrison demanded hoarsely.

"We'll leave them here so you can get them—but don't be in any hurry. Right now, *move!*"

The dark-faced man stared at him a moment longer. He touched his jaw, where a bruise was beginning to swell. Abruptly then he turned and found the stirrup and pulled himself into the saddle. Without a word the four Tarback riders turned their horses, the hoofs scattering dust, and eased off down the draw, lifting to a canter just before they went from sight.

Looking after them, Bob Hunter felt a trembling in the arm he raised to wipe the sleeve across his sweating face. He looked at Chris, half expecting a lecture; but his brother seemed more troubled and depressed than he did angry.

When he saw he wasn't going to get a lecture, Hunter went for his branding iron.

As the days grew longer, so did the number of hours a

homestead rancher put in—and even then there wasn't time enough. The gathering and branding done, their herd had to be moved up in bunches onto the meadows and pine flats of the Ochocos where the cattle could feed and put on shipping fat for the fall drive to railroad. Even though their herd was small, with only the pair of them to do the work, it meant being in saddle by daybreak, and still in it after the sun had moved down below the horizon and the Cascade peaks made cutout silhouettes against a steel-gray sky. It was enough to wear a man, even a young man in prime health. It was worse when he rode with the constant feeling of sharing the range with an enemy.

Though they talked little about it, each knew the other lived from day to day under a growing tension. It was hard to believe that Tarback would let this challenge go—Bob Hunter halfway expected, every time he rode home, to find the place in ashes. The only thing he could think of to hold the Major back from some such punishing move, if the idea occurred, would be that Tarback knew he had even more to risk. If he burnt the Hunter place, he must have known that nothing could keep Bob Hunter from returning the compliment by firing the buildings on his own spread—and Tarback's ranch house, though he seldom spent much time there, was worth a good deal more than the log shack on Willow Creek. Tarback stood to lose in the trade.

For whatever reason, nothing happened at all. The Association's bluff had been called, and for the time being they seemed ready to let it go at that.

So weeks passed. Few people came by the ranch—it was too far up the reaches of the creek, off the wagon road; of affairs in Prineville, that lay fourteen miles away and on the other side of Grizzly Butte, they heard nothing at all until one day when they had a visitor.

It was wholly unexpected. Chris was off somewhere, checking stock; Bob, stripped to the waist and with a bandanna about his forehead to keep the hair and the sweat from his eyes, was putting in an afternoon's work on the ditch that would carry water to irrigate a crop garden and hay field. It was a project that figured large in the Hunters' planning, yet it was one that could only be given odd hours, when more pressing work allowed it.

Hunter had struck a buried slab of lava rock and was trying to burrow around it, uncovering it enough that it could be levered up and pried out by main force. He was sweating hard over the job, cussing a little to keep himself company as he chopped away at loose soil with the spade bit and thought about

67

going to the house for a crowbar. Because of the noise he was making he failed to hear a rider approaching; when he did, he straightened hastily and turned thinking it might be one of Tarback's crew. It was not. It was Jennifer Allen, in a long riding dress and a broadbrimmed straw hat to protect her from the strong sunlight. "Well—hullo!" he exclaimed.

"Hello," she said, smiling, and after that neither seemed able to think of anything to say for several minutes. Only when the big brown horse seemed to grow impatient and started to move around a little, did Hunter break free of the spot where he stood rooted.

He stabbed the spade into the dirt, to hold it upright, and came climbing up the side of the ditch. He remembered his shirt and got it out of the crotch of a juniper and quickly shrugged into it, and whipped off the handkerchief from around his head to wipe his sweaty face. At least he was glad he had thought to shave that morning. Pocketing the bandanna and running stubby fingers through his hair he said, "I wish I'd known you were coming, but it's a nice surprise anyway."

"It was such a beautiful day," she explained. She looked around her, breathing deeply of the tangy air, enjoying it. She leaned toward him then, placed her hands on his shoulders and let him lift her down off the sidesaddle. They stood a moment like that, looking at one another, before he bent and kissed her. Afterward he stepped back, dropping his hands from her waist, and she self-consciously smoothed out the wrinkles from her skirt.

"I brought your mail," Jen told him. "You hadn't been in for so long, and I thought there might be something you'd be wanting." She turned to get it from a saddlebag lashed behind the cantle. For just an instant he hesitated as she read the thought in his eyes and said, quickly sobering, "Don't worry. There isn't one of *those* letters!" He was ashamed at how relieved he was to hear it. He accepted the small handful without comment.

There was, in fact, hardly enough to have bothered with—a couple of catalogs, a letter from a Chicago cattle buyer he had once done business with. It plainly had been nothing more than an alibi for coming, but he didn't let on that he guessed this. He thanked her seriously, and stuffed his mail into a hip pocket of his jeans while he proceeded to button the shirt he had hastily put on.

An awkwardness settled on them. The horse flicked its tail and pulled at a clump of grass. Hunter said, "You sure look good. How are things in town? How's your folks?"

"Papa's fine. Mama's been having her headaches again."

"Sorry to hear it." He knew about those headaches; they were Mrs. Allen's way of tyrannizing over her husband and disciplining a rebellious daughter. They had a particular way of coming on whenever Jen threatened resistance to her parents' efforts to force her to show attention to George Wright, so in a way Hunter knew that he himself was responsible for some of them. But he didn't know what he could do about it.

"And, Chris?" Jen asked, as though glad to change the subject.

"Oh, you know Chris—he's always the same. He's out checking stock, may not get in till late or even at all. He'll be sorry he missed you."

"Me too. In fact, I was taking a chance neither of you would be home."

That led to his showing her the work that had kept him close today. Jen already knew about the plans for irrigating the place, and he conducted her along the course of the ditch, leading the brown horse, and pointed out how the water would flow onto their acres when the plug was cut and opened Willow Creek into the channel. Hunter got a little carried away with enthusiasm, as he usually did when he discussed his plans with this girl—she had a way of listening, with her eyes intent upon his face, that made him feel as though anything he wanted to do was not only possible but beyond failure.

But now her eyes were troubled as she said anxiously, "You know you're working too hard! You worry me. . . ."

"I'm not hurting myself any," he assured her, brushing aside the remark. "There's just a lot to be done, and never enough time."

"Or enough to eat, I'll bet! How long has it been since either of you has taken the trouble to fix a decent meal?"

"We make out. . . ."

"I can imagine!" She looked at the sky. "Must be nearly two o'clock. What have you had since breakfast?"

"Well . . ." The question caught him without an answer. He told her evasively, "I was just thinking it was about time to knock off and—"

"You were just thinking!" Jennifer repeated, mockingly. She took his arm, with possessive determination. "Right now," she said, "we're going up to the house and I'm going to cook you an honest-to-goodness dinner. And don't try to talk me out of it."

"But the house is a mess!"

69

"Then it's probably time I did something about that, too. You know what you need around here, don't you, Bob Hunter? A woman!"

Suddenly they were both very quiet, very solemn. He took her by the shoulders and studied her face—she had taken off the straw hat and it was dangling by its ribbons, and the sun struck full across her cheeks and showed him the shadow of seriousness in her eyes. He swallowed once, and shook his head. "Just what did you suppose I was working for? To be bigger than Major Tarback, maybe? Oh, Jen! When I think what a long way there is to go— But it's worth the waiting," he added. "That is, if *you* think it is!"

For answer she rose on tiptoes and kissed him, and was smiling as she stepped away; her smile was answer enough. She reached up to settle a strand of hair the breeze had freed and whipped across her forehead. "Now," she said, "let's see what I can find in the larder."

He squeezed her shoulder. "I'll fetch up your horse."

He went back and got it, and scrambled into the ditch for the spade he'd left there. When he reached the house, smoke was already coming from the chimney. He turned the brown horse into the corral, washed up at a bench beside the door. He walked inside, and into a fine aroma of beef and potatoes and onions frying together.

Jen had thrown out the coffee that had been heated and reheated until it was the strength and consistency of mud, and started a fresh pot. Soda biscuits were already in the oven; Jen said, "I'm fixing enough so there'll be some left for Chris to heat up when he does get home." Hunter straddled a chair, leaning his arms on its back. It was a sight he had dreamed of: this girl, in his own kitchen, taking over as though she belonged there. It overwhelmed him a little and he was content merely to sit and watch.

But then a thought came that sobered him and turned his mouth a trifle hard. "You haven't told me how things are in Prineville. . . ."

She had her back toward him, but he knew from her slight hesitation that she understood what he had in mind. "They're— quiet," she said.

"That so?" His face was grim. "What happened back in March has been forgotten, I suppose—forgotten and swept under the carpet."

"The lynchings . . ." The curls brushed her neck as she shook her head. "People just don't talk about them any more. Or when they do, they act as though it was a bad job that needed to be done. I've heard some men, who'd kept quiet before, have taken to going around town openly admitting to the name of Vigilantes—almost like it was an exclusive kind of club they belong to!"

Hunter ground his jaws. After a moment he asked, "Did anyone ever hear from the sheriff? Has he offered any excuse for not coming down from The Dalles and investigating this mess for himself?"

This time she turned to face him. Her cheeks held color from the heat of the stove, but her eyes were wide and troubled.

"I guess you haven't heard about the letter. . . ."

"What letter?"

"George Wright sent the sheriff an official report—all I really know about it is what I overheard between him and Papa, afterward. Apparently George told the sheriff there was no way of identifying the men who killed the prisoners. He also said there was a good deal of evidence they'd both been mixed up in some kind of crooked business, though it was probably too late to prove that either. He called it a closed issue. . . ."

Hunter had trouble with his breathing for a moment. He sat there, stunned. "I see," he said finally. "Good old George!"

"I just don't know what to make of him lately," she said earnestly. "He's changed, in these past weeks—even Mama has noticed. He hardly ever smiles, at all; and you can't even talk to him. It's almost as though he had something—hanging over him."

Hunter considered this, could find no answers in it. He shrugged. "Meanwhile, he's gone and fixed things so there'll be no investigation—no nothing!"

She said, "At least, no one at The Dalles seems to have raised any questions."

"Well, *I* could raise some! Maybe I should write a letter, myself!" He came to his feet, took a turn around the room; but then he halted again, shaking his head. "No, damn it! I can't either! I can't do anything without calling George Wright a liar—and probably your father, as well. They'd say I was only acting out of jealousy, to make trouble. I've got no proof—I'd do nothing but make a fuss. And then your name would be dragged into it, and—" His shoulders fell.

Talk was harder, suddenly. They lapsed into a silence that was little broken even after the food was put on the table. Jennifer didn't seem to be hungry; she ate a little but mostly sat and watched him, with a woman's enjoyment at seeing the pleasure

71

she had been able to give her man. And she was right—it was the first well-cooked meal he had had in a long time, and it raised his spirits. Afterward Hunter refused to let her do anything about cleaning up; instead he said, "I've something I want to show you," and led her by the hand to a big pine tree that stood on a slope near the cabin.

"Take a look at that," he said, with a sweep of the arm. "I thought you'd like it."

The land fell away before them in a long, tawny sweep of sage and grass, clear to the western ridges where the Cascade peaks were beginning to lose some of their winter pack of snow. "How beautiful!" she exclaimed. "Honestly, nobody knows how much I love this country! To Papa it's just a place to do business, and without the competition he used to have to face back in Cleveland. As for my mother, I don't think she'll ever see anything but the emptiness, and the harshness, and the dust. . . ."

He swept a place clean and lowered himself beside her. They sat without touching, their shoulders against the tree trunk, motionless and silent for so long that a junco came and settled on a branch just over their heads for a moment, then took off in a scissoring flash of white tailfeathers. Wind hummed in pine needles.

Once, as the girl started to speak, Hunter warned her to silence; they watched a golden mantled ground squirrel, emboldened by the stillness, dart out of the brush a yard from them and, going up on its haunches, pull the stems of grass down with its paws in order to get at the ripe grainheads. They held their breaths, watching. The afternoon about them seemed to drowse in warmth and the sweet cinnamon smell of sun-warmed pine.

After a while he felt the pressure of her head against his shoulder and, looking at her, saw the even rise and fall of her breast and realized she was asleep. A great wave of tender possessiveness poured over him. Long minutes passed, like that, as he studied the soft mouth and the dark-lashed eyes so near to his own. His arm began to cramp a little and he shifted position—not enough to disturb her, but the ground squirrel whipped around to fix him with its beady stare, flicked its tail a couple of times and beat a swift, zigzag retreat into the sage. Following that, there was just the two of them. Hunter picked up a few fragments of bark, shaped like jigsaw-puzzle pieces, toyed with them as he absorbed the stillness. After the unremitting toil of these past weeks, it was a moment of complete relaxation and peace.

He didn't know how much later it was that Jennifer stirred, opened her eyes, and sat up exclaiming, "My goodness! What did I do—drop off and leave you all alone? I'm terrible company!

"I've got to go!" she added, over his protest, as she saw the lengthening shadows and the golden quality of the light. She got to her feet; Hunter rose more slowly. Jen said, "Papa will be furious. It's not right to worry him. I'll have to hurry, now, if I'm to get back by dark."

"I guess you will."

They stood together, then, in the quiet, looking at each other. Suddenly her arms rose, her hands rested on his shoulders. Earnestly she said, "I think this was the most wonderful afternoon I've ever spent! To be together and alone, with no one to bother—to fix your dinner and share it. . . ."

He gathered her into his arms. He said, "There'll be more times like this. Maybe a lot more. Who knows? Even a whole lifetime. . . ."

The brief summer appeared to be hastening to its doom. Winter feed was cut and stacked. After a week of chill rain the skies had cleared again but now they were the skies of autumn, with fluttering wedges of geese being drawn southward across them occasionally, like banners. Cattle came down off the summer ranges, and Oregon cattlemen had their market herds on the trails, some bound for railhead at points as far distant as Cheyenne and Winnemucca.

This was the first year the Hunter brothers had found themselves with a beef crop to warrant joining a drive; on a morning when frost lay in the hollows and golden cottonwood leaves streaked the wind, they latched their cabin and started moving a jag of thirty yearling steers and two-year-olds over the old road across the shoulder of Grizzly Butte.

In the canyon of Crooked River, a trail herd had already been formed—three hundred head belonging to the German, Dutch Schrader, and an equal number in the brand of the Hunters' friend Jim Blake. Because of a pregnant wife and other concerns, Blake himself wasn't making this drive; in return for their handling his interests, he would keep an eye on their Willow Creek property and their breed stock. Also, they would draw day wages from Schrader, who knew every creek and water hole in the dry country east of them and would serve as

73

trail boss Schrader was supplying the cook wagon and had for the bulk of his drive crew, a couple of youngsters named Sam Clifton and Charlie Hewett—neither of them much more than a kid—and three Indians hired off the Warm Springs reservation.

The holding ground, that last night before the actual drive began, was on a flat meadow a half dozen miles up the canyon from Prineville. Everyone's hands would be too full preparing for an early start to allow any time in town; but Hunter, knowing it would be weeks before they would be back this way, used the excuse of picking up the mail and stole a quarter hour, in passing the village, to ride in over the Ochoco Creek bridge with the hope of saying goodby to Jen. To his disappointment, she wasn't at the store and there wasn't time to go looking for her. But Walter Allen had interesting news, which had put the mayor of Prineville in such an expansive mood that he greeted Hunter almost cordially.

"You haven't heard? Word came yesterday, on the stage from The Dalles. The State Assembly over at Salem has finally cut its way through the red tape that's been holding things up. They've voted to let us have our county!"

"You're not joking?"

"It's right here on the front page," Allen said, handing him the newspaper from The Dalles. "Effective January first—with the temporary county seat to be here at Prineville until after the general election in June. The Governor's appointment of the first county officers is promised within the next few weeks."

Hunter scanned the column eagerly. It was news that that part of Oregon had been waiting for, and he pressed for certainty. "I guess there can't be any mistake, this time."

"The only mistake has been that we've had to wait this long. Take my word for it, Robert—now we're no longer to be tucked away in a forgotten corner of Wasco County, this whole part of the country is going to boom. It's like I was telling George Wright, only this morning," Allen went on, blandly indifferent to the effect of praising him to a rival. "The world will soon see what a smart chap George was, to pick this town to hang out his shingle. Prineville's the only real choice for a permanent county seat. It's going places—and a knowledgeable young fellow like him can go places with it. He can be one of the big men of the State!" Allen could hardly have sounded more enthusiastic if George had been his own son. Or—Hunter thought, a trifle sourly—his son-in-law. . . .

Chris, when he heard the news, was inclined to agree with Allen that it was news of prime importance—but for a different reason. In his own quiet way he expressed his optimism: "With any kind of effective county law, Tarback's going to have to head in. It should cut the ground out from under the Vigilantes, or any excuse for going ahead with this damned Stockman's Association. We might even get some action on those lynchings away back in March."

"That all depends," Hunter said dubiously, "on the caliber of the man who gets appointed sheriff."

"At least there won't be any more strong-arming, or shooting of another man's beef. Tarback can't risk it."

"Maybe," Hunter said, but he had a few doubts he kept to himself.

When you were dealing with anyone as complex and devious as the Major, you couldn't be sure. In forming his Stockman's Association and backing it with guns and falsehoods, Tarback had shown he was bent on being the power in control of this Crooked River country. He didn't seem the kind to let a thing like county law interfere with him. . . . But that was the future. Borrowing trouble was a fruitless business.

The drive up the canyon quickly shook down into a routine; but though the country was raw and wild and the hours in the saddle long, the change of scenery and the break from ranch work made it take on something of the nature of a holiday. This was especially true with a pair like Hewett and Clifton in the outfit. The former was a local boy, son of a Prineville homesteader who was drawing wages for the first time. His friend Sam Clifton, about the same age, was a more adventurous sort—rawboned, redheaded—who had lately come over the mountains from the Willamette and whose prized possession was the horse he rode. It was named Muggins and it didn't look like much, but it had powerful haunches and a deep chest and young Sam Clifton declared it could outrun anything on four legs.

Watching the boy spin away from the line of march and go whooping off through the sagebrush after a jackrabbit, risking his neck in order to show off his mount's flat-out speed, Bob Hunter was nearly ready to believe the claim. The gray was fast, all right. Hunter listened to the youngsters' talk of the killing they'd make, after they got back from this drive, with pay in their jeans for betting purposes—Prineville men were notoriously horse-crazy. Such unquenchable high spirits made him feel a little old. It seemed a long, rough haul since he himself was eighteen. Yet it had been less than ten years.

He came under the spell of a mood as they pushed on,

holding to their plodding dozen miles a day. The course bore east, up Crooked River to Beaver Creek and the Silvies, south at a tangent and east from there to Harney Valley where a settlement called Burns was struggling into being, then over to Jordan Valley in the corner where this state adjoined Idaho and Nevada. During the long nights of such a drive—rolled in his blankets by a dying fire, or taking his turn at nighthawking with the mesh of stars overhead almost frightening in their immensity and brilliance—a man could listen to the herd and to the fluting of a wind in the rimrock. He could slowly, laboriously sort out his thoughts:

"Chris? You awake?"

"Yeah, kid . . ."

"I been lying here thinking. Any idea how much we might stand to make off this bunch?"

"Well, according to Schrader, the market's supposed to be about as good as they've seen it. If it holds up till we get there, he told me today we could average out as much as thirty a head."

He repeated it slowly, savoring the sound of it.

"Nine hundred—it sounds pretty good to me," Chris said.

"Yeah. . . ."

But after a moment while the night sounds moved across the stillness, Chris said, "You don't sound particularly excited. A couple of young bucks like us—starting out with nothing much to speak of—I'd say we've been doing all right."

"We've still got a distance to go."

"You in that big a hurry, kid? I hadn't realized." Then, with that rare understanding that existed between them, Chris supplied his own answer: "Or, is it someone else that's in a hurry?"

That brought Bob up onto an elbow, rolling over to try and make out his brother's face in the dim starlight. "Don't blame Jen!" he insisted bluntly. "She wouldn't care how much or how little I had. I don't think it would make the least difference. But, there's her folks. Before Walter Allen could even think of letting her marry me, he's going to have to see a lot more than I can show him: Some money lying in the bank. Or, at the very least, something better than a log shack to take her to—a real house like the one she lives in now, with floors and windows, and paint on the outside . . ."

The futility of it shocked him and he flopped onto his back again and stared at the stars. They didn't look any farther away than his ambitions. But after a moment his brother said gently,

76

"I wouldn't get discouraged, kid. Nine hundred should buy a lot of paint and lumber. And leave something for the bank, too."

At first he failed to understand, and when he did something swelled in his throat and he had to choke out his protest. "Now, wait a minute! We've halves in this, all the way. There's plenty of other things to be done with this money—if and when we get it. There's the commutation fee on that land of ours. There's stock to buy, an irrigation system to finish, permanent fencing to put in on our hay meadows. Nothing in it for you, if I use all our money financing a marriage!"

Chris didn't answer for so long that his brother thought he wasn't intending to. "Well, kid . . ." He spoke casually, but there was something that suggested he had chosen every word with care. "Far as that's concerned, I'm not really so sure I care much about that place of ours—not as much as I reckon you do. Matter of fact, I been getting a little restless stuck in one spot. Oh, I'll stay around awhile, help you get things started. But, one of these days I suppose I'll be drifting. Maybe head someplace where the winters aren't as long. . . ."

Hunter lay very still, looking up at the night stars and hearing his brother's voice echo in his thoughts. He couldn't answer; he couldn't say, "You're a damn liar!" But he knew Chris too well, not to spot the falseness in every word.

He knew how much that Willow Creek homestead meant to Chris. It had all been his baby; it was he who had staked the claim, using the precious, one-time-only homestead right that was one of the rarest privileges a man possessed by belonging to this country. Whatever he said now, and whatever his homeless past had been, there was in Chris Hunter a deep need to sink his roots, a need that was maybe stronger even than it was in his brother.

Yet he would give all that up, write off his share of their spread and all the work and time he had put into it—hand it to Bob and Jen as a wedding present and ride away, if this would help at all to smooth the path for them. That was what he was really saying. And Bob Hunter found his tongue stilled by a sense of gratitude that was too great to find words for, any more than he could find speech to voice his refusal of the sacrifice.

For another thing had struck him, with a breath-stopping force—something that had never really come home until this moment: No brothers had ever been closer, he thought, than he and Chris. It had been the two of them against a tough world. Inconceivable, that anything should come between them—and yet, now, something had.

77

It was the last thing Jen would have wanted; but it was just as surely something inevitable, something she could in no way help. You had to face up to it—when a man and a woman chose each other, other ties came to nothing. That was the way of life, but just the same it sobered and saddened him a little. It left him with some long thoughts about the past years, and some troubling questions about the future that he was still working at when drowsiness came to put his thoughts out of focus, and then blot them out entirely. . . .

It surprised the Hunter brothers to see how Eastern Oregon had been filling up during these years that they had been tied close to their own spread. The trail to Winnemucca, southward now from Malheur Lake and hugging the shadow of Steens Mountain, took them across rangeland that was already on its way to becoming crowded, not only with cattle but even with sheep. One of these days, and not too far off, a drive like this one they were making would be a thing of the past. By then, maybe the Oregon Short Line that was building to a connection with the Union Pacific in Idaho would be finished, to give them a nearer shipping point in the neighborhood of The Dalles.

Fall was well advanced when they trailed into Winnemucca, a season of chill dawns and of yellow leaves streaming from sparse cottonwoods along the Humbolt. The prime market still held firm, however. Within a few hours Schrader and the Hunters had found a buyer for their beef; the deal was made, and a day later they were throwing their cattle into the loading chutes and prodding them into the cars. Schrader had offered the brothers further pay if they would stay with the shipment until it reached the Missouri slaughter house. Riding the caboose to Kansas City, which neither of them had seen, was a temptation; but too much was waiting to be done at the spread on Willow Creek. They pocketed the check for payment of their beef, and the wages they'd earned from Schrader, and started home.

The two youngsters, Sam Clifton and Charlie Hewett, took the jobs on the stock train; they left their horses in a Winnemucca livery stable and climbed aboard the train with their sights set for high times in the big town on the Missouri. They were plenty excited. The Prineville country wouldn't be seeing them again, likely, until spring.

It was on a day of fierce wind and scudding clouds that the Hunters returned to Crooked River. The first to see them, after their weeks of solid traveling, was Jim Blake; they rode into his place in the upper canyon and found him in a shed behind the house, doctoring a horse that had got into some wire and laid open a foreleg just above the fetlock. Blake, working with axle grease and clean rags to daub and bind the cut, greeted the brothers casually—as though it had been a day or two and not a month since he'd last seen them.

"Good trip?"

"Middling." Chris Hunter dug into his windbreaker, brought out the bank draft with Blake's name on it, received in payment for the cattle the latter had shipped with the Schrader herd. Blake gave the figure no more than a glance, nodded as though satisfied, and shoved the paper into a shirt pocket.

"How's the Slash 7?" Bob Hunter asked.

"Same as you left it," Blake said; and with this exchange their mutual obligations were discharged and acknowledged, and a deal was completed.

The brothers watched in interested silence as Blake continued with his work. Wind howled lonesomely along the high canyon walls. Chris observed, "Turned off a mite chilly."

"It's not bad when the sun comes through; right now it looks like rain. . . .

"There's coffee heating on the stove," Blake suggested. "And grub if you want to help yourselves. I'll be in as soon as I finish here."

"Shot of coffee would cut the chill all right," Bob agreed, and the Hunters led their trail-dusty mounts to the corral where there was water and feed. They slipped the bits, leaving the saddles on, and entered the one-room shack where Blake batched it with his crew when he wasn't in town—his wife seldom came here. It was a low-roofed building with wooden bunks built against the walls and a sheet-iron stove for cooking and heating. The wall pegs dripped with the gear of Blake's three-man crew.

The Hunters were seated at the table, taking the chill out of themselves with black coffee, when Jim Blake entered. He threw open his mackinaw, got a tin cup for himself and filled it from the pot. "Hey—I guess you never heard," he said suddenly. "I'm a father! It's a boy—came two weeks ago."

That called for congratulations and some country-style joshing. It was some minutes later that Chris got around to asking, "And what else is new?"

His innocent question was a bombshell. It brought a sudden stillness, and a bleak change to the rancher's expression. He set down his cup and scowled at it.

79

"Things have been happening," he said gruffly. "I guess you knew we're Crook County now?"

"They named it after the old Indian fighter, did they?" Blake nodded. "General George Crook."

Bob Hunter said, "I didn't think this was to go into effect until New Year's."

"It isn't. Still, organization takes time. The pot began boiling as soon as word got out the Governor was getting ready to name the first slate of county officers."

Hunter looked at the rancher, narrow-eyed. He wasn't sure what it was that made him feel he already knew some hint of what was coming. "And has he named them?"

"Sooner than anyone thought likely. Anyone, I guess, except Major Tarback. . . ."

"Tarback!" Chris exclaimed. "What'd *he* have to do with it?"

Blake spread both palms flat on the table, looked from one visitor to the other with bitter anger. "Plenty! He left Prineville the same day the news broke. I think he must have killed a horse or two, in his hurry to get across the mountains to Salem and grab the Governor's ear. Less than a week later the appointments came through."

"And?" Bob Hunter prodded. Blake met his stare.

"You want me to give it to you all in a bunch? All right— listen close!" His voice was harsh as he named them: "County treasurer—Gus Weckler. County attorney—George Wright. Sheriff—Jase Evans. . . ."

"You're not serious!" Chris exclaimed hoarsely.

Jim Blake's grim expression was answer enough. "As for Tarback, he and Tom Ridges will make two of the three commissioners."

Bob Hunter found his voice. "They can't do this to us! Every damn one of them's a Vigilante—all except George Wright; and I've long had suspicions he was playing the Major's game."

"He's got his reward," Blake said darkly. "For a man like George, this appointment can be the first big step in a career. The Major must sure as hell figure he's worth it." The rancher picked up his coffee cup, set it down again. "There's one more name, that I'd just as soon not have to be the one to tell you; but you'll hear it sooner or later."

"And whose is that?"

"Walter Allen. He's to be county judge—and head man on the board of commissioners."

Hunter felt a growing numbness, at the idea of Jen's father

belonging in that company. "You aren't trying to tell me he's gone over to the Vigilantes!"

Chris suggested quickly, "It doesn't have to mean that, Bob. Allen's a good man. He could have been appointed on his merits."

"He could have," Blake agreed, "but it's damned doubtful. It's an open secret, now, that Tarback was into the Governor for past favors, in the days when the Major was a hack journalist running political newspapers over at the capital. I wrote a fellow I know in the Assembly, to see if he thought there was any way we could get these appointments quashed—make the Governor understand just what kind of men Tarback had wished off on him. This fellow said there wasn't a chance. It's done, and anybody's wasting his time to try to undo it."

"But there's got to be something!" Bob Hunter cried. "My God! Isn't it plain enough to everyone, by this time, what Tarback's after? It should have been six months ago, when he used a lynching as the excuse for setting up a phony Stockman's Association. If we wait now till this hand-picked machine of his takes the whole county over, it'll be too late!"

"It may be a little late already," Blake said heavily. "This is a troubled range right now. There ain't too many heroes on it."

"It don't take heroes!" Hunter retorted. "Chris and I are proof of that. *We* stood up to Tarback and the Association— and nothing happened; we never even got one of those damned skull-and-crossbones letters! And surely there's other self-respecting folks in this Crooked River country who aren't willing to hang back and let some bunch of Vigilantes have their way. If we'll only get together—"

"That's just the way Jed Starns was talking, when he heard about the appointments."

"Good for him!" Hunter remembered Jed Starns, that day at Haze's—the timid man with the bony features and the sun-bleached yellow hair who had found the courage to get up on his hind legs and challenge Calvin Tarback. "If a quiet fellow like that can speak his mind, it should teach some other people a lesson."

"That's just the point," Blake said grimly. "I'm afraid they've learned their lesson, all right!"

Hunter felt his breathing go shallow. "What do you mean?"

"I mean that Starns is dead."

"Dead!" Chris looked as though he had been struck. Jim Blake nodded slowly.

"Happened about a week ago. It came as no real surprise. Rumors had been flying like bats, that he was a marked man for sounding off so loud against the Vigilantes. I got worried finally and rode out there to his place by Powell Butte to try and quiet him down. I wasn't in time.

"I found Jed lying on the ground. Looked like somebody used a shotgun on him—the whole top of his head was blowed off. When I rode up quite a bunch of men were there standing around him." .

Bob Hunter snapped, "What men?"

"I think you're ahead of me," Blake answered dryly. "They were Vigilantes. Jase Evans, for one. Bud Morrison and Tom Ridges and a few others. They didn't explain what they happened to be doing on his place; they didn't say a word. But from the look of things I decided it was no place for me! I turned around and left." He added, "Some time later, they brought Starns into town in a wagon. . . ."

"And—that's the end of it?" Hunter exclaimed, incredulous.

"There was no witnesses—nothing to go on, except the rumor. I heard George Wright rode out and looked around a little, but if there was any sign all those horses milling around must have buried it. The town gave Starns a real nice funeral, up on the hill. Major Tarback made a little speech—said it only went to prove why we had to have a Stockman's Association. That it must have been some horse thief done him in."

Hunter's fist clenched hard, resting on the table top. "Don't tell me," he said, "anybody believed it!"

Jim Blake hesitated over his answer. "I'd say it gave them something they could pretend to believe. You've got to understand," he went on earnestly, "whatever we three happen to think or suspect, most people hereabouts are convinced the Major's sincere. And even those who aren't—well, who wants to be the next to get a letter warning him out of the country? Who wants to be next to get the same treatment as Langley and Farrell—and now, Jed Starns?"

There was a stillness. A burnt-through stick of pinewood broke and settled in the stove, with a sudden frying of hot pitch and rush of flames in the stovepipe chimney. Finally Hunter asked quietly, "What about you, Jim? You talking for yourself?"

"I was hoping you wouldn't ask that." Blake lifted a hand and stroked his silky droop of mustache; he looked tired, and older than he was. "I've spent a good many hours working at that question—and I keep coming back to one answer: A man with a family has more than just himself to worry about. Whatever I do, I've got to think first about my wife and son."

"I wonder if you're thinking about them hard enough?" Hunter retorted. "Is it any favor to a boy, letting him grow up knowing his father could have helped to nip an evil before it got out of control and didn't?"

"Bob!" Chris was staring at him in horror; and now he saw Jim Blake's face drain of its color, and mortification brought him stumbling to his feet.

"Hell! I don't even know what I'm saying! I got no quarrel with you, Jim; I know you're no coward. If I had a family, chances are I'd feel the same way." He lifted his hands, let them fall. "Chris, maybe we better hit the trail. We got a ride ahead of us yet."

His brother got up more slowly. "Maybe you're right." Lamely he added, "Thanks for the coffee, Jim."

But Jim Blake failed to answer. They left him sitting at the table, his lean face without expression, his blue eyes staring fixedly at some spot in front of him.

CHAPTER VII

In the saddle again, traveling down the broad canyon with the sun breaking briefly out of the cloud cover to turn an occasional spear of rain into a shining dazzle, Hunter expected a reprimand; but Chris said nothing at all about the way he had spoken to Jim Blake. He did have one comment, and he made it in his quiet, diffident way: "I don't think Jim will hold that against you. And maybe things aren't as bad as they look, kid. In the long run, I mean. A business like this can defeat itself—if you just give it time to tangle in its own rope. When it gets too far out of hand, hell itself won't have it!"

Hunter's reply was sour. "I'm thinking of the hell that can take this county while we're waiting for that to happen. . . ."

At a hitch rail near the barnlike entrance of Hamilton's Livery, Jase Evans was tightening the cinch on his black gelding, the stirrup hung up on the saddlehorn out of the way.

Bud Morrison stood by, impatient and ready to mount. It was Morrison who saw the brothers approaching; his narrow, Indian-dark head lifted. He said something that warned Evans and caused him to turn ponderously. Moving deliberately, the big fellow stepped away from his mount and into the street. "Well!" he said loudly, his voice holding more than a trace of mockery. "The Hunter boys!"

Chris plainly wanted to ride on, but that would have entailed pulling wide and Bob wouldn't do it. He drew up the slack and, with the horse uneasy under him, looked coldly at Jase Evans as sunlight and cloud shadow alternately brightened and darkened the day, and the chill streaks of rain came on gusts of the flowing wind. He said, "Hello, Jase."

"You been away, I hear," the big man said, in that same mocking tone. "I was beginning to think it was for good."

"Disappointed?"

Evans shrugged. "A little surprised, maybe."

The dark-skinned Bud Morrison said heavily, "We didn't figure you for enough nerve to come back, once you got headed the other direction!"

Chris, watching his brother's face, didn't like what he saw in it. He said quickly, "They're only baiting you, kid!"

The latter paid no attention. His stare was on Morrison now and his mouth was hard. "Did you suppose killing one steer was enough to scare us out?" He added: "I hardly thought what happened that day would have looked like we were scared of *you*, Bud!"

The reminder of his poor showing in front of the other members of Tarback's crew turned Morrison's narrow face even darker. Jase Evans took up the challenge, loudly: "Hunter, someday you're gonna find out you can't go cross-grained to the rest of this range, and get away with it forever."

"Oh? Is that maybe what you told Jed Starns?"

The thrust struck home. "Now, wait a minute!" Evans cried, seeming to swell with quick fury. Hunter simply turned away, ignoring him.

A team and rig was coming along Main, having spun across the bridge over the Ochoco. Anyone in the Prineville country would have recognized it—Major Tarback was a superb horseman, but he also liked to keep a red-wheeled, black leather buggy in the stable behind his house, to drive behind a pair of the fine blooded horses he raised. Now, without ceremony, Bob Hunter kneed his mount and put it athwart the path of the oncoming rig. Tarback, on the buggy's seat, had little choice but

84

to draw rein. He was scowling as he demanded, "What do you want, Hunter?"

Moving on abreast of the buggy seat, Hunter saw now that it held another occupant. The storm curtains were up and her face looked whitely out of the shadows where she sat, pressed into the corner, her hands limp on the heavy laprobe across her knees.

Hunter didn't know what there was about Ada Tarback that made her seem a lost and tragic figure. He nodded to her and lifted a hand respectfully to touch his hatbrim. Then, looking at her husband, he said without preliminary, "Tarback, I want you to call off your dogs! I'm not fooling!"

Turning his whole body to do it, because of that stiff neck, the Major stabbed Morrison and Evans with a shrewdly appraising glance. "If you can't keep out of trouble with my riders," he said, "that's not my problem."

"I think otherwise," Hunter told him crisply. "Remember, I used to be on your payroll. I know that the men who work for you follow orders or they just don't stay. So if my steers are slaughtered—or if I don't want to end up like Jed Starns, with a bullet from Jase Evans's gun in my head—looks to me you're the one I want to talk to."

Jase Evans let out a bellow: "I heard that!" He came striding through the shuttle of light and cloud shadow, and as a precaution Hunter quickly pushed his coat aside and placed a hand on the gun shoved behind his belt.

The big man halted in his tracks, and his face turned careful. Hunter was at the same time conscious of a stir about him. By now, he realized, his scene in the street had drawn an audience; he glimpsed Jennifer Allen and her father, who had come out onto the front steps of the store—he was sorry they had to see this but he wouldn't back away from it. Calvin Tarback said sharply, "Leave the gun where it is, Hunter!"

"Maybe you're forgetting—I don't take your orders!"

It was a moment for the Major to show the masterful control that seemed to inspire confidence in nearly everyone except Bob Hunter. An urge to violence flared in the pale eyes, caused a play of muscle beneath the skin of the man's clenched jaws; but when he spoke his voice was level. "I've been very patient with you, Hunter. You've refused to go along with your neighbors' efforts to clean house on this range; what's worse, you've gone out of your way to slander me and the men who work for me. I won't deign to notice what you just said about Jason Evans. As for Morrison shooting one of your steers—he was only trying to

85

carry out the rules of the Association, and went a little further than he should have. I'll pay you right here and now, the full market value of the animal."

He was already reaching for a billfold. Hunter shook his head. "I don't want your money. I'm just serving notice that the Hunters are to be left alone!

"Used to be, a man had a few rights—like not being dragged out and hanged under a bridge, or driven off his own spread by threats. He had a right not to see his beef slaughtered and himself called a cattle thief, because he wouldn't knuckle under to something calling itself a Stockman's Association. Or have his head blown off the way Jed Starns did, for speaking out against the Vigilante machine that's grabbed control of Crook County!"

His voice was shaking as he finished; for a moment he and the Major could only stare at one another, their glances locked. Tarback's voice, when he answered Hunter, seemed almost quiet by contrast but it carried clearly over the hushed sounds of the street.

"Apparently there's no use talking to you—but, in the long run you'll hurt nobody but yourself!" Deliberately, Tarback lifted the reins, with an order for his riders: "Evans, you two get your horses and come along." He waited to see the pair turn sullenly to their mounts. After that he slapped the leathers on the rumps of his team and put the buggy into motion.

Drawing aside, Hunter had a last glimpse of Ada Tarback's too-pale face before the buggy's sidecurtains came between. After that the rig pulled away, to turn at the corner beyond the Jackson House and so pass from sight. Morrison and Evans went with it, the latter showing Hunter a look of plain hatred as he spurred in the wake of the Major.

Only when they were gone did Hunter drop his hand away from the gun. Drawing a breath, he looked around him. He was a little startled to see how large an audience had been drawn to that inconclusive scene. Passing up the rest, he reined his horse over toward where Jen and her father stood.

The girl spoke his name and started forward. At once, Walter Allen's hand closed firmly on her wrist. Whether from anger or from the rain-wet wind, the man's face was red; the thinning hair stood about his scalp in a gray thicket. "I forbid it!" he exclaimed as Jen turned startled eyes on him. "I absolutely forbid you to go near him! You—you heard how he spoke about your father!"

She could only stammer. Hunter said sharply, "Walter, you were never even mentioned."

"You said it was a machine that had taken over Crook County!" Allen retorted, his mouth like a trap. "That would include me!"

Hunter hesitated. "I did hear you'd been appointed judge. But it would never occur to me, for a minute, to think you'd have any part in what Tarback is up to."

Allen refused to be mollified. He still had his daughter's wrist and she had given up trying to pull away; she stood miserably at his side, looking from her father to the man she loved. Spears of rain were falling faster now, beginning to spot the wooden sidewalk and the dirt of the street with wide, dark circles.

"Honestly, Robert!" the storekeeper said. "I just don't know why you insist on making a villain of Calvin Tarback! Are you so eaten up with jealousy? Of him, and of George Wright, and anyone else who manages to lift himself a little out of the common rut?"

Chris was moved to protest: "That ain't just fair . . ." No one seemed to notice him.

"And now," Allen went on, "you're trying to blame Tarback for what happened to poor Jed Starns—when everybody knows Jed was murdered by horse thieves. The same ones you'd want us to believe don't even exist!"

Hunter's cheeks felt stiff, frozen by a cold greater than the autumn chill. He looked at Allen's angry face, and at Jen who had begun to cry. His brother Chris said quietly, "You don't seem to be getting anywhere much with your talking, kid. . . ."

"No, I don't."

He made no move as Walter Allen said roughly, "I see no point standing here arguing—getting soaked to the skin. Jen, go inside." The girl threw Hunter a last despairing look across her shoulder, but she could do nothing but let herself be turned and led away.

Abruptly the clot of people on the street dispersed and scattered as the rain came down harder, in a cold, slashing downpour; the clouds overhead seemed to close together like the lid of a box and the light of the damp day failed perceptibly. A chill wind pummeled the street and drove the blades of rain against a man's face. Hunter pulled his windbreaker more tightly about his throat.

The brothers rode on up the street, their horses restive and uneasy under the rain. Passing Gus Weckler's hardware,

Hunter had a glimpse of the man's ferretlike face peering at him from the store window; he couldn't really see the other's expression but it wasn't hard to imagine a leer of triumph on the new county treasurer. It was the last thing his sour mood needed.

They clattered across the wooden bridge over Ochoco Creek, the pine planks thudding dully under their shoe irons, and pulled up for a moment. The gray water of the creek slid past, dimpled by the rain. Chris voiced Hunter's own thoughts.

"I guess it don't pay sometimes to try and shove your opinions down people's throats. Not if they aren't ready for them."

Not answering for a moment, Hunter turned in the saddle for a look at the village. Its buildings were drab and unlovely in the gloomy light. Wind flattened and shredded the pillars of chimney smoke that rose from every house. A tang of smoke, and of rain-stirred dust, hung heavy about them. Hunter shivered in the chill and his mouth set hard; he swung away, putting his back to Prineville and looking to the trail across the canyon floor toward the abrupt lift of Grizzly, and the higher reaches of the Ochocos that were lost in mist and drifting sheets of rain.

He said heavily, "You tried to tell me, I ought to let this thing defeat itself. Maybe you were right—certainly it don't look like anyone's going to make a dent in it, for all the hollering he does. . . .

"Well," he added, "I've learned my lesson! I hope Allen's right, and I'm wrong; but from now on, when it's anything that concerns affairs in Prineville—I stay out!"

Chris gave him a troubled look. "Now, wait! I don't mean you have to take that attitude. . . ."

The other was adamant. "A man's got more than enough to do," he said, "keeping his own up. If I ever forget that again, I hope you'll belt me one. Now, let's get home!" He shook out the wet reins and lifted his mount with the spur. His brother had no choice but to follow. They struck off at a canter, northward through the driving rain.

CHAPTER VIII

George Wright's quarters—and, consequently, since the new year, the office of Prineville's first county attorney—occupied a dingy room above Weckler's hardware, which was reached by an uncovered outside stairway snaking up the side of the building. For furnishings he had a few uncomfortable chairs, a second-hand desk, and a pineplank case he had made himself to hold his law books. A grating in the floor was supposed to supply heat from the store below, but it worked none too well on a cold January day and George had long since chosen to supplement it with a pot-bellied stove that stood in a box of ashes in one corner of the room.

The stove was working now, the pipe showing a spot of cherry red just where it bent to vanish into the wall; but George was a thin-blooded man and his hands felt numb as he sat at the desk leafing through the pages of a casebook, scowling and restless. Sunlight lay in patches on the floor, and the sky he could see through steamed-over window glass was a fierce blue; but the winter sun gave little heat. Each window frame still held a ring of ice left after the melting of last night's thick deposit.

Seated in a chair near the stove—or rather sprawled there on the end of his spine—young Eddie Wright boredly flipped playing cards at a hat on the floor in front of him. He missed oftener than he hit, swearing each time in a half-hearted manner until George finally lost his temper. "For God's sake! Either shut that up, or find something else to do!"

The other lifted his head. Things had been growing steadily more unpleasant between the two of them these last months, George's deepening deterioration of character meeting a sullen resistance in the boy so that hostility fairly crackled between them. Eddie looked at his brother, now, above the card he held poised. In sullen anger he flung the whole remaining pack, making the hat spin and wobble on its crown. He hitched around on his chair, and through the circle he'd swiped clear on the pane looked out at snow-covered roofs, and the glittering white of Prineville's Main Street below him.

The snow was not deep, but it had been on the ground only a couple of days and was still a clean dazzle, eye-punishing under the glare of the small, cold, winter sun. It had been trampled to slush on the boardwalks and in the street, but in backyards it lay almost unbroken except for the pathways made to outhouse or woodpile, and the occasional wavering line of tracks where one of the town dogs had cut across an open lot. Downstreet, a raw and unsightly heap of charred timbers and rubble thrust through the blanket of snow, marking the site of what until recently had been a block of buildings. The ashes had still been steaming when the snow fell, melting the flakes as they came down; the result was like a black, ugly wound.

Eddie Wright, however, was peering in the opposite direction, toward the Ochoco Creek bridge where his attention had been drawn by the only movement in the frozen landscape. "Rider coming into town," he suddenly muttered. His eyes narrowed, and he shot a look at his brother. He added, slyly, "Looks to me like one of them Hunters. . . ."

He got the result he wanted. George, already returned to his book, looked up sharply and stabbed a finger at the page to mark his place. "Which one?"

The boy shrugged narrow shoulders. "They're too much alike. I can't tell 'em apart from here." Turning again to the window he presently added, "The fellow's stopping at Allen's."

Eddie grinned tightly as he heard an exclamation from the direction of the desk. A book was slammed shut, a chair scraped back. George strode to the window, shoving past Eddie's sprawled legs. He swiped a hand across the glass of the upper pane to clear it, and stared down and across toward the Allen store—at the horse standing there in hoof-chopped snow with a balloon of breath misting from its nostrils, and the man dismounting.

George Wright's face was hard and tight with angry suspicion, that eased only slightly as he saw for himself who the rider was.

Chris Hunter wrapped his leathers deftly around the tie pole, moved around the bay horse and up onto the boardwalk where he paused to kick mud and snow from his boots and look around at the silent town. For a moment he peered in astonishment at that leveled stretch of black earth and char and ashes, downstreet and beyond the intersection, where the familiar silhouette of a row of building fronts had utterly vanished.

"Wonder when the fire was?" he said aloud.

It was no surprise in a town of flimsy wooden buildings, of oil lamps and cheap iron stoves and faulty chimneys, that fires should start and, when they did, that they could sweep through an entire block of buildings before being brought under control. It was the ever-present threat, the doom that hung over every cow-country village like Prineville. Chris Hunter shook his head over it and, turning, walked inside the store.

As he closed the door behind him, the bell on its spring sent echoes through the big storeroom. He thought he was alone, but next moment there was the rustle of a skirt and Jen straightened from behind a counter where she had been stooping to arrange some merchandise on a lower shelf. At sight of Chris she gave an exclamation of pleasure, as if truly glad to see him.

"Hello, Jen." Moving toward her, unhooking the fastenings of his heavy coat, he saw how her eager glance went past him expectantly; then some of the light died in her eyes and her smile failed a little at the corners.

She said, trying to make light of it, "Bob didn't come with you?" But Chris understood.

"Wasn't able to make it this time," he explained, choosing his words carefully. "He's out with the herd, throwing feed. Storm like we just had always makes extra work, especially when you don't know how soon we might get another. There's already clouds piling up over the Three Sisters. We figured one of us better get in and fetch back a few supplies while the trail's open."

Disappointment made her say, with just a trace of hurt, "I suppose you pulled straws—and you lost!" She went on, blurting it before he could answer: "Doesn't he realize how long it's been since I—since any of us have seen him? Not even at Christmas! I thought surely—"

Chris swallowed, looked down at his boots. "I know," he said. "I'm sorry." His eyes lifted again to Jen's unhappy frown. "But Bob's kind of a stubborn guy, and he was plain mad that day, the last time we rode out of town. He said he wouldn't be coming back; and he meant it."

"He's not mad at *me*, is he?"

"Course not. If the truth's told, I think he just doesn't want to make more trouble for you with your pa. According to his figuring, the best way to keep from doing that is to stay clear away—at least, until things kind of straighten themselves out." He swallowed again, uncomfortable and somewhat alarmed, as he saw how the girl's face tightened with hurt and her eyes seemed to mist over. "I'm sorry," he finished lamely.

She blinked a time or two, managed a smile. "It's not your fault. . . . You said you came in for supplies?"

"Yeah." He fumbled in a shirt pocket, brought out a piece of paper and spread it flat on the counter with his palm. "Here's the list. Mostly it's flour we're running short of." The next was a lie: "I got somebody I should see, down the street. Maybe, while I—"

"You go right ahead," Jen said quickly. "I'll have these ready when you come back."

"Thanks."

He was sorry to lie, but glad when the door closed behind him and the cold glare of the winter sun was in his face. Jen had been near crying, and embarrassed over it; he knew she wanted him gone for a few minutes so she could pull herself together. He stood there and swore, under his breath—a single "damn!" He was a slow man to come to a boil, but all at once he was angry—at his own brother. Bob should have made this ride today; it would have done Jen a world of good to see him walk in the store. But no, he had to be stubborn. . . .

Drawing a breath of the January cold, that dried out his nostrils and seemed to sink a blade halfway into his lungs, Chris looked along the street and again saw the black wreckage of the fire. On an impulse, drawn by curiosity, he started in that direction.

The destruction had been complete. Every building on the west side of Main, south from the corner of Third until an empty lot had checked the spread of the flames, was gone. Chris stood and looked across at it, with the revolted fascination destruction always seems to hold. The sound of a familiar voice pulled him around, then, to see the cadaverous figure of Gil Haze, the saloonkeeper, standing in the door of his place of business. Chris returned his greeting, and indicated the blackened rubble. "That's a sad sight."

"Yeah—ain't it!"

Haze had a right to look gloomy, for the largest of the burnt buildings had been his own livery barn. Chris asked, "When did it happen?"

"New Year's—and what a hell of a way to begin one! Somebody knocked over an oil lamp in the drugstore on the corner and, once started, there was no stopping it. We managed to get the horses out of the barn but that was all." Haze lifted narrow shoulders in a shrug. "Come inside before we both freeze to death."

92

The saloon was empty. Following him in, Chris said, "I haven't got much time. I rode in for supplies. Have to be starting right back."

"Have a shot, then, to warm you up before you go." Gil Haze sounded bored and anxious for talk. He moved around behind the bar, uncorked and poured. "That's a long trail."

"It is," the other agreed. "And if you think you got it cold down here in this canyon, you just ought to try crossing old Grizzly." He saluted the other with his glass, lifted it and made a face as the whiskey hit his throat. "Thanks," he said, putting down the empty glass.

Gil Haze used his rag on the gleaming bartop. "We going to get some more snow?" he wanted to know, and they spent some minutes discussing the significance of the mantle of clouds that Chris had seen cloaking the shoulders of the Cascade peaks.

They agreed that it had been an open fall, but that with the coming of January they were in, now, for whatever worst the winter cared to throw at them.

Chris suggested, "I suppose you'll wait till spring to rebuild your barn."

The other stroked his drooping mustache with lean fiddle player's fingers. "Haven't made up my mind yet. I been thinking I might get out of that business. I've just about decided what Prineville needs worse, right now, is an opera house."

"Opera house!" Chris Hunter blinked. "You're fooling!"

"The hell I am! This is going to be an important town, now that it's the county seat; but outside the Union Church, we ain't got a hall that's big enough or suitable for holding public meetings. With a stage, and lights, and a curtain, we could have some real entertainment in these parts. Probably book some shows clear from Portland."

Chris had to grin. "You're planning big enough, for a town that doesn't even own a courthouse."

"Tarback and some of the others are already working on that. They've got a site picked, over east on Third; now they're at work raising the money."

"Aren't you all being a little previous? This location is only temporary, until the county's had a chance to vote."

"True enough," Haze said seriously. "But what's the competition? Cleek, and Mitchell, and maybe a couple of other places—Prineville has it way over all of them. No sense to take the county seat away now that we've already got it. Wouldn't be logical."

"Maybe." Chris took his hat from the counter where he'd laid

93

it. "Well—thanks again for the drink. I better get my stuff at Allen's and hit the road. . . ."

"Oh—one thing, Chris," the saloonkeeper said reluctantly. "Now that Jase Evans has been officially sworn in to wear the sheriff's badge, it might be an idea if you two boys was to kind of steer clear of him. Him and his deputy, both."

"Deputy?"

"That fellow, Bud Morrison. First thing the Commission done was to okay his salary."

Chris grunted shortly. "Sounds like they're all getting up to the trough," he said. "All of Tarback's friends!"

"There's a big change around here," Haze told him. "Meanwhile it's no secret any more that, except maybe for Tarback himself, nearly all the key men in the county government, and in the Stockman's Association, were members of the Vigilante gang that lynched Langley and Farrell. Too late to do anything about that now, of course. If you don't like it, you keep your mouth shut. On the other hand, a lot of men who never had anything to do with them before, are suddenly trying to let on like they always was part of the Vigilantes.

"I'm just thinking about your brother. His name is mud with that crowd—as you well know. You better warn him to be a little careful."

"Bob can take care of himself, I reckon," Chris said, though he didn't think he sounded very convincing. "Anyway, I don't reckon there's much danger of a run-in, not real soon. He's in no rush to get in to Prineville, these days. He's just about washed his hands of the place."

Haze clucked his tongue, shaking his head. And Chris let it go at that.

Walter Allen was at the store when Chris got back there, and there was a courteous exchange of greetings. Jen had his purchases ready. Chris paid, dumped the things into a gunny sack and took them out to strap behind his saddle. The girl had followed; as he was preparing to mount she rather diffidently brought out a package wrapped in tissue paper and tied with a red ribbon.

"Would you give this to Bob for me, please?" And as he took it, with a puzzled look, she explained: "It's a scarf I knitted for him for a Christmas present. I was hoping to give it to him myself. . . ."

"Sorry you didn't get to," he said, a little gruffly, and stowed the package in a pocket of his coat. "Sure, I'll take it to him."

94

He stood a moment with the reins in his hands, frowning over the effort to say something more encouraging. When nothing suggested itself, he nodded to the girl and turned to swing astride. He backed away from the pole and trotted away up the muddy street.

Jen, watching him go, hugged her elbows against the winter chill and thought unhappily of messages she might have sent with him; but decided there was no use sharing her unhappiness. She knew Bob was doing the wisest thing he knew how, under the circumstances. And with his enemies in power, she would not really have wanted to see him here in Prineville however much she missed him.

She turned, then, and saw her father standing in the open door, looking at her. He was squinting against the thin sunlight; from something in his expression she knew at once he had seen the package change hands, had heard what she said to Chris about it. She drew a deep breath and walked into the store past him. Walter Allen stood aside for her and afterward closed the door, his mouth set reprovingly.

"I'll say nothing to your mother about this," he said. "But I hope you understand that I'm very disappointed."

"Disappointed?" she echoed, turning to face him. "But why, Papa? Just because I want to send a Christmas present to a friend?"

"Behind our backs!" he snapped. "I suppose you've been seeing Hunter, too—behind our backs!"

Jen bit her lip. She was not a wilful or disobedient girl; she loved her parents and liked to please them. But this was growing more and more difficult, as the pressures increased that would bend her to obedience where her feelings for Bob Hunter were concerned. "That isn't so!" she cried. "I haven't seen him once, not since you positively forbade it. But, you're being unfair to him—and to me! You have no reason to—to *hate* Bob, the way you almost seem to. . . ."

"I will not be called a crook, and a fool!" Allen retorted, his mouth like a trap. "You can't ask me to forgive him that! Besides," he went on, his manner altering a little as genuine affection softened the edge of his anger, "I want the best for my daughter. Hunter will never be anything more than what he is; and a homestead ranch is no place for you. It would kill your mother and me, to think of you slaving your life away!"

"It's my life," she reminded him.

"But you're still too young to know what you want to do with it. We have a responsibility to keep you from throwing it away and regretting it all the years to come. Why won't you listen to us? Why can't you see what a young fellow like George Wright has to offer? He's from our kind of people—and he has a real future. All you would need to do is give him the least encouragement, and he'd be over here proposing to you in a minute. I can't see what in the world you're waiting for!"

"Oh, Papa—please!" Her eyes brimmed suddenly with scalding tears, her trembling hands knotted. "We've been all over this—so many times."

Walter Allen made an impatient, scooping gesture. He said harshly, "Well, just don't think you've heard the last of it! Some day, young lady, you're going to see the sense of what your mother and I have been trying to tell you. Until then, I don't even want to hear Bob Hunter's name mentioned."

"But, Papa—"

"No, no! No!" He clapped his hands to his ears and brushed past her. He vanished through the curtained doorway at the rear section of the store, leaving his daughter staring miserably after him.

CHAPTER IX

On a Saturday in March, Dutch Schrader walked into Gil Haze's. He had his two young punchers, Clifton and Hewett, with him.

They found places at the bar, and Schrader called for beers. Gil Haze looked closely at the pair with him and asked dubiously, "These two boys old enough to be drinking?"

"We're old enough," Sam Clifton told him, grinning, and Charlie Hewett added, "Hell! We been clear to Kansas City last fall!" Haze looked at him and then at Schrader, who nodded.

"A beer apiece won't hurt 'em any," the Dutchman said. "I'll hold them to that." Haze served them, and Schrader paid.

There was a pretty good crowd. A promise of better weather had brought the range folk out. Winter's back was broken, though patches of snow-ice still lay around and the roads into town, like the village streets, had been spotted with muddy pools

96

that reflected the gray sky, while from roof-edges and eaves, melt water dripped like rain. Tasting his beer, Schrader watched a stud game that was going at a table not far from the bar. As he did, he bristled a little.

The players—all men he knew—were part of what he had come to think of as the Vigilante crowd: Commissioner Tom Ridges, Hack Gorham the blacksmith, and a couple of others. And Jase Evans, of course, with his hat pushed back on his blocky head and the new nickeled sheriff's badge glinting. Just now Evans had been dealt winning cards in this stud game; his pock-marked cheeks were flushed with the liquor he had been drinking, and his crow of laughter overrode other sounds as he flipped over his hole card and dragged in the pot. Schrader, thinking that Crook County's sheriff had most probably led the murderers of Luke Langley and himself dragged Bill Farrell to his death at a rope's end—and more than likely, been the man who shot Jed Starns—felt his mouth draw out long and hard.

. . .

Into a momentary lull, such as will sometimes descend on a room full of men, the voice of Charlie Hewett spoke suddenly: "Anybody know who belongs to the big red horse I seen tied out front?"

Schrader looked at him sharply. He had noticed the horse—a big racer. Someone else answered the question: "Can't you read brands, kid? That's blood stock. It couldn't belong to anybody but the Major."

Along the bar, the Indian-dark head of Bud Morrison lifted. "Like hell it does! That horse belongs to me," he announced flatly. "I bought him from Tarback, out of my wages. And who wants to know, anyway?"

"Why, I was just admiring him," Hewett said. "He's a good horse. Looks like he'd have speed."

"He's fast enough," Morrison told him, after regarding the young fellow a moment with a coldly expressionless stare.

Sam Clifton spoke up with bland confidence. "I got one that could beat him."

Hewett turned on him. "You don't mean the gray? That ewe-necked piece of crowbait you let carry your saddle around for you?" He hooted. "Who are you kidding?"

The other youngster came back at him. "You just ain't seen him let out. I figure he can beat any horse in *these* parts. And if you think that's just blow," he added, his voice rising, "I got a couple months' pay I'm ready to lay on him, even odds!" He was digging in a pocket of his jeans; he dragged out a small wad

97

of coins and greenbacks and slapped them down on the bar, defiantly.

"That's a safe enough bet to make!" his friend retorted, grinning. "You know better than to think anybody'd actually bother taking you up on it!"

Everybody was listening by this time. Dutch Schrader saw smirks of amusement on the faces around them. Any talk of horses and betting and odds could be counted on to draw attention, any time, in this town of Prineville; but the knowing scorn with which Jase Evans and his friends were hearing young Clifton's boasts had an effect on Schrader, and got the better of his judgment. He knew what the boys were up to, and he knew they could be getting out of their depth. Still, at the idea of seeing this crowd surprised and jolted out of its complacency, a perverse impulse made him decide to go along with the game.

"Well, I dunno," he said, his honest German face sober and blandly guileless. "I've seen the gray run. I got a notion it might even beat that blood horse of Morrison's."

Jase Evans pushed his chair back now and put a hard stare on Schrader. "Where is this crowbait wonder?" he demanded suspiciously.

"Outside," Sam Clifton said, with a jerk of his red-thatched head. "I left him tied across the street."

Curiosity brought Evans to his feet and took him to the door where others joined him as he peered through the glass, a scowl on his heavy features. He stood like that for some minutes, observing Muggins; the gray horse stood at the hitch post, the picture of dejection, the gusty March wind streaming his mane and ratty-looking tail. Jase Evans gave a sour grunt and turned back to glare at Schrader. "Mister, you got you a bet!"

Not to appear too eager, Dutch hesitated. "Well, now—"

"What's the matter—you just like to hear the sound of your own voice? Put up your money or shut up! Three to one on the red horse against that scarecrow yonder. Take it or leave it!"

Schrader rubbed a palm across his broad cheeks. "At those odds," he said, "reckon I have to take it. That is, if Morrison's willing to make a race of it—and Gil Haze will hold the stakes. . . ."

In Prineville, it took no more than that to arrange a match between two horse owners. Within minutes the matter was settled, the course determined—a single lap, flat-out, down the long road from Haze's to the river and back. Even those who scoffed at racing the gray against Morrison's blooded horse were eager enough to take the money Schrader and his pair of riders were willing to put up. Clifton and Hewett had their hoarded wages, saved carefully against this opportunity; at odds of three to one, they stood to make a big winning if the gray could only turn the tables.

The crowd poured into the street. Sam Clifton went to get Muggins. The gray horse lifted his head sleepily as he untied the reins, with fingers that trembled with eagerness. "I've got you into the big one this time, boy!" he murmured. "Now it's up to you. You let me down and I'll have to cut off your oats!" He slapped the scrawny neck affectionately—and turned to see Morrison and Evans bearing down on him.

Morrison was studying the gray with an intent carefulness that Sam didn't like. He had a horseman's eye; he had seen past the ungainly look of the animal, had seen something in the width of barrel and the very bone structure of the horse that impressed him. The smoky eyes held danger and suspicion as he told Sam, quietly, "Kid, the red horse had better win!"

"He's gonna have to step some, then."

There was a glint of white teeth as the man's lip curled. "You misunderstand me! I'm saying you better not let no crowbait like this beat out one of the Major's blood horses. Is *that* clear enough?"

Sam stared. He opened his mouth and closed it again, and then a kind of sick anger began to make its way through him. "Are you trying to tell me I got to *throw* this race?" He looked at Jase Evans and a cold sweat broke out along the line of his temples. "Hell, I couldn't! I—I got three months' pay riding on Muggins to win. . . ."

"I reckon you heard me!"

They walked away, leaving him with the threat and the problem. Suddenly he was shaking, and his knees were without stiffening as he slowly led Muggins to the starting line.

All Prineville looked to have come pouring out onto Main Street to see Muggins take on the red horse. Sam caught grins of amusement on many faces as they sized up the gray; he hardly noticed. He was too filled with sick despair. He hauled himself into the saddle and set himself, gathering rein length; Morrison, on the red horse, took his place. He caught Sam's eye with a final warning look, and the youngster tried to meet it but lost his nerve and slid his glance away. A moment later he saw Charlie Hewett and their boss, Schrader, in the crowd massed along the sidewalk. He saw Charlie's grin and wink and a lump of misery formed in his throat.

He didn't know how much his boss had put on the line, but the thought of losing for him and Charlie was suddenly far worse than what it was going to cost himself.

Then they were in position, Muggins and the big red horse shoulder to shoulder and moving about nervously, the road stretching empty ahead of them toward the distant river. The crowd quieted a little as Jase Evans, the self-appointed starter, drew his long-barreled Smith & Wesson and lifted it shoulder high. Wind buffeted the town and raised a tiny leaden surf on the street puddles.

Evans's gun cracked sharply. The crowd's voice swelled as both horses broke forward in a mud-chopping start.

Muggins under pressure, and Muggins standing hipshot at a tierack were two totally different animals. To the sound of the gun, powerful muscles exploded under Sam Clifton like steel springs, carrying him forward with a lurch that would have cracked his neck if he hadn't learned to prepare for it. Muddy water sheeted high and drenched his jeans legs, as shod hoofs struck one of the standing puddles in the road. Then the gray horse was stretched out in a flat run, as the last houses along the street flashed by and gave way to a blur of brown trailside weeds.

The yelling of the crowd was swept away and left behind, and now all he could hear was the drum of Muggins's hoofs and those of that other horse, half a length behind. The red had been taken short, completely outclassed in the getaway; Sam sneaked a look back. He glimpsed Morrison's dark face, and saw in it such a look of murder that his breath caught in his throat.

His hands tightened convulsively on the reins. "Easy, boy!" he panted. "Easy!" Muggins pounded on.

The willows along Crooked River's shallow bank showed steadily nearer, dead ahead; above their leafless thicket he glimpsed the iron superstructure of the bridge. And he remembered, suddenly, everything he had heard about the man who'd been found hanging there, last spring.

That Bill Farrell must have loved life, too. But he'd made enemies and so he had died, horribly. . . .

Suddenly he was sawing at the reins, leaning back against them with all his strength. It was something he had never done in a race and Muggins couldn't understand. The gray horse fought the pull. Sam cursed frantically. "Damn you!" he sobbed through clenched teeth. "You damn fool horse! Will you cut it out?" To withstand the punishment of the bit, Muggins broke stride.

100

At once the red horse forged past, spattering Sam with gouts of mud and slop.

When they reached the bridge Muggins was already three lengths behind and falling rapidly back. Morrison made a right turn and the red horse floundered and nearly spilled him; then he had it straightened out and, as he whipped past Sam into the home stretch, he gave the kid a look and a grin that showed all his teeth, white against the dark face.

Morrison knew! He understood the ignominious struggle that was taking place between the boy and the horse, and the humiliation of it pleasured him. He flashed past, and now Sam, too, had reached the turn; he took it, and up ahead saw the houses af the village and the crowd waiting, and that other horse pounding away from him along the empty road.

His eyes swam with blindness; the wind cut his face and he felt the cold wetness on his cheeks and found he was weeping, in anger and hurt and shame. Under him, Muggins was still trying—Muggins knew he could have beaten the red horse; he could do it still, given the chance. In spite of this inexplicable treachery, even now he could overtake the red. He would run his heart out, if he had to.

Suddenly this seemed a far greater betrayal, even, than letting Charlie and Mister Schrader down. And all at once Sam knew he couldn't go through with it, despite any threats that Morrison and Evans could make—or the thought of that man hanging lifeless from the bridge behind him. Muggins must have sensed the change, in the quick forward shifting of his weight; the ratty gray ears lifted and then Sam was leaning close above the straining neck, crooning into them: "All right, boy! Take him! Show them what you can do. . . ." And Muggins tucked back his ears, and stretched out his neck, and ran.

The wind seized Sam's hat and whipped it away; with the wildly blown strands of his own rusty hair stinging his face, he peered ahead through narrowed lashes and willed Muggins on. Bud Morrison glanced back and saw the lessening of the gap, and his dark face took on a look of pure rage. Suddenly he was swearing at the red, pelting it with the rein ends.

Muggins's nose came even with the red's hindquarters; he was drawing even. For a timeless moment the two animals were neck and neck, while the houses of town and the crowd waiting at the finish line grew steadily nearer. The shouting of the crowd came thinly to them, above the wind and the thunder of their own running.

Then the gray horse was out in front, drawing away.

Hoofbeats echoed off building fronts and the mob in front of Haze's scattered out of the way as they galloped across the finish line with a full length between.

In the solid confusion that followed, Sam Clifton wasn't sure of many things. He was down from the saddle, and Charlie Hewett was pounding him on the back and shouting fair to split his ears. Somewhere in the milling crowd, he could hear Dutch Schrader's voice crowing over the victory; he heard him say, "You better give that red horse back to the Major, Bud. If a boy on a boneheap like the gray could beat him—!"

And he saw again Morrison's hating scowl, and he saw the look on big Jase Evans, and it came over him—like a dousing with cold water—just exactly what it was he had done. . . .

Some hours later, Dutch Schrader was having a drink alone at the bar in Burmeister's as Jase Evans and some others of the Vigilante crowd came looking for him. There were Tom Ridges, and Hack Gorham the blacksmith, and a buckaroo on the Major's payroll who went by the name of "Dallas" and nothing else. Talk ceased as Jase Evans faced Dutch Schrader. It amused him to see how the latter drew away, as far as the counter pressing against his back would let him.

"Having fun drinking up our money?" Jase said, indicating the half-filled glass.

Schrader hastily moved his fingers away from it. But he pointed out, firmly enough, "It was won fair and square."

"The hell it was!" the big man retorted. "That nag had no business beating any of the Major's stock. Morrison should have won his race."

Schrader looked at the faces of the others. He said, "Jase, you wouldn't be a poor loser?"

"Me?" Actually the sheriff was in a high good humor, and he tilted his head back and let out a burst of laughter that caused heads to lift and turn. "Oh, hell no! Nothing like that. Come easy, go easy, is good enough for me. But old Bud, now, he don't like getting beat. He's sore at you, Dutch!"

"I don't know why. I warned him the gray was fast."

"You didn't really think he'd believe it? After all, those boys work for you. He figures you were in cahoots. If it was me, I'd stay clear out of his way a while."

"I'm not hiding," Schrader said. "But I'm not looking for trouble—with him, or anyone. Maybe," he suggested hopefully, "to show there's no hard feelings, you'll let me buy you a drink, all around?"

Jase shrugged and the bartender set out four glasses. But when he brought up a bottle Jase Evans simply reached and took it out of his hand. "Dutch meant to buy us the whole bottle. Hell, he can afford it. And he don't want no hard feelings."

The bartender looked at Schrader, who said quickly, "Sure— the bottle it is." Filling the glasses himself, Jase Evans asked, "What become of them kids, after the race? They disappeared right sudden—and that damn horse with them."

The Dutchman swallowed. "They had chores. About time I was getting home, myself." Over their drinks, the four watched him wolfishly as he pulled out his money—a sizable wad of greenbacks—and settled the tab. But when he would have left they made no move to open a way for him. He put out a boot, tentatively; drew it back again.

Jase Evans said, "I don't reckon this is just real friendly, Dutch. We all four of us got money in that roll. How about a little stud?"

"Like I said, I'm due home."

"Why? It's early yet."

And Tom Ridges added, as though on cue: "Damn it! Don't you understand English, you krauthead? We all of us want a game!"

At that a slow tide of red moved up through the German's throat and into his cheeks. He shot a look around him, as though hoping for help; but other men who had been intently following this talk were suddenly engrossed in private matters, and no eye met his own. Almost a smell of fear was in the room.

Jase Evans sensed this, and it swelled him with a feeling of real pleasure and power. Once he had been a nobody, a mere buckaroo on the Major's payroll. Now he was Mister Evans— Sheriff of Crook County, with all the weight of the Vigilantes and the Stockman's Association behind him. If he wanted to push another man off the Prineville sidewalks—or force him to buy a drink, or hold cards in a poker game against his will— who was going to argue?

It amused him now to hear Dutch Schrader trying to cover his defeat: "I guess maybe I could spare half an hour or so . . ." A word to the bartender put a new deck of Bicycle cards in Evans's hand, the seal unbroken. With the smoothness of a prearranged plan the other three closed on Schrader and herded him, a virtual captive, toward a table near the window in a rear corner of the room.

A townman and a rancher, seated at the table, saw the jerk of Evans's broad thumb; they quickly caught up their beer glasses

103

and vacated it. There were five chairs. Schrader was maneuvered deftly into the corner place, his back to the closed window. The others having seated themselves, Evans split the seal on the pack with one yellowed, horny thumbnail. He shook out the slick, new cards and they drew for deal.

Schrader wore the hangdog look of a trapped man as he watched Tom Ridges pass the cards around, one down and then one up.

"Queen bets," Hack Gorham said, nodding at Schrader. Obediently he dug up his roll of bills, fumbled off a couple and dropped them into the warped wooden center of the table, afterward stuffing the roll back into a pocket of his waistcoat. When the rest had matched his ante, Ridges picked up the deck again as Jase Evans spoke. "I been hearing things about you, Dutch. I hear you ain't been supporting the Association, or paying your dues like you ought to."

Schrader cleared his throat with a noisy effort. "I—"

"It's been reported," Evans went on, "you don't like the way we been clearing the crooks out of this county. You've been heard to say we got what amounts to lynch law. How about it, mister? That really the way you feel?"

The Dutchman looked actually sick, all of a sudden. His head sank forward and he looked from beneath his brows at his tormentors. He touched his tongue to dry lips; his hands were spread flat upon the table, ridges standing out along the knuckles.

Hank Gorham said, "A man should be a little careful who he shoots off his mouth to. Word gets around. . . ."

Schrader raised a trembling hand toward his face, then lowered it again. He spoke at last, a hoarse mumble. "Mein Gott! What are you going to do to me?"

He got no answer for a moment. Jase Evans wasn't even looking at him just then, but past him toward that window at his back. It was being raised, slowly and almost soundlessly, from outside. Evans had been waiting for this, all the time they had been talking. Now, a few inches above the sill, the sash appeared to stick; but it didn't matter—that was clearance enough for a gunbarrel.

A secret amusement altered the angry cast of the sheriff's features; he even grinned a little, and he shrugged his thick shoulders within the sheepskin windbreaker that he wore unfastened and thrown open because of the room's warmth. "Why, who said we were going to do anything?" he countered.

104

"We're just concerned, is all. Tom, deal the cards, will you?"

Schrader looked unconvinced.

Picking up the deck, Ridges began again to pass them out, Schrader watched dumbly as they fell, a third one face up all around. He was breathing normally again but his color was bad and he appeared shaken by the ordeal he was being put through. He looked at the cards as though he couldn't tell one from another.

"Queen high still bets," Tom Ridges said.

The Dutchman gave a shiver suddenly as cold air, creeping through that open slit behind him, overtook and enveloped him. Frowning, he looked around. "Who opened the window?" he demanded, and pushed his chair back, rising to go and close it.

He had taken just two steps when the gun roared. The pane exploded inward. Schrader stumbled back before the shower of glass; his face, as he fell sprawling across the empty chair and overturned it, was a bloody wreckage where the upward-angled bullet had churned into it.

For what must have been a full half minute there was no movement or sound in the room, as the ugly echoes of the gunshot and of tinkling glass subsided. Then trapped breath was released from a dozen throats; and Jase Evans, with no great haste, pushed back his chair and walked deliberately around the table for a look through the window into the alley. A shard of glass squealed under his boot as he heeled about; he shoved his hat forward and scratched the back of his head as he said, calmly enough, "Now, ain't that just a hell of a thing?"

Tom Ridges commented, without moving from his chair: "It just shows, you never know what enemies a man might have. . . ."

The bartender and the dozen other customers were watching, as motionless as though they had frozen that way and forgotten how to move. It was the buckaroo named Dallas who rose now and came around the table to bend over Schrader, briefly. "The guy's dead enough."

"Hell! Can't I see he's dead?" Jase Evans had made no move to touch the body. He lifted his head, put a look over the stunned watchers. "I want a couple of you to get him up to Graham's." Dick Graham, in addition to running one of the four saloons, was Prineville's undertaker. "I'll take a look outside. Not that it's probably much use. Whoever done this ain't apt to be waiting around. . . ." He was beginning to fasten his windbreaker as he headed deliberately toward the street door.

105

A mile out of town, Bud Morrison had been waiting. When the riders drew in he kneed his red horse out of the junipers and fell in alongside Jase Evans. "I guess I fixed him."

"You fixed him good," the sheriff said. "Dead center. He won't be able to give us any trouble now."

"Did you get our money?"

"Right here." The man called Dallas held up the wad of bills he'd sneaked off Schrader's body.

When he was excited, Morrison had a strange, high giggle that sounded odd coming out of that darkly impassive face. He laughed now, one hard palm beating on the pommel of his saddle. The red horse moved a little restlessly under him. Someone passed him a bottle and Morrison helped himself to a long drag. "All right," he grunted, fisting his mouth. "Let's go finish this job."

CHAPTER X

Exasperated, Chris said, "Anybody ever tell you, you got a streak of mule in you a yard wide?"

Only a faint tightening of the muscles at the corners of his mouth showed how much Hunter had been hurt by that. He held his tongue, not wanting to continue the quarrel; he silently kept his eyes on the road unwinding past his mount's ears, and after a moment his brother resumed.

"This is a good country," Chris said. "With a lot of good people in it. And Prineville's a good town; we got friends there. You can't just close them out the way you been trying to do—as though they were all to blame, for the trouble caused by no more than a handful of men."

Hunter shifted his position in the saddle. "Who says I did that?"

"And just how many months is it, then," his brother retorted, "since I've even been able to get you to so much as make this trek into town with me? Looks like, when you wash your hands of somebody, you really mean it!

106

"And what about Jen?" he went on, before the other could answer. "I could almost think you were trying to punish her for something. Certainly that's all you *have* done, with your damned stubbornness. She's the last person in the world deserves such treatment!"

That pulled the younger brother's angry stare around. "I think you know, all right, why I've been trying to leave Jen alone—and don't act like you think it ain't been hard!"

Chris thought that over for a space, in silence. Ahead of them now they could see the pattern of Prineville's streets and lighted houses, under the early evening sky. A low canopy of clouds draping the canyon rims contained a hint of more bad weather.

"Now that I got you here," the older brother said presently, "you going to see Jen this weekend? Or are you going to sneak home again tomorrow without so much as a try?"

"I'm going to see her," Bob Hunter answered. "I've made up my mind I'm going to ask her to church in the morning. I been thinking, it's a while since I heard any good hymn-singing; and let Walter Allen like it or not, I don't reckon he'll be able to say too much if all I ask is the privilege of escorting his daughter to Sunday church meeting!"

"I don't reckon he should, at that," Chris agreed, and he grinned faintly. "Once in a while, boy, you do come up with something pretty cute. . . ."

The chill March dusk was settling fast as they rode into town. Putting in at Hamilton's, they found no one on duty. They waited a moment and then proceeded to take care of their own horses, put them into a pair of stalls and hung up saddles and bridles and spread the blankets. Hunter hefted a pair of saddlebags across a shoulder—"Got my Sunday shirt in here," he commented—and they went next door to the Jackson House to get themselves a room.

The moment they walked into the lobby where, just a year ago, Luke Langley had met his death they sensed at once a strangeness in the atmosphere. Besides the desk clerk, Fred Dailey, a clot of men stood absorbed in some intent conversation that quickly broke off as the Hunters entered. In this odd stillness they crossed the faded carpet and returned Dailey's nod of greeting; Chris asked for and got the key to a room on the lower floor. As yet, no one in that staring group said a word.

To test them, Bob Hunter singled out one of the men—it was the storekeeper and now county treasurer of Crook County, Gus Weckler—and said flatly, "Well, Gus? You think we might

107

get some snow by tomorrow?" The man's narrow face showed no change of expression, except that the mouth seemed to close a little tighter. Deliberately, Hunter walked through the group and turned into the corridor lined with closed doors. Quickly, Chris caught up with him. Chris showed alarm.

"You know what?" he said under his breath. "I think something's going on!"

"Let it," Hunter said shortly. "I never expected anything but bad manners from that Gus Weckler; and as far as the rest are concerned, I don't care what you say—I'm not letting myself give a holler up a drainpipe what any of them do!"

Chris looked at his brother, started a protest and then swallowed it. With a troubled · frown and shake of head, he stabbed the key Fred Dailey had given him into the lock of the proper door and let them in. While Hunter dropped his saddlebags on the bed, shed his hat and went to check the water pitcher, Chris got the room's one lamp to burning. He replaced the glass chimney and stood looking at his brother, the lampglow underlighting beard-stubbled cheeks. "Bob—" he began again. The other cut him off.

"Will you get it through your head, Chris? I am just not interested! I am not fighting this town's battles for it—not if it won't fight a few of its own. Right now all I want is to get washed up and then go out to the eat shack and buy myself a meal somebody else has cooked!" There was water in the pitcher. He filled the hand basin, stripped out of his shirt and was building a lather with the hotel's bar of soap when knuckles struck the door panel, timidly.

Chris, polishing his boots, called, "It's not locked."

The man who entered, and hurriedly closed the door behind him, was a homestead rancher from nearby Ochoco Creek, named Harvey Franks. He had been in the lobby when the brothers passed through it, minutes ago. He put his shoulders against the closed door, now, and looked at the two of them without speaking.

Hunter, who had never held the man as much account, merely glanced at him once through spread fingers and then went back to rinsing and blowing in the water of the bowl. But Chris saw something in the fellow's pinched white face that made him demand, with polishing cloth poised, "What is it, Harve? Come on in—have a seat."

The man seemed to be listening for sound from beyond the door. He slid his tongue across dry lips and said hoarsely, "I ain't staying but a minute." But he advanced to the bed and let

108

himself down onto the edge of it. His hands, laid on denimed knees, twitched. His face looked gray in the thin lamplight.

"You haven't heard, I guess," he said, almost stammering. "I sort of knew, the minute you walked in just now, that you likely hadn't."

"We've heard nothing," Chris acknowledged. "We just got in."

He nodded. "That's how I figured. And I knew, if *anybody* cared about the things that's going on around here, it'd be you two."

Chris looked uneasily at his brother as the latter snorted a little too sharply to have only been clearing water from his nose. To Harvey Franks, Chris said, "Don't mind him. Of course we're interested."

"Well—I understood, too, you were good friends of Dutch Schrader's. . . ."

That brought a reaction. Hunter paused in the act of reaching for a towel, stood with face and hands dripping; his brother slowly lowered his foot to the carpet, the polish rag forgotten. They stared at Harvey Franks. "What about Dutch?" Chris demanded.

"Murdered—this afternoon, at Burmeister's. Somebody shot him through the window. I was there," Franks continued while they stared at him. "I seen it! The bullet come right through the glass. . . ." Suddenly his hands were shaking uncontrollably; he clutched his bony knees to quiet them.

Hunter plucked the towel off the rack at the end of the washstand, strode over to the bed rubbing his face with it, his eyes bleak. Chris prodded the homesteader: "You didn't see who did the shooting?"

"No. But I guess everybody knows it had something, at least, to do with that damned horse race."

"Now—back up a little!" Chris exclaimed. "You've lost us again. What horse race?" And Bob Hunter added, "Maybe you'd better start this thing at the beginning. . . ."

In silence, they listened to the story he blurted out to them, until Chris said, with a shake of the head, "Are you telling us that old gray of the kid's actually beat one of the Major's fast string?"

"Last thing anybody expected, I guess," Franks said. "Except Dutch—and he must have really cleaned up, betting on him. Had him a real wad of the green stuff; but it was gone when we carried him up to Graham's." He looked uneasily around, and lowered his voice as he added: "It's my opinion Jase Evans or one of them others took it off his body after he was dead!"

"Jase Evans!" Bob Hunter echoed, scowling.

"And who else, besides?" Chris demanded.

"Well, there was Tom Ridges, and Hack Gorham, and that fellow they call Dallas . . . I tell you, it was a put-up thing. They made Dutch sit down to a game when he plain didn't want to—and nothing anybody could do but watch it happen. They all but pushed him into that seat at the window, for Bud Morrison to have an easy target. . . ."

"Morrison?"

Caught in a slip, Franks lost color. It wasn't warm in that room, but the lamplight showed a faint shine of sweat on his cheeks. "It's just a guess," he insisted. "*I* don't know who shot him."

"But—I just can't understand it!" Chris exclaimed. "You don't kill somebody, simply because he won some money from you in a horse race!"

"These men do!" Hunter said. He flung aside the towel, picked his shirt off a knob of the bedstead and slipped it on and began working at the buttons. "I'm curious," he grunted, turning again to Harvey Franks. "What does Jase Evans have to say?"

"He ain't been around to say anything—or Morrison, or any of them. They left town right after the shooting; that would have been near three hours ago. Someone said they rode out of town across the Ochoco bridge. The whole bunch."

"Morrison, too?"

Franks knotted his brow. "I dunno as to that." He spread his palms. "I don't really know anything—except I seen a man deliberately murdered. It was the worst thing I *ever* seen. I just had to talk to someone about it. But a man doesn't know when he dares open his mouth any more—not if he's got a wife and three kids at home. Not when almost anybody could be a Vigilante, or on their side—like Gus Weckler and most of that crowd out in the lobby just now. So—I came and talked to you!"

"And what do you expect us to do about it?" Hunter retorted, harshly. When Chris turned to him, starting a protest, he merely swung away from him. He was shoving the tail of his shirt into his trousers when suddenly something made him pause. Slowly he turned back, a bleak thought reflected in his eyes. "Wait a minute! What about those two kids—Charlie Hewett, and young Clifton? Where have they been, during all this?"

Harvey Franks blinked. "Why, I couldn't say. I guess Dutch

110

sent them back out to the ranch. Wait a minute—that's right!" he added quickly. "I remember Jase Evans asking him."

"The ranch!" Hunter repeated. He looked at his brother. "And those others have got a three hours' start on us!"

Chris stared. "You don't think—?"

"They killed Dutch, didn't they?" Hunter retorted. "And *he* only *bet* against them!"

Harvey Franks said, "Come to think of it, I heard a rumor that the Clifton boy had warning he'd better not beat Morrison's red horse. You know how it is with rumors—I don't know how it started, or where I heard it."

Hunter pulled his belt tight, thumbed the prong home. After that he had his windbreaker and his hat, and with his hand on the doorknob turned back to ask Chris, "You coming with me?"

If Chris had any comment to make regarding his brother's change of tune since a short quarter hour before, he decided to swallow it. "Let me get my hat." To Harvey Franks he added, "I'm obliged to you, Harve, for coming to tell us about this."

Franks muttered something. Bob Hunter had the door open. "We'll go out the back. I'm in no mood to argue with any of that crowd in the lobby. And I'm worried we haven't got any time to waste. . . ."

They had already forgotten Harvey Franks. But when their horses were saddled and they rode out into the street, they were surprised to see the homesteader coming toward them through the gusty dark, mounted and ready. "If you don't care, I'd like to join you."

Hunter looked at him closely. "You sure? We're pretty much mavericks around here. Man with a family could make a mistake, just being seen with us."

Franks ducked his head, fiddled with the reins. He spoke almost apologetically. "When I see the way things are, looks to me the time is coming when a man's going to have to stand up and get counted, on one side or the other. If we all think of nothing but our own necks, we're going to end up letting men like Evans and Morrison and Gus Weckler have everything.

"Besides, I'm concerned now what may have happened out there at Schrader's—and me not even thinking about it until you added it up for me."

Hunter shared a look with his brother. "Come along, then," he said gruffly, and shook the roan out into an impatient canter.

Dutch Schrader had settled his ranch headquarters on a shallow bench that held a stand of juniper and a few tall pines.

Some of the timber had been cleared to give materials for his buildings and pole corrals, but the shadows under the trees were piled thick and black. No light showed; the house and barn showed as dark masses in the starless night. Even the sounds of their own horses, as the three riders approached, seemed blotted up in the timber and muffled by the chill, wet-smelling wind blowing along the creek below the bench.

They pulled up, listening and studying the quiet. Chris said softly, "Sounds like horses in the pen, yonder. But where are the boys?" And Harvey Franks suggested, his voice unsteady, "Maybe they're forted up in there, waiting for a shot at us!"

Hunter sent his horse a few yards nearer the darkened buildings, again drew rein. When he still heard nothing he raised a shout, to identify them. Convinced at last that his words fell on empty air, he dismounted and dropped the reins, and moved directly toward the house itself.

There was the blackness of an open door, and no sound from within. Hunter stepped inside and to one side, where he stood debating a moment. Something touched his shoulder; it was a lantern, hanging from a peg. Quickly he cranked up the chimney as he fumbled in a pocket for a match. He snapped that on a thumbnail, touched it to the wick. The wash of yellow light showed him the wreckage of a struggle.

A chair was smashed, a table overturned and the remains of an interrupted meal trampled over the puncheon flooring. There was no sign of blood. Scowling, Hunter turned as the other two followed him inside. "We better look outside," he said. "See if their horses are in the pen."

He led the way out, carrying the lantern now to aid their search. It cast eerie, swaying shadows and a bobbing circle of light as they tramped across the work area to the corral made of juniper poles. Inside, a horse took sudden alarm and went skittering away along the fence with an eye shining in the lanternglow.

Another shape bulked, unmoving, on the ground in the center of the pen, where it lay with its belly beginning to swell and the four legs stiffening. Harvey Franks was the one who exclaimed, "Why—it's that Clifton boy's gray. That's the horse that won the race!"

"That's Muggins, all right," Chris said bleakly. "Someone's shot him. . . ." They stood staring numbly at the slaughtered animal. At last Chris stirred and demanded, in a hollow voice, "Where the devil are those two boys?"

"Guess we're going to have to hunt for them." Raising the

lantern, Bob Hunter turned for a slow look around. Suddenly he stiffened, and his voice was choked as he added, "I guess we won't either. I've just found them. . . ."

"Where?" Franks said, and then swallowed an oath. In mounting dread and anger they walked over to the big juniper and its double burden, that the lantern had revealed.

Both boys had been shot in the back of the head, after being hanged. Looking up at the dead faces, Hunter remembered them alive, on that trail drive to Winnemucca—remembered Sam Clifton cutting off through the sage to demonstrate, proudly, what his old gray horse could do. He said heavily, into the chill quiet: "You see how it goes: Langley and Farrell were lynched because of a killing. Jed Starns got his because he dared to question what was going on. But—where is there any sense in *this?*"

Receiving no answer, after a moment he drew a breath and spoke again, almost in a practical tone. "Dutch must have had a wagon somewhere. I suggest we load them in it and the pair of you take them in to town. I better stay here tonight. I want to straighten up that mess in the house, where the boys tried to fight for their lives."

"Shouldn't everything be left the way it is?" his brother said.

"For who to see?" Hunter retorted, in heavy sarcasm. "The sheriff?" Still troubled by a constriction in his chest, he went on: "There'll be chores, and the stock to take care of. Come morning, I think I better ride over to Milo King's place—he's the closest neighbor, and maybe he'll be willing to keep an eye on things till we can find out if Dutch had any relatives to notify. I'll be in when I've finished whatever has to be done."

Chris nodded as though he only half heard; Harvey Franks, for his part, acted like a man who was too stunned as yet for either speech or movement.

Overhead, the juniper branch stirred in the night wind. Straining hemp fibers protested faintly. . . .

CHAPTER XI

The two men posted outside Hack Gorham's shanty looked as
though they'd as soon have been elsewhere on a cold March
afternoon. The one on his feet, with a gun and holster strapped
outside his red-checked mackinaw, walked jerkily about kicking
at the hard ground, chin tucked into coat collar. The other sat
hunched miserably on the top step with both hands shoved deep
in pockets. Thin sunlight ran briefly along the barrel of the rifle
laid across his knees, then faded as broken clouds fled down the
canyon sky, pushed before the wind and letting down an
occasional white streak of falling snow.

The building sat well back from the street and from the
unpainted board shed Gorham used for his blacksmith's shop.
No thread of smoke rising from the chimney, Hunter noticed.
He ran a hand across unshaven cheeks and narrowly considered
the place, while the roan horse under him edged over a step to
have a pull at weeds lining the ditch. He sensed the stillness that
hung upon the village. He thought, Sunday afternoon; and yet it
seemed no ordinary Sabbath calm. Or perhaps he merely felt
nothing should be normal, after the terrible things that had
happened yesterday. . . .

He turned in the saddle as two men he knew came toward
him, boots thudding the sidewalk. He asked, "What's happening
yonder at Gorham's?"

They halted, as though the question startled them. One slid
his glance away, but after the faintest hesitation the other
explained, "Hack's laid up. He's been hurt."

"Hurt? How?"

"Why, they tell us he was putting a shoe to a horse, sometime
last night. And the animal got out of hand."

"Last night. . ." Hunter repeated. "You sure of this?"

"It's what they told us," the man insisted.

" 'They' wouldn't be Jase Evans, by any chance?"

Not waiting for an answer, he gave the reins a twist that lifted
his horse across the sidewalk directly in front of the pair. One of

114

the men shouted after him: "You can't see him, Hunter. They ain't letting anybody in. . . ." Ignoring the warning, he sent the roan across an empty lot clogged with weeds and a few remaining patches of old snow, straight toward the blacksmith's house.

At once the pair stationed there came alert, the one in the red mackinaw coming around to face him while the second, slighter figure stumbled to a stand on the top step with the rifle in both hands. Iron hoofs spurting snow underfoot, Hunter's mount held straight toward them; the empty windows of the house, and the cold chimney, gave no indication of life within.

Hunter saw the faces, now. The man in the mackinaw was the Tarback rider they called Dallas; the other was George Wright's kid brother, Eddie. They let Hunter come on within twenty feet or so and then Dallas raised his voice in a sharp challenge: "You ain't needed here. Head the other way."

He ignored the warning, letting his horse move ahead until he was quite close to the wooden stoop of the shack. There he reined in. His manner was mild enough as he asked the scowling Dallas, "What's this about Hack Gorham? A horse kicked him?" He shook his head. "Hell, he's been a blacksmith too long to let a thing like that happen!"

The buckaroo seemed caught off guard, a shade uncertain how to handle this. So far he had made no move to touch his gun. He pointed out gruffly, "A man only has to get careless once, Hunter."

"Guess that's true enough," Hunter admitted. He added, "How's he making out? What does the doctor say?"

"He don't need no doctor. If you got to know," Dallas snapped, "we're here to keep nosy gents like you from bothering him."

Eddie Wright, up on the steps, felt impelled to add his bit: "We got our orders, mister! Now, you go along!"

Slowly, Hunter turned his head and looked at the boy. Eddie had been growing too fast this past year; he had almost a man's growth now but his frame needed filling out, and his bony face—still unformed and undefined—was that of a youngster in his teens. He stood with legs spread and narrow shoulders slightly forward, the shotgun leveled across his middle. Hunter looked at the weapon and said coldly, "Don't point that thing at me, boy!"

Eddie's head jerked a trifle; his cheeks pinched up, his mouth pulled into an odd shape by surprise and anger. Looking straight into Hunter's eyes, he cursed him—foully.

115

It was an easy reach, from the saddle to the youngster standing on the steps. Without warning Hunter's arm swung and his palm struck the boy in an openhanded slap, hard across the face. Eddie's head was rocked back on his shoulders; his hands loosened their grip on the shotgun and Hunter simply plucked it out of his fingers. He flipped the weapon, caught it in firing position and with the same motion swung about in saddle and let the double barrels drop into line on the face of the staring Dallas.

"The same goes for you!" he snappeed. "Leave your gun where it is!"

Dallas had been caught flatfooted. He stared at the greener's twin tubes, and then he looked up into the face above them. He seemed to see something there that he had never expected—something that held him motionless and kept his hand away from the gun and holster strapped about his middle.

Hunter nodded, in satisfaction. Letting the reins drop, he stepped out of his saddle with the shotgun clamped and steady under one elbow. "I'm having a look inside," he announced. "I aim to find out just what it is you don't want people seeing in there. Don't give me any trouble!"

They said nothing. He tramped the three wooden steps, shoved past Eddie Wright whose staring, wind-whipped face showed clearly the mark of Hunter's fingers. Pushing inside he closed the door behind him.

There was no lock, nothing but a simple latch; he snicked that on and then looked around him, still holding the shotgun. This one main room, serving as both living quarters and kitchen, showed a bachelor's messy clutter. Dirty dishes littered table and sink. There must have been a fire in the stove that had only recently gone out, for the house felt fairly warm.

At first glance it appeared deserted. But then he became aware of labored breathing, that carried him across the room and to the door of a lean-to bedroom at its far end. And there he found Hack Gorham—fully dressed, lying on an old iron bed with his face toward the slanted ceiling and the front of his shirt drenched in blood.

Watching the rise and fall of the massive blacksmith's chest, Hunter could well imagine it was this tortured sound that had driven the guards outside, preferring to wait in the cold rather than endure it.

He leaned the shotgun against the wall and, coming nearer, saw now that someone had made a clumsy attempt at a bandage. It had done little good, and bandage and shirt and

116

bedclothes were soaked. The wound could only have been made by a bullet, and at close range. Sight and smell of the blood had Hunter fighting back a warm, sickening rush of nausea that clogged his throat; but he touched the man's shoulder, spoke his name.

At his second try he got a faint response. The closed lids stirred and a murmur broke from the slack lips. He could guess what the hurt man was asking for. He went out into the other room, found water and brought a dipper of it back with him. Gorham was past swallowing, but he seemed aware and grateful for the little that Hunter managed to get past his parched lips and onto his tongue. His mouth worked and his eyes came open and settled on the man leaning over him.

"Hack, who did it to you?"

The eyes wavered, lost focus and moved away. Urgent determination put Hunter on one knee beside the bed, where he could grip the dying man's shoulder as he tried to push his words past a barricade of fading senses. "One of those youngsters, wasn't it, Hack? He got to a gun and used it trying to save his life. And when they both were dead your Vigilante friends brought you home and dumped you here, and they've got a guard outside to keep anyone from talking to you while they wait for you to die.

"Are *those* your friends, Hack? Who don't care what happens to you, so long as their own tracks are covered?"

His fingers dug into the heavy muscle that plated the man's shoulder; it gave limply. The lips, under a wiry stubble of beard, moved and for a moment speech seemed to be trying to break forth. Then the ruined chest swelled convulsively; the lungs emptied and Hunter dropped his hand and rocked back upon his heels, knowing that he looked at the face of death. . . .

Time stopped. He didn't know if it was a minute or an hour later when his head lifted sharply, but then he was coming to his feet as he heard a tumble of angry voices approaching the shack. Boots struck the wooden stoop outside; a hand tried the door. When it failed to give, someone swore and a shoulder struck the panel. At a second blow a long, clean split cleft the wood for half its length, and the latch was wrenched from its screws. The door sprung inward to bounce off the wall. Jase Evans came bursting in, with others close behind him. They piled up there when they saw Hunter in the lean-to doorway, facing them, shotgun cradled against one hip.

Evans blinked at sight of the gun, and then his eyes lifted to Hunter's and his mouth pulled out into an ugly shape. He had a

117

gun in a holster strapped to his leg, but in the face of that shotgun he was keeping clear of it. He said heavily, "You just won't leave things alone, will you?"

Hunter returned his stare, the shotgun unwavering, and letting no sign of fear touch his face. He looked at the men in back of Evans, seeing Dallas who must have been the one who ran to fetch help in this emergency, and Tom Ridges and Gus Weckler and others of the Vigilante crowd. He told Jase Evans, "I've been watching a man die."

"Oh." He thought it was a look of relief that moved across the sheriff's eyes. "Then he's dead, is he?"

"Yes—finally. It would take someone with Hack Gorham's strength to last the night, the shape he was in!" He added: "Which one was it, managed to get his hands on a gun before you grabbed them? Charlie Hewett? Or more likely, the redhead. . . . Because, it was no kick from a horse put that hole in him! That took a .45 caliber bullet!"

Jase Evans's thick chest swelled. Without turning his head or taking his eyes from Hunter he spoke an order to the men behind him: "I want to talk to this bird. The rest of you wait outside. . . ."

There seemed to be no questioning his will. After the briefest hesitation the others withdrew with a shuffling of boots and a backward turning of heads. Evans swung the broken door shut and they were alone in the chill the crowd had brought in with them.

Evans appeared no longer concerned about the shotgun. He walked past Hunter and into the lean-to, the other moving aside for him. Evans stood a minute looking at the dead man and then, apparently satisfied Hunter had reported correctly, came out again. He flung his sheepskin open and hung both thumbs into his shell belt. "All right," he said. "Let's have it plain. So you think you got some notion how that happened?"

"I know damned well how it happened!" Hunter snapped. "After what I found at Schrader's last night."

"And supposing I told you that, before we strung 'em up, that pair admitted they'd been planning to grab off a big bunch of the Major's prime saddle stock? They and Dutch had it all set up between them. Us Vigilantes got wind of it and nipped the thing in the bud."

"Don't waste your breath!" Hunter snapped. "We both know why they died—because young Clifton had the nerve to lick Bud Morrison in a horse race!"

The sheriff's pock-marked cheeks settled and became as

118

expressionless as his eyes. A stillness and a challenge hung between these two, for a long moment. Then Jase Evans said again, quietly, "All right. Suppose you have it your way. What do you think you're going to do about it?"

"Maybe it don't look like there's much I can do," Hunter answered levelly. "You and Tarback and your crowd have put this town, and this range, under a reign of terror. It's reached a point where you can kill a man—or a boy—on any kind of a drunken whim and the decent element can only stand aside and let you do it. But there's a limit, Jase—and as far as I'm concerned at least, you and your Vigilantes passed that limit yesterday. I've made up my mind: From this moment, I'm fighting you. And I don't intend to quit!"

The sheriff's mouth twisted into a smile, but his eyes retained their stony chill. "You'll be alone, bucko! All alone!"

"At the start, maybe. But, someone has to start it."

Jase Evans sneered at that; still, there was a first faint hint of uncertainty in him as he stood and watched the other walk deliberately to the door and throw it open.

Out in the yard, a dozen heads turned and lifted menacingly as Hunter emerged. He looked them over, a deliberate surveyal—almost as if he were memorizing faces: These he knew, were the nucleus, the hard core of the Vigilantes—the nothing men, the followers who let the authority of Jase Evans and the Major give them a spurious importance. Malcontents like Tom Ridges and Gus Weckler, trash like Bud Morrison and Dallas who, because they had the backing of the powers-that-be, were able now to feed stunted egos and terrorize their betters.

There was one face that didn't belong: Hunter looked at Eddie Wright, who stood glaring at him with all the hatred the boy's thin and bony face was capable of expressing. Suddenly Hunter felt a surge of something almost like pity for Eddie's big brother George; suddenly he thought he understood something of George's problem, and of his recent puzzling behavior.

He broke the shotgun, pulled the unfired shells and with a contemptuous gesture dropped the weapon into a patch of dirty snow in front of the boy's scuffed boots. Afterwards he walked deliberately down the plank steps, moving unarmed among his enemies, and got the reins of his horse. He swung astride and as he pulled the roan's head around one of the group moved silently, scowlingly aside. They were uncertain of him, unwilling to make a move without some kind of an order that

119

didn't come. There was no sound now as he kneed the roan and sent it walking away, across the snow-spotted and weed-choked open.

He looked back once and through a few pencil-streaks of drifting sleet saw Jase Evans in the doorway of the shack, also staring after him. When he turned away, it took all his will to keep from kicking the horse into a run.

Carried forward by the heady impetus of outrage and anger, Bob Hunter rode straight to Allen's, dismounted and tramped the low steps to the double door. His hand was trembling when it seized the knob; only when the door failed to give to his wrenching twist did he remember that it was Sunday, and of course the store was closed.

He stood there with the snowflakes streaking down, staring about him at the gloomy afternoon as he debated. When he ran a hand across his cheeks and felt the scrape of beard stubble, it occurred to him he hadn't shaved or thought of his appearance in twenty-four hours or more.

His saddlebags, with clean clothing and a razor in it, would still be in the room he and Chris had rented at the Jackson House. He returned to his horse, led it over to Hamilton's Livery and put it up. Later, in the hotel room, he got out his razor and, using the cold water in the pitcher, scraped his jaws clean. He toweled and was just buttoning into a clean shirt when, suddenly, the door opened and Chris strode inside.

His face was white. He closed the door and kept his hand on the knob as he stared at his brother. "My God!" he exclaimed hoarsely. "I been hunting this town for you. Then it occurred to me you just might be here."

"What's the trouble?" Hunter's own feelings had calmed, by now. He spoke quietly enough.

"Trouble! You're asking me? After what you've been up to?" Chris pulled off his hat and scaled it onto the bed. He ran rope-scarred fingers through his hair. "You must have lost your mind!"

"You mean, standing up to Jase Evans?"

"Trying to tackle that Vigilante crowd, all by yourself!"

Hunter looked at his brother in silence, for a moment. He shook his head. "I don't understand you," he said. "I really don't. Yesterday you bawled me out for turning my back on people—just because I was disgusted at the way they let themselves be buffaloed by a bunch of thugs."

"That don't mean you should go and make yourself a target!"

120

"I could almost think," Hunter said, choosing his words with painful care, "you'd forgot the look of what we cut down from that juniper, last night at Schrader's."

"Of course I haven't forgotten. God, no!" Chris flung out a hand, a helpless gesture. "Maybe it does seem to you I'm talking different, since yesterday; but I've had my eyes opened. I saw the reaction when we brought those boys in. And I'm convinced now the people here aren't taken in any more by Tarback's lies—they're simply scared out of their wits!

"So, it appears you were right after all, and I was wrong. Because if they won't do anything to help themselves, there's plainly nothing anyone else can do for them."

Hunter heard this in amazement. Suddenly the grim humor of the thing struck him. "Almost funny, isn't it? Here you want to quit—just when I'm finally fighting mad!"

"Bob!" Urgently, Chris put a hand on his brother's shoulder. "Please listen a minute. For your own good!"

"Take your hand off me!"

Hunter saw Chris lose color, as though he had been struck. The hand fell away. Hunter said, as their stares clashed, "As far as I'm concerned the chips are all down. If I ever want to look at myself in the mirror again, then I've got to fight this thing!"

"But—*how?*"

He shook his head. "Maybe I haven't figured that out yet. But if you won't fight with me, all I can say is you better get on back home where it's safe, and take care of the chores!"

Chris blinked and the color rushed back into his face; his voice shook with anger. "All right, damn it! I'll do that!" He grabbed his hat off the bed, heeled about and strode to the door. But with his hand on the knob he turned again, for a final plea. "Bob . . ." He tried again. "Bob, don't throw yourself away!"

"I'll worry about that!"

Chris saw the cold iron in his brother's face; he wrenched the knob and went out, dragging on the hat. After the door's slam died, Hunter stood a long moment staring after him.

Never before had these two parted in anger. Suddenly Hunter drove his fist, hard, against a brass bedpost, swung away to stare sightlessly at the window. Outside, the brief squall of snow and sleet had passed, but the clouds pressed low and laid a premature dusk upon the canyon. The dying day was no more bleak than his own thoughts.

At the Union Church, the first evening hymn had been sung and the preacher, clad in rusty black, was opening the Bible to locate his text when Hunter spoke, from the back of the room. He had entered silently and unnoticed during the singing. He said now, coming a few steps down the center aisle, "Reverend, would you let me put a word in at this meeting?"

Heads turned. Up on the platform, Adam Nealy blinked in consternation. As Hunter patiently waited, he fiddled with his spectacle frames, cast a nervous glance over his startled congregation and then again at the intruder. "Why—I don't know . . ." Then, reluctantly: "I suppose—if it's something important—"

"*I* figure it's important." Hunter made his way down the aisle as a stir of dismay and anxiety ran, like a wave, along the wooden benches. He kept his eyes straight ahead, looking to neither side until he had mounted the platform, to the pulpit Adam Nealy vacated for him. Thanking the minister with a word and a nod, he turned then to look over the people who nearly filled this raw, range-country meeting house.

Individual faces seemed to leap at him: Harvey Franks, with his wife and a trio of squirming kids, all of them threadbare. Jim Blake, and Mrs. Blake beside him holding the baby that must be almost six months old now. On the third row he saw Walter Allen nervously chewing his mustache, and there was Jennifer seated between her mother and George Wright. Hunter ignored the cold disapproval in the older woman's stare, and George's narrow scowl; he let his eyes rest, instead, for a long moment on Jen Allen's face—a sight he had been denying himself during all these months of winter and belated spring. Her expression was troubled; her eyes clung anxiously to him and her hands were in her lap, knotted tight, as she waited— with the rest of the silent, hostile room—to hear what he had come to say.

About to speak, he caught sight of Ada Tarback seated all alone on a far, rear pew, and he nearly faltered. Her face was partly hidden by a shawl, but Hunter sensed again in her a hint of something tragic. He well knew that every word he spoke would be a direct blow against the woman's husband, yet strangely he felt she would approve.

He straightened his shoulders, placed rope-scarred hands on the edge of the pulpit. He drew a breath.

"I can imagine there's some who won't much want to hear this," he heard himself saying—and it didn't sound like his own voice. "All the same, I mean for you to listen!" Bodies stirred on the long benches; a wave of hostility beat at him. But though

122

anger honed the edge of Bob Hunter's temper and roughened his voice, he tried to remember where he was and control his manner.

He said, "I'd just like to know how long we're going to put up with it! Over a year we've stood by, while men got hanged for crimes they didn't commit, or driven out of the country by lies, or simply murdered for talking out of turn. Now there's three more dead, since yesterday morning—and we all know who killed them, and why. Maybe you figure this ain't exactly the place to discuss such things; but what better place is there? Who's going to care enough to put an end to what's happening, if not us? And you and I *can* end it, if we only will—because these men are afraid of us!

"I mean it," he insisted, seeing the disbelief in their faces. "We could have stopped this thing anywhere along the line— before they started sending out their unsigned letters, before they browbeat everyone into joining their Stockman's Association, before they grabbed control of the county government. Deep down, these Vigilantes are afraid of what will happen, once we decide to call them to account. If they weren't, why did they let Hack Gorham bleed to death, without a doctor? Why, unless after killing Schrader and those two boys, they sobered enough to know they didn't dare give anyone a chance to talk to him—maybe make him confirm what we'd already guessed!

"If we ever again want to see a decent order of things, here in this Crooked River canyon, then it's our job to set matters straight. No one's going to do it for us; it's up to you and me. And we'd better start right here—tonight!"

This was his challenge, he paused for breath, and to let it sink in. But if he had really hoped to rouse an answer, he saw now that he was to be disappointed. Here and there, one or two of his audience showed frowning interest. Jim Blake had a thoughtful look, but his wife put a hand on his sleeve and earnestly whispered something, and Hunter could see the man's expression change. He sought out other faces, for some hint that his argument might have struck any kind of response. And found nothing.

Bitter disappointment drained through him, leaving him with defeat and a weariness that seemed to weight his body and his tongue with lead. He tried to say something more but the words were suddenly not there; the seconds dragged out, and at his elbow now he heard the preacher uneasily clear his throat.

Hunter found he was gripping the sides of the pulpit until his palms ached. He pushed away from it, straightening his shoulders.

"I've spoke my piece," he said gruffly. "I guess it wasn't as nice to listen to as something out of the Bible. I reckon I might as well go along and let the reverend get on with his service." Still, a moment, he waited—still hoping. But whatever gave me the idea, he asked himself in the heavy silence, that just because I felt so strongly, I was the one to lead these people into a fight—or push them, either, in a way they don't want to go?

He turned, stiffly, and descended from the platform. His eyes met Jen's; he thought he saw a shine of tears in them. After that he was striding resolutely up the aisle, past rows of people who averted their glances and let him go in painful silence. Only one other face turned toward him; in the far corner of that back row—the pale, haunted features of Ada Tarback. He felt her stare follow him as he got his hat from a table, where he had left it, and pushed out the door into the chill spring night.

CHAPTER XII

He woke in his room at the Jackson House to find a square of dazzling sunlight on the floor by the bed. But if the sky had cleared brilliantly overnight, his mood hadn't. He lay for minutes staring at the spiderweb of cracks in the ceiling plaster, weighing his problems and almost ready to concede that Chris had been right and he had wasted his time by even staying in town. Afterward, dressing and shaving, he found himself reliving every minute of yesterday, culminating with that disaster at the church meeting; his eyes were sober when he shrugged into his windbreaker and left the room.

Entering the lobby, he stared as Jennifer Allen rose from a sofa in a corner. They looked at each other a moment; then Hunter broke free from where he stood and hurried to her. She held out her hands and he took them in both his own. "You been waiting?"

"Only a little while," she assured him quickly. "I had to see you!"

Hunter stammered, "Me, too. I—" A hotel lobby was a public place, but a quick look assured him they were alone in it. Hungrily, then, he drew her to him and their kiss answered a long need. "It's been so long!" she exclaimed, her breath warm against his throat.

"I know . . ." He let her go; she stepped back and, taking his hand again, drew him down onto the sofa. Her eyes, shining with the pleasure of seeing him, sobered quickly enough as he asked, "And how's my girl been?"

"Lonesome, mostly." Her eyes lowered. "And yet I could almost wish now you'd stayed away! Last night at the meeting—the way they treated you—it was humiliating!"

He shrugged. "No more than I should have expected, I guess. What did your folks have to say?"

"Not very much," Jen told him. "Feelings were pretty strained. George was angry, of course; and Mama was indignant as could be. But Pa would say absolutely nothing. I don't honestly know what he made of it all."

"It was a fool thing for me to do. Trouble is, I don't really know where to take hold of this thing!"

"But, then—" Anxiously she searched his face. "Well, after all, why does it have to be you?"

"You sound like Chris." Hunter ran his palm down across his face, tiredly, and shook his head. "And I can't answer you— except that it has to be someone. And I'm the one whose conscience is hurting. . . ."

Fred Dailey had entered the lobby. The desk clerk said good morning and then, remembering, added, "Package here has got your name on it, Bob. Must have been left on the desk, sometime last night."

"A package?" Curious, Hunter went over. Dailey handed him a packet, small enough to slip into his coat pocket. It was wrapped in brown butcher's paper, with his name crudely printed on it in pencil, and tied with a cotton string. He examined it, puzzled; snapped the string and turned out the contents.

A foot-long piece of new yellow hemp rope uncoiled in his hands. Beside him, Jen exclaimed in a puzzled voice, "Why, what in the world—?" And then: "Look! There's writing. . . ."

A square of cardboard had been put in with the rope. The same hand that addressed the package had printed, in bold, crude letters:

LEARN TO KEEP YOUR GODDAM MOUTH SHUT, OR YOU CAN HAVE THE REST OF THIS!

Naturally, there was no signature.

A sound from Jen turned him quickly. Both her hands were pressed against cheeks gone white with shock; she swayed, moaning a little. Alarmed, Hunter dropped the piece of rope onto the counter and took her shoulders in his big hands, saying, "Jen! Don't!"

All at once she was sobbing, hysterically. He shook her, then caught her to him and held her tight with his cheek against her hair until, slowly, her storm of terror subsided. Fred Dailey had picked up the note and was reading it, narrow-eyed, with Hunter looking at him above the girl's dark head.

He shook his own head and said, in a bitter voice, "What the hell good am I doing, anyway? All I've managed so far is to get the one person I really care about scared half to death!" Dailey laid the note down again without comment, his face impassive. That was the way of it in Prineville now, Hunter thought darkly. Even a man like Fred Dailey, whom he considered a friend, would not commit himself.

"I'm sorry," Jen murmured, finally, and pulled away from him, dabbing at her cheeks with the heels of her hands. "I'll be all right now. But—what are you going to do?"

"About this? I dunno yet." He shoved note and rope and wrapper into a pocket of his windbreaker. "Right at the moment I think I better take you home. If you'll pardon me a minute . . ."

In his room again, he opened his saddlebags and took out his wooden-handled six-shooter. He checked the loads and shoved the gun behind his belt and then pulled the skirt of his windbreaker over it. From now on, he knew, he must never make the mistake of going unarmed. If he hadn't been before, he knew that after this he was a marked man.

He returned to the lobby, where Jen stood waiting. He took her arm and escorted her out into the crisp, bright morning.

It was Monday, and early yet; the town was quiet. From the planing mill came the cough of a steam engine and the whine of a blade biting into raw timber. A spring sky, scoured clean of yesterday's overcast, stretched its deep blue canopy above the canyon rims. A few rags of snowdrift lying in gutters and shaded spots were leaking rivulets; icicles dropped diamonds of melt-water from eaves and building overhangs, where the sun struck them and made them flash.

126

Jen was troubled and silent as they walked side by side toward the Allen place—a prosperous looking two-story house a block from Main. At the gate Hunter stopped and said, "Be better if I don't go any farther. You're feeling all right now, aren't you?"

"Of course," she said, turning to look earnestly up at him. "I'm only ashamed I acted the way I did. But—Bob, dearest! You know how much I've been dreading the day when you'd get one of those terrible letters. . . ."

"I know." He touched her cold cheek. "But you're not to worry. I promise I'll watch my step with them. On the other hand, I can't back away."

Her eyes blurred with tears; she shook her head a little against his hand, with a helpless look. Then suddenly she turned and fumbled open the gate and hurried up the path to the house.

Hunter stood and watched until the big door closed behind her. He was sure he saw a curtain move at an upstairs window and thought of Mrs. Allen, no doubt watching the two of them with icy disapproval. He gave the window a defiant stare, just on the chance, and afterward heeled about and strode off the way they had come.

He had had nothing to eat, and though he felt no great appetite he was about to enter Poindexter's on the search for breakfast when he ran into Gil Haze coming out. The saloon owner looked grim. He drew Hunter to one side; lantern jaws working at a toothpick, he said in a low voice, "I hear you got one of them letters."

"News sure doesn't take long to get around, does it?"

"It don't, for a fact." Haze's jaw muscles worked and the toothpick rolled from one corner of his mouth to the other, beneath the lush fall of mustache. "But I felt pretty sure this was coming. Maybe you hadn't heard about the meeting at Tarback's house last night?"

Hunter said carefully, "There was a meeting?"

"So I'm told. I think you got 'em worried, boy! From the few echoes I've picked up, I gather the meeting had mostly to do with you."

"Any idea who was there?" Hunter asked.

"I got a notion you could name them as well as I could." The saloon owner brushed a fist across his mustache. "With my own ears, though, I been hearing Gus Weckler talking big, this morning. I heard him say, 'If that Bob Hunter don't watch his step, one of these days he'll be going up the hill—feet first!'" Haze nodded with his gaunt head toward the rise, north of

127

town, where scattered crosses and mounds of earth marked Prineville's cemetery.

Bob Hunter's mouth drew out long. "Weckler!" he repeated with disdain.

Haze shrugged narrow shoulders. "The man's a rat. You ask me, Prineville would be a better place without him. Anyway, I thought you should know what's afoot."

Hunter thanked him solemnly and watched the man ambling on down the sidewalk with his curious, longlegged gait. Absently he sank a hand into his coat pocket, felt the crumple of wrapping paper and the hardness of new rope.

All at once he stiffened; his head lifted as a vagrant thought slowly crystallized into near certainty, honing an angry spark to light his eyes. "By God!" he said, aloud. "I wonder . . ." Hunger suddenly forgotten, he whirled to stare a moment along the street. And then he began walking, and his firm stride lengthened with a swiftly growing purpose.

He gave only a glance to the morning stage, northbound for The Dalles, that stood made-up and driverless in front of Allen's store where it would pick up the mail sack. A couple of passengers—a stock buyer and a cattleman's wife—stood with tickets ready and luggage at their feet, waiting to enter the coach. Hunter went past on the other side of the street and turned in at the hardware store just as Gus Weckler, unaware of him, finished unlocking the big door.

"Open for business?" Hunter asked.

At the sound of his voice, the storekeeper jerked about with keys on a ring chiming in his hand. Something he appeared to see in Hunter's face made his own thin cheeks drain of color. But he bobbed his head, unspeaking, and shuffled into the store ahead of the other, who followed him in and heeled the door shut again.

Weckler's thin lips writhed into a parody of a professional smile. "You were interested in something?"

"That's right," Hunter said bluntly. "Rope! I don't doubt a minute you can match this for me." And he brought it from his pocket as Weckler's face slowly died. He saw how the store owner cringed and tried to draw away; suddenly furious, he caught the man by a shoulder and thrust the length of yellow hemp into his face. "By God, I think I can find the very piece this was cut from—and some of the same paper it came wrapped in. And when I do find them, friend, it's all I'm going to need!"

Flinging the now terrified Gus Weckler aside, he set about his grim search for evidence. It took hardly any time. A brand new rope coil hung against the far wall and he saw it at once. He was just starting for it when he heard the door's quick jerk and slam behind him.

Turning, Hunter swore. His man was gone.

A few strides carried him back, to wrench the door open. Gus Weckler was moving with the speed of terror, pounding at a run along the sidewalk. Reaching Hamilton's Livery he paused and looked back, only to see Hunter coming after him and quickly closing the distance. So he abandoned that hiding place and scurried on, to take the steps of the Jackson House. He lost moments there fumbling at the door, but got it open and darted inside.

Relentlessly, Hunter pressed the chase. The hotel lobby was empty when he entered it, but running footsteps echoed plainly down the long corridor that split the building. He followed, not hurrying too much—the man couldn't really hope to get away from him.

He came out into a back lot littered with trash and broken furniture. He was in time to see the door of a privy at the rear of the lot pull noiselessly shut.

Hunter drew the gun from behind his belt. If Weckler happened to be armed, he was a rat who would turn and bite when cornered. A few paces from the closed door, Hunter took his stand. "All right, Gus," he said sharply. "Come out of there!"

He thought he could hear breathing, like that of a trapped animal. His voice sharpened. "Those walls won't stop a bullet! And I won't wait!"

A moan of anguish broke from the man inside the privy. "All right—*all right!*" The door opened a crack. Hunter seized it, flung it back with a crash. Weckler came stumbling out, his face shiny with fear. He stammered, "I haven't got a gun!"

"Well, I have," Hunter told him bluntly.

"Please! You—you wouldn't *shoot* me?"

There must have been something reflected in Hunter's stare that made the other quail. He subsided into trembling terror; his mouth worked convulsively. Bob Hunter seized him by his coat and gave him a shove in the direction of the street. "Start walking!"

The passengers had entered the stage coach. The driver came out of Allen's with a limp mail bag over his arm, which he tossed up onto the seat and then scrambled after it. He was settling to his place, separating out the ribbons and ready to kick off the brake, when Hunter came herding his man across the muddy thoroughfare. Hunter lifted his voice: "Hold it! You got another fare for The Dalles."

The whip looked down from his place, a scowl on weatherbeaten features. "I'm late already. Ain't time for him to buy a ticket."

"He'll pay at the other end—he's good for it." With no more argument, Hunter worked the door handle and then all but threw Gus Weckler into the coach. The woman screamed faintly and the other male passenger cursed and moved his legs as the storekeeper sprawled across them. Hunter slammed the door. Weckler, squalling in outrage, thrust his head through the open window. "Somebody, help!" His cries broke the town's quiet. "Get the sheriff! Don't let him do this to—"

Reaching, Hunter got a handful of his clothing and pulled him down against the window sill, hard. Weckler all at once subsided. Bob Hunter told him in a tone that held no compromise: "You're going, all right. And you're not coming back! I mean, not ever! Try it and you'll have me to settle with—you understand?"

The man was shaking. Two rivulets of sweat ran down his grooved cheeks, and through the twist of collar he held Hunter felt a painful swallow swell the man's throat. Convinced that Weckler had lost all his fight, Hunter released him and stepped back to throw an order at the staring driver: "Any time." The whip said something under his breath. But it was no matter of his, and with a shrug he lifted the ribbons and yelled his four-horse team into motion.

They went into the collars; the coach lurched upon its thoroughbraces, flinging Gus Weckler against the rear seat. That was the last glimpse Hunter had of him. Grit and mud spurted under shoes and tire irons and after that the coach was rocking away up the street, to throw back a brief thunder as it struck the wooden bridge over Ochoco Creek and then be swallowed up by the wide canyon bottom.

Hunter, watching it out of sight, suddenly found himself alone in the middle of the street with a gun in his hand.

The whole thing had been unplanned, an outcome of pure, white-hot anger, and the aftermath hit him hard—left him nearly aghast at his own behavior. He looked about quickly, and saw a dozen people silently watching him. Yonder, in front of his store, Walter Allen stood and stared as one thunderstruck.

Shoving the gun behind his belt, Hunter walked over.

130

Morning sun flashing off the lenses of silver-rimmed spectacles made the storekeeper scowl horribly. Hunter expected an angry outburst, and he spoke first. "Well, you've just lost your county treasurer!"

Allen started to answer, shook his head and let loose a gust of held breath instead. He rubbed a hand across his mouth, let it fall again. Another look around the sunbright street, with its drying ruts and dripping icicles; he said heavily, "Come inside."

In silence Hunter stood by while Allen locked the doors, pulled the shades, and put the CLOSED sign into place. With a jerk of his head the storekeeper indicated the curtained doorway at the rear.

Hunter had not been back here since that morning, over a year ago—the day following the lynchings that started the Vigilantes on their road to power. Now Allen dropped into the barrel chair at the desk and scowled at him from under lowered brows. "I want an explanation."

Hunter brought a handful of rope and brown paper from his coat pocket, dropped them on the desk. "Did you know about this?" he demanded.

Almost reluctantly, he thought, Allen picked up the bit of cardboard and read the crudely penciled letters. He stared at it for a long moment, then let the hand and the note drop into his lap and continued to stare, unmoving, at nothing.

Hunter said, "Both the rope and the paper came out of the stock at Weckler's. I accused Gus of writing the note and he panicked—I figure, from a guilty conscience." He added, "I heard Gus was making threats at me, at Tarback's last night."

"I wouldn't know about that," Allen said dully. "You'll recall I was at church. . . ." He stirred himself, then, enough to put the note on the desk beside him and point to the worn leather armchair opposite. "Sit down, Robert. How about a cup of coffee? *I* could use one."

It was brewing in a pot on the back of the wood stove; Hunter had been aware of the pleasant smell and it reminded him that he hadn't eaten. He got a couple of china cups off the shelf and filled them, both men preferring to take it black. Afterwards he seated himself and watched as Allen had a sip or two, seemed to find it tasteless and set his cup impatiently aside. His hand shook, Hunter noticed.

Still thinking of the church meeting, Walter Allen blurted, "That was quite a speech you made. . . ."

"It was a damn fool waste of time. I don't know what ever made me think it would accomplish anything."

"You could be mistaken. You hit pretty close to home." Allen lifted a hand and ran it through his graying hair. "Gus Weckler's not the only one with a bad conscience," he said. "I can't tell you when I've had a night's sleep! I'm not a bad man, Robert," he insisted with tremulous earnestness. "I haven't done anything I could blame myself for. And yet—that's not the point! There's the things a man *should* do, and doesn't—when just standing by makes his guilt. . . ."

Very slowly Bob Hunter lowered his coffee cup, unfinished. Gone quite still, he watched this honest and tortured man struggle with the burden he was trying to get off his soul.

"All I can say," Walter Allen went on, after a moment, "is that I've meant well. But I believed in Calvin Tarback, and I was foolish enough that it tickled my vanity to have people calling me 'Judge.' "

Hunter pointed out carefully, "I never did think, or say, that you were a part of what was going on."

"I know—and I thank you for it." Allen lifted his shoulders, let them fall. "But the fact is, I *am* a part of it. And I'm in a trap."

"No man's in a trap, if he refuses to admit it."

Allen shook his head. "You just don't know! They'd kill me, Robert. Like they kill every man who dares to cross them!"

"Even a judge?" Hunter exclaimed, incredulous. "They wouldn't dare!"

"I wish I still believed that! There's a lot of things I used to believe, Robert. Once I actually thought what was being done here would prove good for Prineville—by showing the world we were able to keep order, even without any real help from The Dalles. Once the Stockman's Association took control, I truly hoped there'd be no more of the kind of violence that touched off those lynchings last spring. I was told, and I'm still convinced of it, that some of the men they warned out of the country were shady characters we could well do without; and if a few innocent men also suffered—well, justice is never perfect."

Allen looked down at the hands lying in his lap, and they twitched a little, nervously—very much as Harvey Franks's had twitched, as he sat on the edge of the bed at the Jackson House and told the Hunters of Dutch Schrader's murder.

"When Jed Starns got killed," Allen went on in a lifeless tone, "I really thought it was outlaws who'd killed him. I'm ready now to admit what you said must have been right—Starns had his head blown off because he opposed the Vigilantes. Today, I

132

can only wonder how I ever wanted to be associated in office with men like Jase Evans and Gus Weckler and Tom Ridges. . . ."

Hunter finished his coffee and set the cup on the floor beside his chair, before he said, "I'm curious to know what's changed your mind—and when."

"It was a couple of things that happened yesterday. Seeing the bodies of those two youngsters they murdered—and then you, last night in meeting. That took courage, Robert!" He wagged his head soberly. "You must have known nobody was going to stand up and agree with you. But I know at least you got *me* to thinking. Finally—and too late. . . ."

"Why too late?" Hunter challenged quickly. "We've got a chance to fight back, by breaking the machine to pieces. Weckler's gone. Maybe we can get George Wright away from them, and—"

"No—no!" Walter Allen held up a restraining hand. "You don't suppose they'll stand by and let—"

He broke off, his head jerking. Hunter had heard nothing but Allen was staring at the doorway, with frightened eyes; now he got to his feet, went over and brushed aside the curtain. Since he himself had locked the front door, it was obvious there could have been no one in the storeroom. But when he turned slowly back his face was ashen, and all at once Hunter knew he was talking to a person unmanned by terror. He waited.

Allen said, in a voice that was hoarse and shaken, "After all, I've got to think of my wife and daughter. So, I'm leaving—getting out! It will be a disappointment for Mrs. Allen," he admitted, his gray lips twisting in a smile of tired cynicism. "She's enjoyed it too, hearing her husband addressed as 'Judge.' Still, she never really liked this country; she should be happy enough going back to Ohio, or some other such place. It means starting over, of course. At fifty-three. . . ."

"I think you're making a big mistake," Bob Hunter said. He might as well not have spoken.

"My business here," Allen continued, "the building and the stock, and the good will—they should be worth something, of course, even in a forced sale. But all that takes time; and meanwhile, there's Jennifer." His face twisted in pain. "Robert, I love that girl—nearly more than life itself! I can't bear to have her caught in the midst of this!"

"You think she'd run from trouble?"

"I think she'd go if you were to take her!"

Suddenly Allen came back to drop into his chair, pulling it

133

close to Hunter's. He leaned tensely forward and his whole manner was eager and conspiratorial as he blurted what was in his mind. "Robert, I've known a long time that you wanted to marry my girl; and it would fit her wishes, too. Oh, I'll admit her mother and I have tended to favor George Wright, but—well, he's in too deep with the Vigilantes for me ever to trust him again. So, if you and I should come to an understanding—"

Hunter interrupted, saying coldly, "I don't reckon I follow you at all. I can't afford to marry anyone."

Allen indicated a small iron box beside the desk. "In that safe I have three thousand dollars ready cash. I'll give every cent to see my daughter safely away from here. Portland—California —it doesn't matter, any place that suits you. And if you find that isn't enough to make a start, just let me know. . . ."

He was waiting, eagerly, for Hunter's answer. For a moment the other man could only stare at him in disbelief. Slowly then he shook his head.

"Walter, I'm sorry. I couldn't do it—it's too much like being *bought* to marry Jen! I'm glad you've maybe decided you have no more objections, but if there's to be a match, I've got to make it on my own. I hope you understand."

It hurt, to see the man wilt. Walter Allen slumped slowly back in his chair, a stricken look on him. "I understand," he agreed finally, nodding. "And it's to your credit. I suppose I'm just a foolish old man, worrying about his daughter's happiness. Since you're her choice, I can also see there's not much likelihood of happiness for her, after she's watched you get yourself killed trying to fight these Vigilantes. I wonder if you've thought of that?"

All too poignantly, Hunter remembered the stricken look on Jen's face, the moment's hysteria that had seized her at the ugly sight of that rope lying on the desk. But he thrust the thought away.

"She wouldn't want a coward, either!" He pushed to his feet, in an access of impatient energy. Looking down at the tired and dispirited man in the other chair, he said flatly, "It's something I can't help. I've taken on this fight. I have to see it through."

Allen looked at him from under lowered brows. "How?" he demanded bluntly.

He started to answer, thought again and shook his head. "I don't know, Walter. Right now, I honestly don't know. . . ."

CHAPTER XIII

There was a lot of distance to this Oregon stock country, a lot of miles separating its scatter of cattle and horse growers and sheep outfits. After three days, Bob Hunter had begun to feel the futility of trying to cover it all singlehanded, which was what he almost seemed determined to do.

Yesterday his own horse had gone lame and he was riding one of Shoe Peg Hamilton's iron-jawed livery animals; now this one too was beginning to play out, along with its rider's patience and temper. The day was a bitter one. All around the horizon, veils of distant rain shook down from the broken, greasy-looking clouds that plastered the sky. The wind was enough to tire a man and horse, pushing erratically from changing directions so that a rider had to shift his weight to meet it.

Having watered his animal in a low swale, where he'd found a collection from recent rains, Hunter came up into the wind again and topped out on a long flat covered with sage and rabbit brush and a few junipers. Directly before him, horses were running, their hoofs raising thunder from the porous soil and building a column of dust, to be touched to yellow gold by the sunshine that poured through a vagrant rift in the clouds. Riders were working them. Hunter pulled up to watch the mounted men cut back and forth through the clumps of spiny brush, whooping and swinging coiled ropes.

A pole corral, its wide wings thrown out on either side of the open gate, waited. Once the gather had been pushed inside, he again rode forward.

Gate poles were being slid into place and the dust had already fairly well settled. It being high noon, one of the horse handlers was putting a fire together while somebody else broke out the makings of a range meal. The rest were taking advantage of an idle moment to check a saddle girth, or build a smoke, or size up what they had in the pen. All this activity suddenly ceased as they caught sight of Hunter.

There were four different outfits represented here, pooling

135

their efforts and their crews. He had at least a nodding acquaintance with every man present—and a nod was exactly what he got from them. Drawing rein he thumbed his hat back from his forehead and looked around, in a silence with a thread of suspicion in it as they waited, apparently, for Hunter to speak first.

"You boys got some nice stock there," he offered.

Someone said grudgingly, "We think so."

There was no friendliness, no invitation to light down. It was a reaction he had met before, in these last few days of riding, and Hunter drew a breath and straightened his shoulders. He said bluntly, "I know you want to get back to work; and I'm pressed for time myself. So I'll tell you what I came for."

"We know what you came for." Vern Larkin, a rancher with a six-man crew on his payroll, moved forward a pace or two. He had to tilt his head and squint into a dazzle of sun-shot cloud, as he looked up at the man in the saddle. "We've had word you were riding around the country trying to drum up recruits for a fight against the Vigilantes. We figured you'd be getting to us sooner or later."

Hunter prodded him. "And?"

"We've decided we're staying out. It ain't healthy or sensible to do anything else. Look, man!" he persisted, when the other would have interrupted. "None of us is any happier than you over the turn things have taken lately. We all liked Dutch. As for those boys of his—the redhead was a stranger, but we knew the Hewett kid, and he was sure as hell no horse thief. Makes you kind of sick, to know what happened to a couple of youngsters like that."

"Then, damn it—!"

Larkin remained adamant. "I said, we're staying out! If anyone else showed signs of backing you, it might be worth considering. But you've been turned down everywhere—and it doesn't leave us any choice. A man has to think about himself, and his family if he's got one. Surely you can see that!"

Hunter stared at him. "What I see is, that's the attitude that makes it certain nothing at all will be done!"

Someone insisted, "Hunter, we're just being reasonable."

"Then maybe it's time somebody started being unreasonable for a change!" But words would not breach a stone wall. He took a breath, and let his eyes rest on each man in turn. "You all of the same opinion?"

They wouldn't answer him directly. They let their glances slide away, and one started fiddling with a fraying end of a catch rope, as though suddenly intent on fixing it. It was the kind of evasive, half-ashamed look he was becoming almighty tired of, but he knew it masked a set stubbornness that was unshakable. For he also knew the argument none of these men would make openly: *If I stick my neck out, how can I tell which of my neighbors is secretly a member of the Vigilantes? Or which of them might betray me in an effort to buy safety for himself?*

"Will you take some advice, Hunter?" Vern Larkin asked with serious earnestness. "You're stirring up hard feelings, and that's about *all* you're doing. If you don't ease off, you could find yourself in trouble."

"Believe me, friend," Hunter told him, "that's where we all are right now!"

He lifted the reins. A fine smell of coffee and beans came from over at the fire; he looked that way a moment. But no one suggested he drop down and join them, and he was too proud to ask for an invitation. It wasn't, he told himself, that they actually wanted to be rude. The risks involved in associating with him were too dire just now. They were all standing there wishing he would be gone, and take his troubling presence and conscience-stirring arguments to bother someone else.

"Thanks for your time," he said gruffly. "I won't be back."

He pulled the rent horse about and used the rowels, putting his back to these men. He rode stiffly straight, not favoring them with another look, and presently a dip in the sage flat lost the corral and the penned horses and the crew behind him, and left only a brown smudge of dust drifting against the clouds.

"I've had a plenty," Hunter told the horse, in a tone of sour disgust. "Let's head for town. . . ."

He was in Hamilton's, wearily stripping off saddle and gear, when a town kid came dashing in and offered him a piece of paper that evidently contained a note. "For me?" Hunter demanded. "You're sure?" By the time he had it unfolded the youngster had vanished again, out into the smear of crimson sunset that filled the dusty street.

Hunter read the words twice, slowly. The message, neatly penned, was brief enough: *I must talk to you, at once. Come to my office.* It was signed: *George Wright.*

For a long minute he stood frowning, searching for a clue. He couldn't imagine George Wright having business with the man who was both his rival, and also an avowed enemy of the machine to which he belonged. One bizarre thought Hunter dismissed as quickly as it occurred to him, because it obviously made no sense: The enemy would have no reason at all for wanting to suggest terms—not at this stage of a fight he was clearly losing.

The puzzle was no clearer by the time he had finished with the horse; still, he could hardly do any less than find out what George had in mind.

He racked his saddle and went out of the stable and a few doors along the street to the building that had once held Gus Weckler's hardware store—it was locked and shuttered now, its stock and fixtures having been auctioned off in a sale George Wright had managed on behalf of the vanished county treasurer. Some of the tiredness and discouragement had slipped away from Hunter, to be replaced by a growing curiosity that carried him up the outside stairway, to the door whose pebbled glass held Wright's name in stenciled letters. There, as he took hold of the knob, some last voice of caution warned him he didn't really know what lay on the other side; but the thought was no more than half formed when the door swung open under his hand.

He halted abruptly, on the threshold.

In George Wright's chair, behind George's desk, Calvin Tarback was making himself comfortable, thumbs tucked in the armholes of his waistcoat. Seated on a straight wooden chair beside him, young Eddie Wright had his elbows propped on the desk, both forefingers poked through the trigger guard of a Colt revolver, and was idly twirling the weapon around his fingers. The two of them stared at the man in the doorway

Hunter turned his head then and found Jase Evans leaning meaty shoulders against the wall, arms folded on his thick chest and a heavy-lidded droop in his eyes. Dying sunset stained the windows. Aside from these three, the room was empty.

Looking at Tarback, Hunter said, "George isn't here?"

The man's blond head made the smallest movement of negation. "No."

"I guess he didn't write this either?" He held up the note that had lured him here. Tarback flicked it with a glance.

"Is it likely you'd come, if I'd signed my own name to it?" Thumb still hooked into waistcoat, Tarback crooked his forefinger—a summoning gesture. "Come in."

When Hunter made no move to obey, Eddie Wright suddenly quit twirling that revolver and let the butt slap against his palms. He said, "You heard the Major." Something like the clenching of a fist tightened inside Hunter's chest as the huge bore of the .45 settled on him, a point-blank aim. All the juices seemed to dry out of his throat; he tried to swallow and suddenly couldn't.

But he managed to step into the office.

Tarback nodded to Jase Evans, who straightened from his lean against the wall. "See if he's got a gun. If he has, get rid of it." Evans stepped to Hunter and his big hands went over him, found the six-gun in his holster. Turning, Evans simply tossed the weapon out the door and over the stair rail, into the dirt twenty feet below. Afterward he closed the door and moved away from it, coming around until he faced the prisoner.

Bob Hunter could see nothing, just then, but the unwinking eye of that gunmuzzle yonder, and the face of the boy who held it. He found his voice, and said hoarsely, "You better take that thing away from the kid!" No one moved, no one said anything. Hunter felt a bead of cold sweat break out and run down his ribs under his shirt. "Damn it," he cried. "He'll use it!"

"Oh, I don't think so," Calvin Tarback answered calmly. "Not if you behave yourself." But Hunter knew what he could see in those wild and undisciplined eyes, and his blood ran cold.

"What do you want with me?" he demanded in a voice he knew was too loud.

Tarback unhooked both thumbs, sat forward and laced his fingers together. "Wouldn't you say it was time you and I did a little talking? Where we can say what we mean, without any third parties listening?"

"I don't think we have anything to say to each other."

"I think we do! You've been making a nuisance of yourself, Hunter. And I want to know just how far you expect to get with it!"

Hunter pulled his eyes away from the gun, and met the Major's cold stare. He took a slow breath. "Tarback, I'll *never* quit fighting you! Not now!" The dam inside him broke suddenly; the words came pouring out. "You want it plain? Well, there it is! You started out with the scared remnants of a lynch mob, who had to follow you because you knew their guilt, and because you were the only one big enough to save them. You used these Vigilantes of yours as the core of a Stockman's Association, which gave you the whip hand over an entire range. And then when the big chance came, and you got to the Governor with your list of appointments, you ended by putting all of Crook County in your pocket.

"I kept asking myself, *why?* And do you know what I've figured out? I don't think it's money you want at all. You already had that. No, I think it's the itch for power that drives you, Tarback—something in you that has to see other men crawl. . . ."

139

Tarback's watching eyes showed no slightest change of expression. He rubbed his thumbs softly together. "Go on," he said quietly. "Suppose you tell me some more about myself."

But Hunter shrugged. "Sorry. That's all the farther I've got. This much, though, I think I do know: A hunger for power is something that keeps growing, the more you feed it. And sooner or later, it has to go too far. Sooner or later, someone's going to stop you!"

"You, perhaps?"

"In case you hadn't noticed," Hunter answered bluntly, "I'm sure as hell making a try!" Suddenly he was fed up with this scene. Anger carried him around, putting his back to that six-gun Eddie Wright had started twirling again between his hands. He covered two steps toward the door when Tarback's angry bellow sounded.

"Come back here! I haven't finished what I want to say!"

"I've heard all I want of it."

He kept walking, what seemed an endless, treadmill distance to that closed door. Then the knob was in reach. He put out a hand for it.

Tarback cried, "*Stop him!*"

Working the knob, he pulled the door open. From the tail of his eye he saw Jase Evans drawing his gun. But that wasn't the weapon whose sudden report smashed the stillness of the room.

The bullet took Hunter between the shoulders. Slammed hard against the edge of the doorframe, he clung there, gasping, numbed by the shock of it. And, somehow turning, he got a long look at the tableau—Evans and the Major frozen motionless, and Eddie Wright just bringing the smoking gun down level again.

His world grew black, swam once more into gray and splintery light. He still felt almost no pain, but he knew his senses were fading when the fingers holding the edge of the doorframe began to lose their grip. Anger, and a great effort of will, pulled him upright; all conscious thought came suddenly to a focus on a single object—that gun Jase Evans had taken from him and thrown into the alleyway at the foot of the steps.

It would still be lying there. Suddenly, the idea of getting to it was an obsession.

He pushed away from the door, setting first one foot and then the other in front of him. He was outside on the landing; the stairway's rough railing was under his hand. Grabbing at it convulsively, leaning on it, he tried to will strength into his legs and consciousness into a body that was rapidly slipping out of control.

Eddie Wright's second bullet struck and his left leg doubled under him. He realized he was spilling head first down the steep stairs, helpless to save himself. And then he knew nothing.

CHAPTER XIV

When after long minutes there was no answer to his ring, George Wright was about to turn and walk away; but the big door swung open then and Jennifer Allen looked out at him, unspeaking. Her face was white and solemn. Taking off his hat George cleared his throat and asked heavily, "Where is he? I'd like to see him, Jen."

"It won't do any good. He hasn't regained consciousness. But—all right. This way."

He followed her through the strange stillness that lay upon her father's house, up the stairs to the second story and along the hall. At the open door of a front bedroom she stood aside for him; he entered, and haltingly approached the man who lay on the bed.

Bob Hunter seemed scarcely alive. His eyes were closed, the skin of his face looked like wax; his breathing was so shallow the movement of his chest hardly lifted the covers. Behind George, Jen spoke in a voice that sounded heavy with worry and fatigue. "He hasn't stirred since we put him there yesterday. He was shot twice. The doctor says the bullet that went through his chest may have touched a lung."

Across the room a man stood at the window, hat in hand, looking out at a gaunt and leafless cottonwood. He turned now; George almost failed to know him. Chris Hunter's face seemed like scraped bone, and his eyes held a feverish burning that had never been there. It was almost more than George Wright could do to meet his stare, and it took a moment for him to speak.

He said, with an effort, "I was over at Mitchell. I got back an hour ago. I only just heard. I—" He swallowed, trying to clear the leaden obstruction from his throat. "I honest to God don't know what to say!"

Chris Hunter's arms hung limp at his sides; his fists worked slowly, clenching and opening, as though with a life of their own. He said nothing. George tried again.

"I don't suppose there could be any mistake? There were four of them in the room. . . ."

"Eddie had the gun," Chris answered coldly. "He was carrying it when they came down the steps. He was yelling his head off, bragging that he'd killed that sonofabitch Bob Hunter. A dozen people have told me they heard him."

George looked at the floor. Chris went on: "Tarback got to work and hustled the boy out of sight before anyone could think to do anything. Nobody's seen him since. I figure they sneaked him out of town, to hide him somewhere until things blow over. Until we know whether it was murder, or whether Bob will live."

The other man lifted his eyes again, and they were anguished. "I'm asking you to remember, Chris—he's only a boy. Not eighteen! Whatever he did, he's not responsible."

"I'll *try* to remember it," Chris Hunter said, through lips as stiff as the lips of a mask. "I make no promises!" His eyes burned with the new, feverish purpose that had taken possession of him. Abruptly, Chris Hunter stepped around George and strode from the room, his solid stride sounding along the hallway until it was muffled by the stairway runner, descending. George took a long breath, and looked at Jen.

"Today is the worst day I've lived," he told her. "I never did like Bob Hunter—and I don't think I have to tell you why. But, I'd have done anything to keep this from happening!"

Her eyes probed his. "Can you honestly say that, George? Are you sure there isn't anything you might have done, while there was still time? What Eddie did," she reminded him solemnly, "came of following too blindly after Major Tarback for too long. And when it comes to that—just what kind of an example did *you* set him?"

The quiet reproof hit hard, whipping color into his sallow cheeks; yet he knew he had no answer. Guilt silenced him. He put out a hand, dropped it again without touching her. He looked at the face of the man on the bed—as near to dead as a living face could look. And when he lifted his eyes again to the girl, what he saw in hers held a finality that bunched his jaw muscles and tightened his hand on the felt of his hatbrim.

142

He turned and walked out of that room, and defeat settled more heavily in him at every stride.

At the bottom of the stairs he found Mrs. Allen, a prim and disappointed woman who might have resembled her daughter some indefinite time ago. Reading the grim look in his face she said, "You've talked to Jennifer . . . This has all been most upsetting. She and her father both insisted on bringing that young man here—and I suppose he does need more attention than the doctor would have been able to give him. The Lord knows none of us want him to die!"

"Just don't let this discourage you," she went on, laying a hand on his arm. "For the moment Jennifer's completely taken up with playing like a nurse. I think it may even have given her some notion she's in love with this Bob Hunter. But surely, if we're patient—"

George Wright shook his head. "No," he said. "It was never any use; if I ever thought so, I know differently now. She's made her choice—she made it long ago. And it's not me!"

Mrs. Allen shook her head, but she had no more encouragement to give. Somber of expression, she could only stand aside as he stumbled from the house.

Jim Blake was no drinking man, but he had some business with another rancher, and he had hunted him to earth in Kelley's Saloon. Hence he was seated at a table in Kelley's, facing the door, when Chris Hunter entered. Something made him break off talking in midsentence, and the other man too kited about in his chair for a look.

Calvin Tarback stood at the bar with Jase Evans and Bud Morrison flanking him, the badges on their two coats gleaming dully in the light of a cloudy afternoon. The Major looked into the bar mirror, saw Chris Hunter in it. He put down his brandy glass and turned with that erect, stiff way he had of moving. More slowly, the pair with him pivoted about. Morrison still held his glass; Sheriff Evans hung both elbows on the edge of the counter behind him and peered at the newcomer, big hands dangling empty.

In a sudden stillness, Tarback said, "I heard you were looking for me, Hunter."

"I've been looking. What were *you* doing—hiding?"

"From you? Is that likely?" the Major retorted, and the men with him shared a scornful laugh. In a serious tone Tarback added: "I'm told you hold me to blame for what happened to your brother. It was not my doing, Hunter."

143

Chris lifted a shoulder. "I guess maybe you didn't pull the trigger." He walked forward, closing half the distance to the bar. He moved his feet apart and stood with his weight distributed. "But you don't think I'll go after a kid that didn't have the sense to know what he was up to!"

"Don't threaten me!" The Major's voice was suddenly rimmed with ice, as cold as the stare that locked with his accuser's. "Not if *you* have any sense."

"I've never killed a man," Chris Hunter said doggedly. "And I reckon you've planted a few. No difference! I'm telling you now, as plain as I can make it: If my brother should die, you'll be seeing me again. And that's a promise!"

His voice rang for a moment in the quiet, while a dozen onlookers held their breath. And, leaving it at that, he turned sharply and started for the door.

Where he was sitting Jim Blake couldn't see the Major's face, but he saw the sudden lift of his shoulder and the movement of his arm. Too late he started to his feet; a warning cry was locked in his throat and next instant was drowned in the thunderous clap of sound from the gun that had appeared somehow in Major Tarback's hand. The bullet that struck Chris Hunter in the back of the head picked him off his feet, flung him forward onto his face with arms and legs flung out carelessly like those of a rag doll. A small blue cloud of smoke formed and dissolved in front of Major Tarback.

He turned, then, to address the shocked, still room. "You all heard this man threaten me."

"Sure they did," Jase Evans said quickly. "A clear case of self-defense."

Horrified, Blake found his tongue. "Self-defense! Why, he had his back turned!"

"Trying to sneak a gun," the sheriff corrected him blandly. "I was watching him—I knew what he was up to." And Deputy Morrison added, "That's how it was, friend. It's how the law saw it."

"*The law!*" Unarmed, himself, Jim Blake stared at Calvin Tarback, at the smoking gun in his hand, and the badges on the pair who stood at either side of him. He looked at the murdered man—a glance only, before he hastily turned away. Suddenly, the inevitability of it all struck him like a punishing blow.

So it had come to this, as it was bound to have done. He had been warned—like everyone else—and had simply closed his mind to the warning, for convenience's sake. And now a better man than himself had paid the penalty.

144

He stood there and a great wave of guilt descended on him, bore him under. His lungs felt crushed, incapable of breathing.

It was a murmur of voices this time that dragged Bob Hunter reluctantly back from dark regions of lethargy and unawareness, where the mending of ravaged tissues carried out its slow work. He opened his eyes, puzzled, and for a moment panicky until he remembered again where he was. He lay gathering the threads of consciousness, and became aware that the voices had ceased. Turning his head on the pillow, he saw Jim Blake and Jen standing in the doorway, watching him.

They exchanged a glance and then the man was coming toward the bed. He loomed blackly against the morning light filling the east window at his back. "Bob!" he said. "You're awake. . . . Can you hear me?"

He tried to nod and, looking again at Jen, saw the white mask of her face was stained with the marks of weeping. "What's wrong?" he demanded, in a voice that seemed scarcely loud enough to reach beyond his lips. "What is it?" And then he supplied his own answer: "It's Chris, isn't it? You've come to tell me he's dead."

Jim Blake's solid figure seemed to rock back upon its heels. "How—how could you know?"

He couldn't really explain, and he didn't try. He fought against the overpowering sense of loss, found the strength to ask, "What happened? And when?"

"It was yesterday," Jim Blake said. "At Kelley's. . . ." The story poured from him then, and left Hunter staring at the ceiling directly overhead with eyes blinded by pain. A hand crept into his own, where it lay limp upon the blankets; it was Jen's, consoling, and his fingers tightened on hers convulsively.

"No one will be ashamed if you cry," she murmured in a broken voice.

But there were no tears in him. Dry-eyed, he looked at nothing. He heard his own voice say, "Chris! He threw himself away—for nothing!"

"Maybe not quite *all* for nothing," Jim Blake said. "Maybe not quite."

It took a moment for the words to reach him. They pulled his stare toward the rancher's face, focussed it there in a puzzled frown. He said gruffly, "What do you mean by that?"

Jim Blake rubbed a palm across his heavy mustache. He had never looked so grimly serious. "Bob, you told me all along I couldn't always play it safe, just because I had a wife and a baby

145

to think about. You said a time would come. Well, what happened to Chris—and to you—finally made me see it was the time! Too late to do Chris any good; but I knew, all right, when I stood there and saw murder committed, and then heard the only law we have in this county tell us that nothing was to be done about it. From that moment, the time for standing aside was finished!"

Hunter absorbed this, but all he could answer was, "Like you said—it's a little late."

"But I'm not the only one!" Quickly the rancher looked around, found a ladderback chair and pulled it over, dropped his hat on the bed. Jen remained in the doorway, watching, as Blake leaned forward eagerly to tell his news.

"There are a few more of us, Bob. We got together for a meeting yesterday evening, in the office down at the grist mill—besides Bill Stewart and me, there was John Combs, Sam Smith and Adam Nealy . . ."

Hunter stared. "The preacher?" He saw the other nod.

"This is in earnest, Bob. Only five of us, to start; but that's because we mean to keep things quiet while we organize for battle. Once we're started, we'll see it to a finish."

A bitter skepticism turned Hunter's mouth hard. "You really think you can sell this country on fighting the Vigilantes? Go ahead! I tried it and I got nothing but saddle sores. Believe me—you can talk till you're hoarse. You'll be lucky if they so much as listen!"

Jim Blake drew a deep breath. "I know what you mean—because I was one of those that wouldn't listen. I'm ashamed, now, at the way we all stood by and let you try to carry this alone, and I'm sorry for what it took to wake us up. I can only hope we've at least learned by your experience—that we know where you made your mistakes.

"It's clear we'll never lick the Vigilantes by urging ordinary people to go to war against them. Our thought is that there's one way it can be done: with the ballot box! Do you realize we've got an election coming up? In June—a little less than two months away. It's the first chance Crook County will have had to choose its own officials. The Vigilantes won't be looking for a contest. We've got to put up a slate of our own—and then round up the votes to ram it through!"

Hunter said dubiously, "Two months isn't much time. Not against a machine as solid as this one."

"It's maybe not as solid as it looks. You chased Gus Weckler out of town. Walter Allen's washed his hands of the Major, and

146

I got an idea George Wright's had about enough." He remembered, then: "But, hell! I guess you haven't heard about Eddie! Either one of you. . . ."

Jen said, "Why, no." And Hunter added quickly, "What is it, Jim?"

"They brought his body in this morning. He was found out in the sage—shot with the same gun he tried to kill *you* with."

Jen uttered a gasp of horror. "Oh, no! Not that boy—!"

He nodded grimly. "Most people I've talked to say it was suicide—he thought he'd done murder and couldn't live with it. Myself, I wonder. What's more important, I wonder what George is going to think."

Hunter said, "I know damn well what George will think: That his kid brother was murdered, to keep him from embarrassing the Major!"

"Either way, it's one killing too many! Just think back a moment: Luke Langley and Bill Farrell. Jed Starns—Dutch Schrader—Hack Gorham. Sam Clifton and Charlie Hewett. And Chris. . . ." Blake surged to his feet. "Bob, this range just can't take any more! And meanwhile, the machine's lost its county treasurer and its attorney and—" He looked apologetically at Jennifer. "If you'll excuse me saying so—its judge. That's all been directly due to you, Bob, one way or another. You've shown us it can be done. Now it's time to finish the job. . . ."

Before Hunter could speak, Jen stepped in, saying quickly, "No! Right now it's time to quit talking, so this man can get some rest. Honestly, I mean it!"

Blake was immediately contrite. "I'm too full of my subject," he confessed. "I'm sorry." He put a hand on the hurt man's shoulder. "You get mended, Bob. I'll be in again. I'll keep you posted."

The talk and the effect of the news had drained Hunter's strength, more than he knew. He could only nod. His eyes were closed before the other two were out of the room; he let tiredness have its way with him.

In the lower hall where their words could not reach up the stairs to Hunter's room, Jen turned on Blake; her face was troubled, her voice edged with suspicion. "Why did you come here? Did you *have* to tell him all this?"

He stared. "But we need his help, Jen! I was going to ask him to let us put him on the ticket—to run against Jase Evans."

"For *sheriff?*" Her face drained white; one hand moved to

147

her throat. "Oh no, Jim! *Please!* I know this sounds selfish, but—I almost lost him once. The next time—"

"If we just win this election," he explained patiently, "there doesn't have to be a next time."

She shook her head. "I know that if you tell him he has to run, he'll do it—and kill himself trying. Can't you see? Just now he should forget all this, and be thinking of nothing else in this world except getting well again. Oh, Jim!" She made a helpless gesture and her eyes shone with tears. "Hasn't he done enough? Hasn't he *given* enough?"

It was a moment before Jim Blake answered, nodding. "Of course, Jen. You're right. It's up to the rest of us now. Sure, we'll find someone to run for sheriff—even if I have to do it myself! The only thing, I'd purely hate it if Bob somehow was to get the notion we deliberately passed him over."

"If he ever does think that," she promised, "I'll see that he's put right, Jim."

His teeth, beneath the dark mustache, flashed in a smile that lighted his face. "In that case you've got a deal!" he said, and left her.

CHAPTER XV

Down here in the broad canyon's shelter, spring came on at a faster pace than on the high sage and juniper flats, exposed the way they were to the full sweep of wind and weather. Hunter could watch the season's progress from day to day, as the sky above the palisade rims cleared and clouded and the cottonwood branches outside his window swelled with new-minted foliage. His hurts, mending, kept pace with the tedious passage of dragging time. Both were slow processes.

He was up now, able to spend hours a day in a rocker by the window and to move about some in the little second-story bedroom. Under Jen's tender and selfless care there was no reason he shouldn't recover from the bullet that had nearly killed him; but convalescing roweled him with angry impatience, as he thought of all the labor that needed doing on the Willow Creek spread—though he knew that neighbors were taking care of the immediate chores, and better than he could have done himself. Even harder was his knowledge that the fight against the Vigilantes, that he had come to think of almost as his own personal vendetta, was going ahead without him.

Not entirely without him. Jim Blake and the other leaders knew Hunter's feelings, and they made it a point to keep him abreast of developments. On some days there would be a regular procession of grim-faced, spurred and booted men up the stairs to Hunter's room in the Allen house, bringing him news and hearing his suggestions; Mrs. Allen stood by and watched bleakly but made no protests, while her husband became more worried and more apprehensive and his mustache grew ragged with nervous chewing. Walter Allen didn't see how the Vigilantes could possibly be beaten without gun-play and violence making a bloody shambles of the streets of Prineville.

Jim Blake felt otherwise. He told Hunter one May morning, "We're almost there. We figure there's maybe eight, nine hundred votes in the county, and we're nailing down as many as we can. Some won't commit themselves, but I figure we're already safe for nearly three hundred—with a couple weeks still to go. Al Lyle's doing good work for us, up north in his end of the county; I'm sure we'll put him in the State Assembly with no trouble. And here around Prineville and in the canyon, there must be close to sixty, maybe seventy men we can count on if things should come to a real showdown."

"It sounds good," Hunter agreed. "But damn it, it's got to be *sure!* If we lose, and the Vigilantes take reprisals, we'll never get anyone to buck them again." He slapped a knee impatiently, and swung himself to his feet. Jim Blake, eyeing his unsteadiness, started to reach out but Hunter shook his head; with a hand on the back of the rocker he said, "I can't sit here any longer. I got to pull my share. Watch the door," he added, in sudden determination, "while I get my clothes on. If Jen knew she'd try to stop me. But I'm going over town—just to see if I can make it there and back. . . ."

He was weak enough, and a little lightheaded at first; the ground looked far enough away as to make him almost dizzy, trying to reach it with his boots. But although Jim Blake hovered at his elbow, ready to lend a hand if he needed it, Hunter quickly found he owned reserves of strength he hadn't suspected. The thin sunlight and the welcome scent of a May morning were invigorating to a man shut in and immobilized so long. He had gone less than a block before he knew he was mended and whole and ready to live again.

It took scarcely longer than that for him to sense the change around him. This was not imagination. Men who had tended to avoid him in recent months hailed him now and even came from across the street to shake his hand and congratulate him on his recovery. There was no longer anything furtive about them as they stood on the open street and discussed with him and with Blake the progress of the campaign against the Vigilantes. Prineville, once a town afraid to speak its mind, had found its voice and its courage again. And Hunter could tell Jim Blake was pleased and proud for him to see this.

He was a little proud himself. No one could deny that much of it had been his doing.

They entered Gil Haze's; it was a slack moment and the saloonkeeper was seated at a table tuning up his fiddle, a soulful expression on his face. Seeing Hunter on his feet again, he insisted on hurrying behind the counter and setting up a schooner of beer all around. But he quickly sobered. He said, "Jase Evans is in town . . ."

Hunter felt the quick stab of Blake's regard; but he made no comment as Gil Haze continued: "There's been some bets laid as to what's going to happen when you two meet up. Now, don't look at me!" he added quickly. "I ain't saying you should fight him! I'm just telling you what I hear, because I think you should know. And what I hear is that Jase was in Wright's office that day and helped set you up for Eddie Wright. And he was standing at Tarback's elbow when Chris was killed."

Hunter set down the empty schooner, saying nothing; his face was white and his hands trembled a little as he wiped them on one of the towels hanging from a row of hooks along the front of the bar. Jim Blake said, "For Pete's sake! Will you lay off him, Gil? The man's barely on his feet. It's no time to hit him with things like this!"

"He's not bothering me," Hunter said quietly. "Do you suppose I've thought about anything else much, these past weeks?"

Blake stared at him. "You looking for a private showdown with Jase Evans? And the Major?"

"I'm not looking for it," he answered, in the same tone. "I don't forget that we're fighting to establish some kind of respect for the law here in this Crooked River country. I hope the law can do what's needed to settle for Chris. But, if it can't—" He left that unfinished, lifting his shoulders, and suddenly there seemed little more to say.

A few minutes later Jim Blake said it was time to start back

150

for Allen's—no point in stretching a man's reserves too far the first day. Actually Hunter felt much sounder than he would have expected; very shortly, he thought, he'd be ready for a full day's saddle work again. "I guess you're anxious to get back to your place," Blake said as they walked back up the street.

He hesitated over an answer. "I guess so," he said finally. "Though it's going to seem awfully empty, with Chris gone—it'll take time getting used to that. But right now, there's other business: I figure I've sat around long enough, while the rest of you carried on this campaign without me. It's still my fight; I still want a part of it."

"Plenty of time to think about that," Jim Blake started to say, and then turned sharply as a storm of hoofbeats blew up behind them.

A group of eight riders drew rein in a grit-spattering stop, Jase Evans and the dark-skinned Bud Morrison in the lead. Evans's tough-jawed animal acted for a moment as though it meant to climb the sidewalk; but the pair of them stood their ground, and as the horses settled the sheriff lifted a gloved hand and punched the hat back from his forehead.

The nickeled badge gleamed from his coatfront. Like all the men with him—and unlike Blake or Hunter—he was armed, a rifle under his knee and a holstered six-shooter strapped about his waist. He looked directly at Hunter and showed his teeth in a humorless grin.

"So! I heard you were up and on your feet again."

"You did? What about it?"

A grunt broke from the man's thick chest. "Nothing. Except it's just too bad the little bastard couldn't have shot straighter."

"Is that why Eddie was killed, Jase?" Jim Blake demanded.

The big man's raddled cheeks tightened as Evans swung on the rancher. "I dunno what the hell you're talking about!" he retorted, too loudly. "He killed himself. Got ahold of some bad booze and it sent him out of his head."

And Bud Morrison added blandly, "He always did fight his likker!"

Bob Hunter, his fists tight clenched, was having trouble controlling his breathing. "A seventeen-year-old boy? A drunkard, and a suicide?" Disgust pulled at his mouth. "You and Tarback should damn well be proud of yourselves, for that!"

That brought the sheriff's stare back to him. It seemed to measure the effects of the bullet that had wasted him, and stripped pounds from a frame that could not well spare them.

151

Evans said heavily, "Looks like my hunch was right. While there's even one of you Hunters alive, it's one too many!"

Shaky and weaponless as he was, Hunter almost forgot himself then. He actually started to step forward, an arm rising to shove the head of Jase Evans's horse out of his way; but Jim Blake managed to lift a blocking shoulder in front of his friend and his own voice cut in, forestalling him. "That was a plain threat, Jase!" he warned the big man. "I'll be holding you accountable."

"Who to?" the other challenged, his attention diverted as Jim Blake had probably aimed. "You, maybe? And that bunch of amateurs you got trying to work against us?"

"Call us amateurs if it gives you a laugh," Jim Blake answered coldly. "You just might be laughing different, one of these days."

"The same day you figure to take this off of me and pin it on your own chest!" Evans touched a thumb to the sheriff's badge on his coat. "That's the day I'm gonna have to see! Maybe," he added scornfully, "you think you got anybody worried—any more than a bunch of feist dogs snapping around our heels!" He looked at his followers. "You know what they've taken to doing, now? They *spy* on us!"

"That's a lie!" Jim Blake snapped.

Seeing his random thrust had struck angry color into the man's cheeks, Jase Evans elaborated. "Sure, they do! They spy—they got places where they keep men posted, just to watch the roads and learn where we ride and what we're up to. You see the mill, yonder—" He pointed to the big bulk of the grist mill, rising on the bank of the river south of town. "I understand there's always one of 'em up there a-peekin' at us, these fine moonlit nights." Lips spreading in a grin, he added, "That's all they are—nothing but a bunch of lousy moonshiners. . . ."

Bud Morrison laughed his high, jeering giggle. "Moonshiners! Best name for 'em I've heard yet, Jase!"

Jim Blake had turned several different colors; Hunter could see him trembling, and a nerve in one ashen cheek was leaping. He cried suddenly, "You figure that's a hell of a joke, don't you? Go ahead—enjoy it. To us, one name's as good as another. We might just take that one and ram it down your throats!"

The grin on Jase Evans's loose mouth lost its edge for just an instant. But then he laughed aloud and in the same moment yanked the reins. The horse backed and turned under him, the knot of riders pulled away and went spurring away up the street, leaving a film of dust and the sound of their hooting laughter.

The two friends looked at one another, and Jim Blake struck his palms together in an angry gesture. His voice held the edge of frustrated emotion. "That's damned hard to take!" he muttered. "But maybe it shows me a little of what *you* must have felt, all those months when you couldn't make anyone listen to you."

Hunter shrugged. "Don't let him get under your skin—he enjoys it too much! Now we got the job started, we can't let anything keep us from finishing it. . . ."

George Wright brought his rented livery rig into the tangled shadows of a clump of brush and halted there, listening to the hushed breath of the night. It was nearly still, except for a faint chill movement of air through pine boughs and brush. The stars were all out but, fortunately, there was no moon. He suspected they would be having a late-season frost by morning.

He wrapped the reins to a grab-iron and stepped down from the buggy. The horse was plucking at the bush, nibbling young leaves and making slight tearing noises—surely it was possible to hear them, easily, as far as the house, whose high gabled roof he could see against the stars. Anxiously he caught at the halter. The horse didn't like that and tried to pull free, tossing its head against his grip; it shifted its hoofs in the dry litter underfoot and the buggy rocked, creaking. George, sweating a little, cursed the animal under his breath.

Suddenly he froze.

Someone was approaching, and for a moment his imagination magnified this and convinced him he had been discovered or betrayed, and enemies were coming in from every side. But he got over his brief panic and knew it was only one person, moving toward him from the direction of the dark rear of the big house. Moments later he glimpsed a woman's cloaked figure and stepped forward into the open; she saw him there, and veered to meet him.

She was almost sobbing. "I thought you wouldn't come. I've been waiting so long . . ."

"Out here? In the cold?" She was shaking; he could feel it as he touched her arm.

"I couldn't spend another hour in that house!"

He took a hastily packed carpetbag from her chilled fingers, and led her to the buggy. She also carried a beaded reticule. Stowing the luggage inside, George said anxiously, "Nobody saw you?"

"He isn't home," she assured him quickly. "I've been alone all evening."

"So we're in luck, then!" George helped her in, went around and climbed to his own place. He took the reins and with a slap at the horse's rump got the buggy into motion.

Ada Tarback pressed against him and he could feel the long, punishing shudders that went through her. He said, a little anxiously, "I hope you haven't taken a chill. . . ."

"No—no," she said faintly; but he thought he heard the click of her teeth as she sought to hold her jaws quiet. A moment later her voice came again, muffled and tentative. "You wouldn't have—you know: A—bottle?"

His jaw set hard and for an instant he felt an engulfing certainty that this whole thing was a terrible mistake, doomed to disastrous failure. He looked straight ahead, his hands firm on the reins. "No bottle, Mrs. Tarback. You're through with all that. Remember?"

"Yes, George. I'm sorry." After a bit she added, "Only, I'm terrified! I'll be all right if only—"

"You'll be all right," he assured her in a firm tone. "You have my promise." It appeared to serve. She touched his arm and then dropped her hand away again. She rode in silence beside him, with the trusting timidity of a frightened child. Pity rose and for an instant choked him.

It was late and most of the village slept. They passed among darkened houses and met no one until the moment when they crossed the wooden bridge across Ochoco Creek. There a single rider met them, coming at a canter, hoofbeats mingling briefly with the sound of the buggy wheels rolling over the planks. George Wright stiffened and the woman beside him caught her breath as she averted her face; but under the darkness of the buggy's hood there was no reason to believe the man could see enough to recognize either of them.

Yet, neither could George tell who the rider might have been. Whoever it was he would be bound to remember, later, the rig he had encountered at this unexpected hour, with the two people in it. Unfortunate; but it could not be helped, and it certainly would not turn them back. The buggy settled into a steady gait along the stage road leading north toward The Dalles. The night grew colder about them, the breath of horse and passengers shone frostily in this starglow.

A couple of hours deeper into the hills, where timber crowded the trail, George Wright drew out of the stage road and into a grassy patch of clearing near a creek. "This should be far

154

enough, " he suggested, breaking a silence that had lasted a long time. "What do you think?"

"Whatever you say," the woman told him. But she added anxiously, "If you're really sure . . ."

"I'm sure he won't be after us tonight. Even if I'm wrong, we can't get away from him by running—he could always outrun a rig like this one. No, we'll stop." He wrapped the reins, stepped down and came around to help her alight. She did so, stiffly, and clinging to his arm. She was plainly near exhaustion. "Are you hungry?" he asked.

"Yes—no. I really don't know!" She shook her head hopelessly.

"I brought some food. I'll have a fire started. One thing I know, at least: It's cold!"

Ada Tarback decided she wanted nothing except, perhaps, some coffee. He was equipped to supply it and did so, building a fire and then, with a bachelor's efficiency, brewing up a mess from materials he had in the buggy and water from the creek. Afterward they sat and stared at the hypnotic leap of the flames, and the sparks that streamed above the seething coals. The night appeared to draw in close about them.

George looked at the woman, huddled in her cloak. "Do you have money?" he asked. He had to repeat the question before she seemed to hear and roused herself to answer.

"Enough, I think. I didn't want to take any more from him than I simply had to!"

"Let me see." She let him have her reticule; he counted the bills and coins he found in it and handed it back, explaining as carefully as he would to a child: "If you're careful with it, that should be enough to get you where you're going—but there's not much leeway. I'd be pleased—"

"No," she said. "You've done enough. I'm afraid already of what this may mean for you, George—when he finds out. . . ."

"He may never find out," George assured her. "If he does, I'm not afraid of him." He reached more wood for the fire. The green pine popped and sizzled with exploding pitch; sparks poured toward the trees overhead. "You're the one I'm concerned about. You're sure there's no way he can trace you?"

She shook her head, staring into the flames. "I doubt if he'd bother. Once, perhaps; but not now. And I don't think he knows about these people of mine in St. Paul. If I can only once be free of him—"

"Not only of him, Mrs. Tarback," George reminded her.

"I know what you're thinking," she answered quietly. "I'm

155

not an alcoholic—not really. It's just that sometimes, when you see no other way to escape . . ." She didn't finish.

Ada slept, near the fire, with the laprobe from the buggy for a blanket. George Wright maintained his vigil and kept the blaze going until finally he, too, nodded, to awake at gray dawn and look about, shivering, at the silver sparkle of frost covering earth and rock and down timber. Mist rose eerily from the creek that flowed by their campsite. He arose, stiff in every joint, and shaking with cold in every limb set about gathering materials to rebuild the fire. He made as little noise as possible, knowing the woman was exhausted by the ordeal of flight from her husband's house and needed rest against the journey that lay ahead.

She woke rested, despite the primitive discomfort of their camp, and as she went to the creek to wash and try to put some order into the tangle of her fair, faded hair, George prepared a real breakfast. They were silent, talking little. The sun rose and the air quickly lost its chill as the May morning grew older. Still they remained where they were, and some hours afterward a sound of heavy wheels and of a four-horse team carried across the stillness. When at length the stage came into view along the road, northbound, they were waiting and ready, Ada Tarback's carpetbag beside them.

George stepped forward to hail the coach. "Passenger for The Dalles," he called up as the driver brought his vehicle to a rocking halt. The man gave them both a suspicious, puzzled scrutiny but he gave no argument. He took the fare George handed up to him, waited while George helped the woman into the coach. There were only two other passengers; he placed the carpetbag on the seat beside her. And as he moved to close the door, she leaned and her hand rested on his for an instant.

"Must you go back there?" Her eyes were dark with concern.

"Yes." He nodded. "I really must. There'll be no place for me in Prineville, when this is over; but I at least want to see the finish. You know my reasons."

Her nod answered him. "God bless you!" she murmured and withdrew her hand.

George Wright stepped back as the impatient whip yelled up his horses. The young man stood and watched the coach roll off through the trees, until the red pine trunks swallowed it and the timbered ridges blotted up the sounds of its passage and the bitter dust slowly settled. After that he returned to the buggy, with the horse already waiting between the shafts. He climbed aboard, flipped the leathers, and put the rent rig once more in the direction of Prineville.

It was perhaps an hour later that a sound of approaching horsemen came from ahead of him. Four riders took shape against a haze of yellow trail dust, which thinned and settled on the trunks of crowding timber as the men drew to a walk at the sight of the buggy. George Wright pulled in and let them come toward him, with Major Tarback at their head.

Tarback made a good figure in the saddle. He was as carefully dressed this morning as George Wright was used to seeing him, but for the first time in the latter's memory he appeared to have been in too great a hurry to use a razor. His cheeks showed a faint shine of beard stubble; his pale eyes were furious.

To one of his men he said, "Is this the rig you passed on the bridge?"

The man hesitated. "It could have been, Major. It looks like it. But one's about like another; and, at that time of night—"

George Wright interrupted. He managed to keep his voice cool enough as he said, "There's no need arguing. This was the rig."

"You admit it?" Tarback's face was iron, his tone incredulous. His chest swelled on a breath. "Do you admit that my wife—?"

"She was with me. She isn't now. That's as much as you'll get from me, Tarback," he added coldly. "Don't waste your time."

As he met the big man's stare, there was a movement among the other riders. At once George Wright brought his hand out of a pocket of his coat, and showed them the snub-nosed Colt he had been holding. He tilted the muzzle squarely against the Major's chest and he said, in icy warning, "If you think I won't use this, you're badly mistaken!"

The movement stilled as they all looked at the ugly weapon. Tarback peered into the round black eye of its wide bore and his voice held a different note as he said, "You listen to me!"

"No—*you* listen!" George Wright interrupted. "Your wife has left you. She finally got as much as she could take. She's gone where you'll never see her again, at least not if I have anything to do with it!"

One of the men with Tarback looked meaningly at his boss. "I think there's ways we could get it out of him, Major."

George never took his eyes from the big man's face. "You want to tell them to try?" he suggested mildly. The gun in his

157

hand rose a trifle, the muzzle unwavering.

Tarback seemed to hesitate. His face altered color a trifle and the muscle beneath one eye twitched a time or two. But he didn't challenge the gun, and instead took his frustrated anger out on the thought of his wife. "That lush!" he muttered savagely, and shrugged. "Without me, she'll end in the gutter!"

"I don't think so," George said calmly. "But if she does, it will be you that put her there. I wouldn't want that on my conscience. To say nothing of Chris Hunter. Or—" His face hardened.

"I think I see now," Tarback said after a moment. He put on a look of sober understanding. "You blame me for what happened to your brother. George, you should know me better than that. I swear! No one in the world could be sorrier. . . ."

George Wright looked at him. He spoke one word, then—a tired obscenity. And leaving it at that he slapped the leathers that he held in his left hand, explosively, and started the rent horse forward.

Taken by surprise the riders let him go; but when he had traveled no more than a few yards, Major Tarback suddenly gave vent to an angry yell. He kicked with the spurs, sent his fine horse after the buggy; he spun in a flurry of dust and came around facing George, crowding him so that the younger man instinctively pulled in again. The gun lay in his lap but he didn't touch it.

Peering under the buggy's hood, Tarback's face was congested with anger. "You hold on! No one turns his back on me until I'm finished!"

"Finished?" the other repeated. He shook his head. "Tarback, maybe you don't know it yet, but that's exactly what you are—you and your machine, both! I know you like to sneer at the men who are working against you; but, wait a few weeks!"

The other man straightened up in the saddle. His mouth worked, the lips tight under the mustache. "No!" he said hoarsely. "You're wrong! By God, I'll flatten them!"

"Me too, then," the lawyer said. "By lying to protect my brother, I earned my share of the blame for everything that's happened. Now Eddie's gone—and I mean to tell Hunter and Blake that if there's any way they can use me, I'm with them to the finish!"

A moment longer their eyes clashed. Deliberately, then, George flicked the reins, starting on again; and this time the

158

Major drew aside and let him go. His men, a little distance away, waited in silence, judging his mood and puzzled by it—uneager to break in on whatever he might be thinking.

The buggy moved ahead through the timber. Sunbright stillness swallowed it up.

CHAPTER XVI

Any man just up from a sickbed would have found the journey to the Upper Deschutes a punishing trek by horseback, yet it was a remote corner of Crook County's sprawl and with the issues at stake its votes could not be overlooked. Bob Hunter knew some of the stockmen who ran their cattle in that lava-studded region of timber graze and lush river meadow, and he'd volunteered to take the canvass there. He found that rumor had preceded him.

These men already seemed to know about the campaign being waged against the Vigilante machine by the group that had defiantly adopted the scornful name of Moonshiners placed on them by Jase Evans. Hunter's story reached receptive ears, and he told it with an eloquence he hadn't known he possessed. Now he rode slowly back toward Prineville, nearer physical exhaustion than he liked to admit—but carrying a dozen pledged votes for which three days' steady saddle work hadn't been too high a price.

With election less than a week away, nothing else seemed of any real consequence by comparison.

This was a lonely trail, a mere wagon track through the thick juniper forest. A turbulent wind came out of the overcast, wearing on man and mount alike, and in his present shape it had got to Hunter. He rode with head down, chin sunk into coat collar and boots shoved deep in stirrups, determined to tough it out. Yet his senses were anything but alert; so it was that he didn't even hear the flat report of the rifle, knew nothing at all of danger until the rent horse suddenly stumbled and went down.

Breath gusted from him in a grunt of pure surprise. Somehow

159

he fell clear and lay prone beside the dying animal, dazed while that new-healed bullet hole in his chest throbbed to the pound of his heartbeat. He had no idea where the bullet had come from. He could only suppose it had been meant for him and that some pressure of the wind had put the ambusher off his target and made him kill the horse instead.

Another gust moved across Hunter, plucking at his coat and sending his hat rolling on its brim and covering him with a stinging sheet of blown dirt. Abruptly it died; the gritty sand pattered away to silence in the branches of the junipers. Now the rifle let go again. And this time he heard it, even as the saddle horn close beside him exploded into splinters. There had been no echo, the sound of the weapon being sopped up by the crowding trees; he almost thought he caught the snick of the lever action as a fresh shell was cranked into the breech. Jarred into action, Hunter gathered his wits and rolled slightly to reach for the saddlebag behind the cantle. He got the flap open, dug inside and brought out the revolver he carried there. As he drew it free, the rifle tried yet a third time.

Now, for once, he saw the smoke, melting against juniper branches a little ahead and to his right—plainly, whoever had been waiting for him should really have held off a shade longer. Perhaps, though, he'd been too eager to get the job done. . . . Hunter threw the gun over and fired hastily, thought he heard a scrambling behind that twisted treetrunk. At once he was on his feet, rolling across the body of the horse as he dived for the nearest cover.

He made it, to crouch clutching the six-shooter in one hand while he pressed the other against that throbbing hurt in his chest. The pain eased after a bit. He hauled himself to his feet then, placed a shoulder against shaggy bark, and listened to the windy stillness, as he looked about him.

The juniper forest crowded thick to narrow his view—curious, scruffy little trees, thick at their bases but twisting abruptly to a point, and no two precisely alike. Pungent scent of dull green needles hung about him as Hunter checked the loads in the six-shooter. Five bullets left. . . .

He was sweating a little, still shaky—any of those near misses with the rifle could have been his finish. Anger helped steady him, as well as the knowledge that being set afoot out here could prove almost as fatal as if the ambusher had used better aim. It occurred to him, then, that the other man would have had a horse, and that it must be tied somewhere fairly close. Which meant there might be a chance, his luck holding, for him to circle and find it.

Certainly, it beat staying in this one spot, growing more tense with every minute that passed.

Edging away from the tree where he had taken cover, he was prepared for anything but there was no answering movement, no sound. It seemed to Hunter the very air throbbed with waiting. He tried to keep a screen of trees between him and the place where he had last spotted the rifleman, but suddenly he wasn't quite sure where that was. Lost by now was the single straight slash of the wagon road—the only real landmark; the forest swallowed him, so completely that one direction all at once looked very much like another. He was beginning to realize it would be possible for a man to get badly turned around, after traveling no more than a few short yards.

A sudden flicker of movement caught a corner of his eye, pulled him about—it was only a chipmunk, but it had given him a bad start. He could almost hear the twanging of his nerves. He stood watching the little rodent scamper from sight, and now a jay burst, squawking, out of nearby branches and took off, a flash of blue feathers against the drab sky. His gun arm jerked uncontrollably, and he felt sweat break out along his hairline; he cursed softly. As the stillness gathered once more, he settled his breathing, renewed his grip on the gun. And he prowled ahead again, blindly searching.

All this while, he knew he was listening for a sound of hoofs that would tell him his ambusher had gained the saddle and was riding away, leaving him there. But now the wind had risen and was swaying the treeheads, rattling in dry growth, interfering with his efforts to listen. Once he went down onto his ankles, trying for a look below the mass of branches; he saw only more twisted gray trunks and crowding brush and was starting to straighten again when suddenly he froze.

Not twenty feet from him, and slightly to his left, the figure of a man edged into view. His back was turned giving Hunter a moment's glimpse of jeans and leather jacket and shapeless, sweated hat, and a rifle carried at the balance. Almost before he could realize what he was seeing, the man was gone again—as silently as he'd come, simply melting into the tangle of scrubby timber. He hadn't so much as turned his head, and apparently he hadn't seen Hunter. But the latter, aware of his exposed position, lost no time fading again into cover. He was frowning darkly as he stood and assessed the state of things.

161

At least, now he knew! He wasn't the only one searching in this maze of trees—plainly, the ambusher was just as carefully and deliberately stalking *him,* meaning to finish the job he'd started. From this moment, the one who let himself be carelessly seen was the one who wouldn't walk away.

Hunter had the momentary advantage and yet it took real persuasion to send him out there after his vanished enemy; he was sure he must be making noise enough to carry above any sound the wind made in the tree branches. When he reached the point where the man had vanished, sure enough there was a line of boot prints in loose gray soil, disappearing into the farther trees. It would be too dangerous to go blundering directly after them. Instead, with nerves stretched out like fine wires, he swung wide and started off in a flanking movement he could only hope would bring him in on the man's blind side, without losing him entirely. . . .

A dry branch snapped without warning. He jerked in that direction, and there was his man—legs braced, shoulders hunched and head lowered against the stock of the rifle. Hunter saw the dull glint of the barrel pointed straight at him, and he dropped rolling for cover quicker than he had ever moved in his life. The rifle cracked and a length of shaggy bark was stripped away from a juniper's trunk, above his shoulder. On his knees he returned two quick shots. The rifleman floundered back out of sight, leaving him with the mingled roar of the weapons ringing in his head.

It was then that he became aware of thrashing movement somewhere behind him, and a horse's whicker. The ambusher's horse—startled by the gunfire and fighting its tether! Quite by accident, Hunter realized, he had managed to place himself between the man and his mount.

Wasting no time, and not bothering any more to cover his sound, he was up at once and plunging in that direction. He leaped a rotting log, scrambled through a waist-high thicket of bitterbrush and there, ahead of him, had a glimpse of a red hide. Satisfied that the animal was securely tethered, he spun then and braced himself—and here came the owner of the horse, legs pumping high as he ran with careless and frantic haste to save himself from being set afoot. For the first time Hunter saw his face, but that blooded red horse tied among the trees had already told him who it would be.

Bud Morrison saw him; the rifle, carried at high port as he ran, swung over for a snapshot. Hunter ground his teeth and worked the trigger of the Colt. His bullet stopped Morrison like running into a wall. The man was flung backward, the rifle spinning from his hands, and smashed into a thick clump of sage. He sprawled there, half supported, his arms and legs flung wide and his head thrown far back, dark face turned to the sky.

Lowering the gun, Hunter fought the sickness that was trying to churn up through his throat at this, his first kill. The half-formed question that tore at him was: Why? Had Calvin Tarback put out the word to get him? Or had this been Morrison's own idea? Suddenly he thought he knew. Acting coldbloodedly, on orders, it was hard to believe the man wouldn't have done a better job of it. Instead, for reasons best known to himself, he'd been too eager. He'd hurried it, and so missed what should have been a sure thing.

Well, a strange man like Morrison could have deep capacities for hatred. Plainly he'd resented Bob Hunter, ever since that day a year ago when he'd been disarmed and bested in front of the Tarback crew. And it had led him to this. It all ended here.

What bothered Hunter particularly, as he drew a shaky breath, was realizing that his horror over having killed a man was strangely flawed by some other feeling. He considered the emotion and then, almost incredulous, put a name to it: Yes—it was disappointment—a nagging regret that this couldn't have been Tarback, or even Jase Evans, lying at his feet! He shook his head, rather shocked at himself. For he was remembering something he'd told Jim Blake—that personal vengeance was one of the very things they were trying to do away with by bringing respect for the law to this part of Oregon.

Well, he thought, a man couldn't always discipline his feelings. Nor could he down completely the savage satisfaction of knowing that one of the three who had been there the day Chris was murdered had paid for his part in it. . . .

Bob Hunter was still staying with the Allens; even though it was a couple of weeks that he'd been well enough to be up and around, and in no need of any special attention, they'd refused to listen to any suggestion that he could as well as not move to a room at the Jackson House. Waking now in the spare bedroom, on a morning of bright June sunlight with a pleasant breeze stirring the window curtains, he enjoyed the luxury of lying at ease for long minutes while he took inventory of his hurts—and discovered they were gone. Last night, after still another punishing day in the saddle, there'd been only a vague hint of ache in the vicinity of that healed chest wound. This morning he knew he was mended, as completely and undramatically as that.

Not a sound came to him from anywhere in the house—only a twittering of sparrows in the tree outside his window. Lying there, mind pleasantly empty of thought, he wondered vaguely what time it was and set himself to recall his plans for the day—and remembered, with sudden jarring awareness, just what day it was. At once, all the laziness was shocked out of him and he flung the bedclothes aside, sat up reaching for his clothing. Dressing hurriedly, he strapped on the gunbelt and holster he had got into the grim custom of wearing. He went down through the silent, empty house and let himself out.

The sun was warm. Overhead an armada of huge white cumulus clouds, rank on rank, sailed the ocean of sky that arched above the canyon rims. Sun-and-cloud shadows filled the deep bowl where the village sat. Oregon had brought out its finest weather for Election Day.

Anyone familiar with Prineville would have sensed at once that it was no ordinary day. Approaching Main, Hunter saw the unusual number of saddle horses and rigs tied along the street—unusual even for a Saturday, which this was not. There was a clotting of idle men in the vicinity of the Jackson House, where a flag was hung to indicate the lobby had been taken over and the polls set up here. The village stores and saloons seemed to be doing a good business, but there was a general sense of calm and orderliness. That could be a false impression, though.

Someone hailed him from across the street at Allen's. It was Jim Blake, and when Hunter went over to join him there he thought the man who was running for sheriff against Jase Evans seemed confident, but also strangely sober. "Any news?"

The other hesitated, then suggested, "Let's step inside."

The store was full of people. Walter Allen, as nervous and distracted as ever, turned from his customers long enough for a nod of greeting as they went through. When they brushed aside the curtain at the small door at the back, they found Jennifer and George Wright in the cubbyhole office together, talking.

Jen flashed Hunter a warm smile and slipped off her book-keeper's stool to give him a quick good-morning kiss. George, leaning against the rolltop desk with arms folded, looked away. His own greeting was cool, if polite enough. He and Bob Hunter, because of things that had happened and especially because of the longstanding rivalry over Jen, could perhaps never be really friends; but Hunter for one held no grudges. George seemed to accept his loss of the girl; and having once broken with the Vigilante machine, he had worked as hard as anyone in the campaign to defeat it.

He said now, roughly, "Well—in a few more hours, we'll know."

"It will take longer than that," Hunter corrected him. "Several days, at least, before all the returns are in from places like Mitchell, and the Upper Deschutes and the Haystack country."

George didn't agree. "That matters only if the count is close. We all know the bulk of the votes are right here, around Prineville. If either side can manage to carry them by a wide enough margin, then what happens out in the rest of the county won't make too much difference in the final count."

Jen said indignantly, "If women only had the vote, there wouldn't be any question about it at all! It's the men who've let those people run things to please themselves. Believe me, *we'd* have put them right out!"

She was so much in earnest that the three of them exchanged faintly embarrassed looks. There would be a woman's suffrage measure on the ballot, but they knew it had little chance of passing. The time just wasn't ripe yet for anything so radical; but knowing how strongly the girl felt, nobody wanted to be the one to say so.

Bob Hunter asked, "Is it possible at all to tell how things are going, so far?"

"It's not too hard," Jim Blake said, and again Hunter had a feeling that the man concealed a deep concern behind his quiet manner. "We've kept close check on the men entering the polls. We think we know in most cases which way they're voting."

"And how does it look?"

"One-sided. Too damned one-sided; that's what has me uneasy. Our own people have been pouring into town since early morning, and they're still coming in. Looks like we could have close to a hundred per cent turnout if it keeps up—in which case I think there's a good chance of putting our slate over, maybe two-to-one against the Vigilantes."

Hunter said, "So what's wrong with that?"

"What's wrong with it is, I can't figure out what Tarback's crowd thinks they're up to! We know they're in town, yet so far not a single one of the leaders has showed up at the polls. I'm getting the notion that they don't even intend to."

"You think they're boycotting this election?"

The other nodded. Jen exclaimed, "But how can they expect to win *that* way?"

Blake answered her somberly. "They probably know they've already lost. Which doesn't mean they're quitting—not

165

after riding the high saddle around these parts for all these months. Not that bunch, and not that easy!"

Hunter's eyes narrowed as he thought about this. "You say they're here in town?"

"Twenty or thirty of them are down at Haze's, right now. They've taken the place over."

"Why Haze's? Gil Haze was never any friend of the Vigilantes!"

Jim Blake shrugged. "His saloon stocks the best liquor. . . ."

George Wright eased off the edge of the desk he'd been leaning against. "I suppose I know that crowd better than anyone else." His voice was gruff, as though it embarrassed him to remember. "I'd say we haven't heard the last of them. Before they'll admit they're beaten, they'll make some kind of move."

"You aren't suggesting they'd try raiding the polls?" Hunter said sharply. "Destroying the ballots?"

George's answer was a shrug. Jen started to protest: "Oh, but surely—!" and then went silent as she saw, from the faces of the men, that it was really that serious.

Jim Blake stroked his mustache thoughtfully with thumb and forefinger. "We take nothing for granted. We've got our friends alerted and they'll be around town until we're all satisfied these Vigilantes aren't up to something. If they are, they may find out that us Moonshiners—" and his mouth quirked with dry humor as he used the name Jase Evans had hung on them "—aren't ready to quit, after working as hard as we done to win this election. . . ."

The talk broke up. Minutes later Bob Hunter walked out onto the street and stood looking toward Haze's a minute in grim speculation. A white galleon of cloud drifted briefly across the sun and shadow flowed over the town, touching him with its chill. It clung to him like a premonition, as he crossed toward the Jackson House to cast his ballot.

In an atmosphere of tension the hours lengthened, the steady influx of men coming in off the range to vote continued. A few brought their families, but mostly they came alone; and having voted, they stayed. There was little drinking, little tendency to use Crook County's first election as an excuse for celebration— the stakes were too high. And as the hours passed, the anxious questioning as to just what might be going on down there at Gil Haze's became more intense.

Hunter was in Poindexter's restaurant, finishing off a plate of steak and potatoes and listening to the talk around him, when he saw Jim Blake enter and pause to have a few earnest words with four men seated at a table near the door. They were members of the Moonshiners, and Hunter watched as they hastily reached for their hats, leaving their meals unfinished. He slid off his stool at the counter as Blake caught sight of him; it didn't take the latter's urgent signal to bring Hunter over, to join him out on the sidewalk.

"Something's happened?"

The other nodded. "Gil Haze just sent his swamper out with a message: Things are getting ugly, down there. Now Jase Evans and the rest are likkered and talking about putting a torch to Prineville."

Hunter stared. "They can't be serious!"

"Gil thinks they are.

"I'm calling our men together," Blake said grimly. "I figure this could be the showdown!"

CHAPTER XVII

Taking the ultimate revenge on a town that had dared reject them was, at the outset, the rather off-hand suggestion of Jase Evans: "We ought to burn the damn place down!" he'd said, into one of those silences that occasionally fall upon a room full of men. He was pointing out the window, at that emptiness across the street where the rubble from last New Year's destructive fire had been finally cleared away. The foundations for a couple of new buildings had been laid, one of them to be the opera house that lately had become Gil Haze's pet project. Stacks of lumber and bags of cement under tarpaulins stood about. "Like yonder," Evans said. "Once we got her started, nobody'd ever put her out. By God, she'd make a pretty blaze!"

Whether or not he was serious or only voicing a half-drunken fantasy, his words roused a quick response among the score or better of sullen men who made up his audience. It was enough to put a shiver of dread into any sober listener, and this was when Gil Haze collared the old man who cleaned his spittoons and kept his floors swept up, and sent him off secretly with an anxious message for Jim Blake, or for anyone else he could find to relay it to.

Returning from the back room into the bar, he found Jase Evans waiting with an ugly look on his face. "Where the hell you been?" the big man shouted. "I'm waiting for another bottle."

Haze stared coldly back at him, showing him no fear. The whiskey was in the big fellow's voice, in the shine of his eyes and in the looseness of the sweaty, scarred cheeks; the sheriff's badge hung crookedly to his shirtfront. But if Evans was drunk, it was only enough to make him dangerous. Gil Haze, who had endured considerable bullying from him during these last months, now refused to take any more. He shook his head and said, "You're going to have to wait quite a while. Or else go somewhere else for your bottle. This bar is closed."

The sheriff's heavy head settled a little between thick shoulders. His eyes narrowed meanly. "Since when?"

"Since right now," the saloonkeeper answered. "Me and Emily just closed it." Evans looked at the ivory-handled revolver with the filed-off front sight that hung from its nail on the back-bar. His stare turned narrow, a shade cautious. "You've all had more than you need," Haze said flatly. "You'll get no more here."

Jase Evans cursed him. What more he might have done Gil Haze was spared knowing, for just then the slatted saloon doors were pushed open and Major Tarback entered.

Tarback was a changed man. Some there were who said the deterioration in him had dated from the night his wife departed from Prineville, leaving under mysterious circumstances that gossip couldn't uncover; others held it had been a more gradual thing, taking hold as he saw the tide of power commence to turn against him. His familiar air of confident superiority had gone a little out of focus. As he walked into the saloon now and looked about at these followers of his, there was a carelessness to the hang of his clothing. His cheeks showed odd lines and hollows beneath their stubble of unshaven beard.

Plainly, he was in a mood of suppressed ferocity as he demanded, "What's going on here? A little early to celebrate, isn't it? We haven't won this election yet."

Jase Evans had turned to lean against the bar, facing him. *"Won* it?" He laughed shortly, coarsely. "Are you serious?" And Tom Ridges, teetering his chair back on two legs, added, "Tarback, we've lost—even before the votes are counted."

168

"That's a lie!"

"It's a fact," Jase Evans retorted. "Though you seem to be the only man in town that don't know it. Have you looked around any? The place is crawling with them stinking Moonshiners and their friends. I still can't see how they ever managed to scare up such a backing!"

Tarback seemed beside himself. "I tried to tell you! I said all along they were a threat, but you didn't take it seriously. Not even when Morrison was killed by that sonofabitch Hunter!"

"Who the devil would have thought any of them really owned the nerve to buck what we had here—and get away with it?" Evans turned away, shrugging, with the manner of one who dismisses a loss.

Calvin Tarback was not ready to admit the loss so easily. He raised a pointing finger, which trembled slightly as he stabbed it at the other's back. "They haven't got away with anything!" he exclaimed. "Not yet, by God! I tell you, we can't let it happen."

Over at his table, Tom Ridges made a face. He said wearily, in a voice that held little trace of the respect he had once shown this man: "Come off it, Tarback! We're licked cold. . . ."

Tarback swung, in that stiff-necked way of his, to stare at the man as though he couldn't believe anyone would speak to him in just that way. And Gil Haze, who had been watching all this with stringy arms folded on the polished wood of the bar, spoke into the stillness. "You should of been here a minute earlier. These guys were talking about putting Prineville to the torch. . . ."

He saw the man's face alter, those pale eyes taking on incredulity as they speared the saloonman. Tarback demanded hoarsely, "Who was talking like that?" In answer, Gil Haze tilted his head in the direction of Jase Evans.

"That one started it."

Jase Evans came about to meet the Major's stare. For a moment Tarback seemed beyond speech. His hands pulled up into fists and his voice shook. "You'd better have been joking!"

"Who says so?" Evans glared at his employer. "I figure at least we should show the town it made a bad mistake, thinking we'd be as easy as this to get rid of!"

"I'll kill the first to try it! Damn you, this is *my* town!"

"Was, maybe. Hasn't it leaked into your skull yet what's happened? You're finished here. We all are!"

Tom Ridges seconded this: "And if some of us figure we'd like to sniff kerosene burning before we leave, there ain't a thing *you* can do about it!"

Baited from two directions, Tarback swung his head like an angry bull. A most alarming thing happened to his face then. Something like a shudder passed through it, a spasm of the jaw muscles that shook his whole head and made the cords in his throat stand out tautly. A fleck of white showed at the corner of his lips. "Scum!" he spat. "Filth!"

He took a step forward, another. Jase Evans, perhaps unconsciously, drew back until his back muscles pressed against the bar. Tom Ridges, bolt upright in his chair, couldn't seem to pull his eyes from Tarback; but the man seated next to him rose hurriedly, with a startling scrape of chairlegs. As he did he dislodged an empty bottle and it toppled to the floor, to go rolling in a wide circle.

Calvin Tarback looked over the whole silent group. "Who are you to defy me?" His voice began as a hoarse whisper but it grew quickly louder. "I remember a drunken lynch mob that this town would have spat on. I remember how you came begging for help, until I took charge and troubled myself to make the lot of you respectable. Not only that: I set you on top of the heap—on top of a whole county. Yes, and I put county money in your pockets, and power in your hands. And do you think now you have the nerve to turn against me?

"*Do you?*"

Stunned by this tonguelashing, no one met his challenge—no one spoke. There was not even a sound of breathing, so that when a growing shuffle of boot leather became audible in the dirt of the street outside, it came distinctly in the quiet. It was the buckaroo, Dallas, whose curiosity took him to a window. "Major!" he cried explosively. "It's the Moonshiners—my God, it must be all of them!"

Chairs were tipped over in the sudden trampling rush to the door and windows at the front of the room; only Gil Haze remained where he was, as though incurious. Stunned, gone motionless, they watched the mass of armed men filling the street. For so many—surely, at least seventy—they made very little noise. There was no disorder, no shouting; they came with a deliberate, quiet purpose. Some took cover behind stacks of yellow lumber in the vacant lot across the way, but the rest spread out boldly along the dusty street facing the saloon and halted there as though every move had been planned. Trampled dust settled out and an odd stillness fell. The high clouds pushed their flowing shadows across the scene and the sun glinted on hand guns and rifles carried openly and ready for use.

Inside, at the bar, Gil Haze was quietly at work taking down

170

bottles and glassware and moving them under the counter. His precious fiddle quickly joined them in a place of safety.

Jase Evans, unable to bear the tension, bawled a challenge. "You, out there! What do you damn Moonshiners think you're up to?"

The voice of Jim Blake countered: "Is Tarback there?"

"Speaking," answered the Major, after a moment's hesitation. "What do you want?"

"Depends on just what that crowd of yours is cooking up. If it's a showdown, then we're ready. Come on out if you've got the guts to face us!"

Jase Evans swore under his breath and pulled his gun. Immediately came Gil Haze's warning: "Watch it!" Heads turned. The saloon owner had his elbows propped on the bar and the ivory-handled six-shooter leveled in both hands, ready for a target. He said, "I ain't having my place of business turned into a battlefield. Take it outside if you want to fight. But the first man that fires a shot in here won't live to fire a second!"

Jase Evans told him harshly, "Stay out of this, Haze—or by God, you'll regret it!"

"I've stayed out of it too long," the other retorted. "That's the only thing I do regret!"

The revolver swung in a slow arc, threatening anyone who might defy the warning. One or two who had started to imitate Evans's move toward a gun, now held themselves carefully motionless. "Well?" came Blake's shout, prodding them. "What's it to be? We're waiting!"

Evans, seeing how the saloonkeeper's gun had immobilized his followers, exploded: "Hell! The man's bluffing. He won't use that thing."

"You think not?" Haze countered mildly. The gunmuzzle swiveled and came to a point squarely on the big fellow's chest. "In that case maybe I'll start with you. You're too good a target to miss. If you doubt it, tell your friends to go right ahead and begin shooting. Just any time. . . ."

As he saw the hollow eye of the gun staring at him, big Jase Evans looked as though the air had been trapped inside his lungs. He changed color and suddenly there was a faint shine of sweat among the ancient scars that marred his face. The others, anxiously watching, saw his bluster vanish.

Outside, it sounded like Bob Hunter this time, calling, "Gil Haze! You all right?"

Haze didn't let the point of that gun vary an inch as he shouted back his answer. "I'm fine as frog's hair, Bob. But some

171

of these other fellows are beginning to act a little uneasy about the whole thing. I got a notion they'd like to get out, if they only had a chance."

This seemed to provide a hurried consultation. Then Jim Blake, again: "All right—that's fair enough. They can go, for all we care. We could probably make a case against the lot of them, but we'll settle for four. We want Tarback, for the murder of Chris Hunter. And Evans, Dallas, and Tom Ridges—for their part in the killings of Dutch Schrader and of Sam Clifton and Charlie Hewett. The rest, we're willing to forget. But those four are under arrest."

"By what authority?" Major Tarback demanded. "I see no sheriff's badge on you, Blake—not yet."

"We'll let the court worry about my authority. We're determined to see you stand trial, and we won't have it any other way. And it will go hard on anyone who tries to interfere."

Len Meeks, the laborer from Stewart & Pett's mill who had always been out of his depth in this Vigilante crowd, suddenly tore himself away from the window. He flung a frantic look about the room. "Hell, I got no business in this!" he cried. "*I* ain't killed anybody. I was there when they lynched that murderer under the bridge, but I never done nothing myself.
. . ."

"You heard the offer," Gil Haze reminded him dryly. "There's a rear door to this place. Anyone that wants to leave is welcome to use it."

"Oh, no!" Big Jase Evans shouted. "Nobody's walking out!"

"After they been called filth and scum," Haze pointed out, "what reason they got to stay?" He looked at the Vigilantes, many of them showing the first clear signs of wavering. "I hope you realize you're in luck! More than a few of you have had a part, at least, in things you could rightly swing for; and yet they're giving you the chance to walk away with clean hands. I don't think they'd have to ask *me* twice!" He added, "Just leave your artillery here on the bar. . . ."

On the tail of his words a good half dozen started a sudden rush for that rear door, leading through Haze's storage room to the alley and safety; and after that the stampede was on. It took less than a minute. Chairs and tables were shoved aside. Guns clattered onto the counter, drowning Jase Evans's bellow: "You bunch of dogs! You dirty yellow dogs!" All at once no one was paying the big man any kind of heed.

Among the last to break and start for the exit was Tarback's man, Dallas; he had taken no more than a step when Haze's

revolver swung and pinned him, turning him motionless. Haze
shook his head. "Huh-uh! Not you, friend. You're supposed to
stay—remember?"

There was just the four of them left, then, stranded by the
receding tide of routed Vigilantes: Dallas, Tom Ridges, Jase
Evans, and the Major. As swiftly as that, the organization that
had ruled the Crooked River country, unhindered and almost
unchallenged, simply ceased to be.

Haze couldn't resist the impulse to gloat a little. "Well,
Major," he said pleasantly. "Looks like your following's kind of
dropped off. What's that they say about fleas and a dead dog?"

Calvin Tarback had stood through these last few dreadful
moments with an impassive dignity that disguised whatever
emotion he was feeling. Now he turned, slowly, moving his
whole upper body, to favor the saloonkeeper with a brief look
of such fury as to make Gil Haze tighten his grip on the
revolver.

Outside there was some confusion now—apparently the
fleeing Vigilantes were being intercepted and searched for
weapons before they were allowed to scatter. But this was
quickly done. And, narrowly observing the four penned into the
saloon with him, Haze said dryly, "The next move is yours.
They aren't going to wait forever while you decide whether to
fight or give it up."

Tom Ridges, a six-shooter weighting down his fist, was
prowling nervously from window to door and back again,
peering out at the besiegers as though judging the chances of
making a fight of it. The puncher called Dallas, with escape
thwarted by Gil Haze, had given way to panic that showed in
such violent trembling that his legs wouldn't hold him. He had
dropped into a chair beside an overturned table; his hands, his
head, his whole body shook as the spasms went through him.

A murmur of growing impatience sounded from the street.
Now Jim Blake's voice, again: "Tarback, you've got just two
minutes to decide to surrender. . . ."

A look passed between Jase Evans and the Major, a signal
that both seemed to understand. Dallas and Ridges appeared to
have been dismissed as too unimportant to bother informing
them of what had been decided. Deliberately, Tarback turned
his back on them, and on the danger waiting in the street; he
started instead in the direction of that other door beyond the
bar. Quickly Gil Haze, who had laid his six-shooter on the
counter in front of him, snatched it up again. "No you don't!"
he warned.

Tarback halted, turning to him and shaking a snub-nosed revolver out of somewhere in his clothing. And at the same moment Jase Evans was in motion.

Evans had swung wide, to come at Haze from an angle making it impossible for him to cover both men at once. The saloon owner stumbled backward, instinctively trying to keep the pair of them within his range of vision; it was this move that saved his life. As his gaunt shoulders struck the backbar, Evans's gun bellowed. His bullet smashed the mirror inches from the saloonkeeper's head. And the latter, reacting, swung his own weapon and shot the big man in the chest.

The shock of the bullet must have flattened any ordinary man. It drove Evans back three scrambling paces, while his head jerked with neck-popping force and his hat tumbled onto the floor. He dropped his smoking gun but caught himself somehow, to stare in surprise and disbelief at Gil Haze; then, dying, he looked for Calvin Tarback. But the Major was already gone, vanished through that door beyond the bar leaving his companions to their fate. The big man's face showed his knowledge of this ultimate betrayal.

Afterward, all expression was wiped away and he swayed and fell, straight forward, the way a tree falls.

Outside, the crowd had been released by the sound of shooting and was already storming the swinging doors. Calvin Tarback heard the double gunshots that still numbed his ears. Never pausing, he plunged on toward the alley door that had been left standing wide by the last of the Vigilantes to go stampeding through. He reached it, and halted a moment as he considered the quickest route by which to reach a horse that would take him out of this town, where everything he built had come crashing down about his ears.

Evidently the Moonshiners—damn them!—had not expected anyone else would be escaping by this route. The alley behind the saloon lay silent and empty, unguarded. . . .

Except for one man.

Tarback saw him, then, standing all alone in the shuttle of flowing cloud shadow and sparkling sun. A rifle was leveled across his middle, in both hands; his voice was harsh as Bob Hunter said, "Drop the gun or use it, Tarback—either one you please. I sure wouldn't need much of a reason to put a bullet through your guts!"

Stopped in his tracks, Tarback looked at the rifle and then at the other's face. The shadow of his hatbrim struck across

174

Hunter's eyes but he could see enough to know there was no challenging that rifle. Nor would words have any effect on this man, not with the body of murdered Chris Hunter between them. Knowing he was beaten, Tarback swore and flung the snubnosed gun away from him. "All right," he said harshly.

Hunter came toward him, the rifle still ready and his hand clamped tight around the trigger action. Now Tarback *could* see his eyes, and of a sudden sheer terror broke through him. His empty hands groped upward; his voice shook with the fear that stopped his breathing: "My gun is on the ground! Hunter, for the love of God—!"

The rifle barrel touched his shirt front; the eyes in that other face probed his. For that moment Tarback felt certain he was a dead man. But then the fury in Hunter seemed to lose some of its edge, and something came to discipline the raw danger in his stare. His hand relaxed on the rifle action and a long breath filled his chest.

"There's no need for me to kill you myself, Tarback," he said. "We'll have a court and a jury now to take care of that. The world will see that Crook County's through with your kind of lynch law." He gestured with the rifle barrel. "Now, turn around and walk back inside. . . ."

Another summer lay upon this land: upon the Cascade peaks that still held a few scraps of their winter snow, upon the high desert where dust pillars walked and played out among the juniper stands and the rimrocked canyons of dry rivers, on Prineville with its brand new court house. At the homestead ranch over north of Grizzly Butte, sunlight made a dazzle on roof shingles, and on the water that filled the completed irrigation ditches. Bob Hunter turned in the saddle. "How do you like it?"

Jen said: "It's just wonderful!"

"I did what I could."

Flowers had been planted by the slab porch; there was even a glimpse of lace curtains at the open window. Hunter, dismounting, held up his arms and she let him lift her down from her own horse. Standing close, she looked up and saw the sober look on his face. "What are you thinking?" she asked softly.

He shook his head. "I can't help thinking it would be pretty near perfect, if only—"

"I know—Chris. But he wouldn't have wanted us to spoil a

175

day like this one, with feeling sad about him."

"No," he agreed, after a moment. "No, he wouldn't, would he? Not old Chris. . . ."

"Never in this world."

She stood on tiptoe to kiss him gently. And Hunter slipped an arm around his bride, and drew her close.

VL-1/10